That Summertime Sound

A Novel

Matthew Specktor

MTV Press

New York City

First published in the United States of America in 2009 by MTV Press
A Division of MTV Networks
1515 Broadway
New York, NY 10036

Distributed by powerHouse Books
37 Main Street, Brooklyn, NY 11201 / (212) 604-9074

DESIGNED BY ERIC FROMMELT

First Edition
August 2009 / 10 9 8 7 6 5 4 3 2 1
Printed and bound in the United States
ISBN: 978-1-57687-520-9

MTV Press and all related titles, logos, and characters are trademarks of MTV Networks, a division of Viacom International Inc.

Yes, Virginia

I

Bring It On Home

1

Nowhere At All

Invisible Dan drove the car, a green Volkswagen Jetta that hurtled along I-80 in the middle of the night. We'd just coaxed him into fifth gear—he'd never driven a stick before—and now allowed ourselves to drowse, drifting on the edge of sleep as we whisked through central Pennsylvania. The Promised Land was still two hundred miles away. Columbus, Columbus, Columbus. Was there a word more beautiful in all the language than this one, which bespoke whole worlds of firstness, freshness, discovery? Westward we flew, as the word made a rosary under my breath, the engine's hum and the seat's vibration lulling me deeper. Then a truck slid past on the left and Dan panicked. He ground the gearbox and stomped on the brake,

"Shit!"

The car spun a full 360 degrees. Dust kicked into the air and Dan screamed as we fishtailed over to the shoulder and stalled. We sat there a stunned second. Then Marcus, dear old Marcus, leaned forward and took charge.

"Easy there, hoss." He bent across from the backseat to show Mr. Invisible once more how it worked, the H-shaped pattern of the gears. "Like this."

"Like that?"

"Yeah—"

The gearbox ground again, the car sputtered. We were at forty-five degrees in the middle of the interstate, angling across the yellow line.

"Try again." Marcus's nicotine-streaked fingers pointed towards the stick. "One more time."

"Um—we're in the middle of the highway."

"So what?" This was Marcus in a nutshell. No matter that he'd eaten six hits of acid since sundown, was staring out at a world that might've been teeming with green insects as he saw it. Nothing bothered him, everything was cool. "We're fine."

You'd buy anything he wanted to sell you. In a sense I'd already bought. I should've been lounging by my parents' pool in California, instead of trapped in a car full of tripping lunatics hurtling towards the Corn Belt. We were headed towards Ohio for an entire summer. Who else could've convinced me the Buckeye State was Paradise, that its people were as gods in their colorful extremity. You know it's true, he'd told me. Come on.

"Look." He gestured once more. "Just depress the clutch there and then let go, hoss. Slowly."

Cluhutch. The way he said it, sitting on the 'u' there for a moment, drew the word out into a squelchy Middle American parody, hillbilly Elvis deluxe.

"There, see?" He spoke otherwise with well-mannered precision. His accent was unplaceable, people sometimes thought he was English. "See how easy that is?"

The car shuddered. Marcus said,

"Again."

It was two-thirty in the morning. He and Lena, the car's owner, had both driven earlier shifts and now claimed they were tripping too hard to drive. Maybe they just wanted to torture us, Invisible Dan and I, the outsiders. We were perpendicular in the center of the primary interstate that cut across the northern half of the U.S. Yet so what? The highway was silent. The road was a moon-slicked ribbon that cut between head high stalks of—corn? Wheat? I had no idea. Ohio might have been Kansas for all I knew, for all I could distinguish the local agriculture on sight. I was from Los Angeles, after all. Everyone I knew, the New Yorkers and New Englanders I'd met during my freshman year at Harper College, yearned to be there instead in January or July. They envied my Hollywood birthright. I'd grown up with famous people peering into my crib, folkie musicans and Laurel Canyon royalty. My father was a producer. I ought to have known all there was to know about exaggerations and lies. So why on earth was I going to Columbus, instead of going home? Why take Marcus at his word?

"Goddamn it!" Invisible D pounded the wheel with his palms. It was easy to forget he was here, this crop-headed and morose Bostonian who looked like Peter Parker's still-more-innocuous twin. "Will someone please help me?

Please?"

Lena leaned forward. "Oh honey," she breathed, laying her hand gently on Dan's nape. Her eyes were enormous. "You need me to drive or something?"

He flinched. Poor Dan!

"No, no." He gritted his teeth manfully, there in his blue Oxford shirt and tan khaki pants, those things that amounted to a form of reverse camouflage where we were. It was 1986, and the rest of us wore paisley shirts and second-hand love beads, fisherman's caps and gabardine trousers: thrift store paraphernalia we'd scraped up in the decaying industrial towns of western Massachusetts. "I'll do it."

He turned the key in the ignition and this time, finally and with Marcus's help, got us running again. He reached back and brushed the spot on the back of his neck Lena had just touched, rubbing it tenderly like a bee sting. We headed west. The stalks in the fields were all ominously still, the sky a darkling, monochromed silver. Dan was in love with Lena. That was his excuse for going. What on earth could've been mine?

****

"Tell me again," I said when we sat down in the booth. "Tell me again about Lords—"

Lena rolled her eyes and cast her head back, a pantomime laugh. Marcus sighed. This had been a few hours earlier, when we'd stopped for dinner. We were west of Springfield and east of the Allegheny River at twilight, crowding into a semi-circular booth in yet another junky truckstop, one of the generic diners we loved. Already I was pestering them.

"What?" I said. "What is it about Lords of Oblivion that's so tiresome?"

Lena chuckled. She and Marcus sat in the middle, with Dan and I on the outside.

"Nothing," she said. Behind her the window was a scar-streaked purple. "It's your enthusiasm."

"My enthusiasm?"

How beautiful she was, Lena with the creamy skin and the jack-o'-lantern orange hair. It was dyed this week in a shade called Great Pumpkin, sweeping crossways over her forehead, cut in a stylish bob. Her face was long, Slavic. Her eyes were dark. I'd have been in love with her too, if her worldliness didn't quash all hope, if I'd been able to find myself worthy.

"Yeah." Her nostrils flared, hazel eyes sparkled. "They're just a band."

"Just a band?" I looked to Marcus. "Tell her."

"I have told her." His own eyes were button-like, black. His lips twisted in amusement. "She doesn't believe."

This word, too, twisted out in a strange, almost sinister fashion. It seemed ironized, as if the very notion of belief was behind us now, was somehow dated and silly. We were nineteen, and all of us had just finished our freshman tour at Harper. Marcus was my roommate. He and Lena had been friends since high school. Now we were on our way to the Emerald City, as he described it, the Epicenter: The Heart of the Heart of the World!

"What's not to believe?" I searched him. "What?"

Lena just winked at Marcus. She'd never contradicted him, yet never fully supported his claims either. Opposite me Dan was having none of it, just pushing around specks of sugar with his plastic straw, staring down at the wood grain table. He didn't give a shit about a rock 'n' roll band, his heart was being torn in two. Marcus dug in his shirt pocket and pulled out a tiny square of blotter paper. He stuck it on his tongue a moment, then washed it down with milky, silty diner coffee in a thick-handled mug. Flashed a peculiar smile that meant so many things: trust me, on the one hand; you fool, on the other.

"They'll never get it," he said. "So why try?"

"Why try? Isn't that the whole point? Isn't that why we're going?"

Marcus just smiled. But indeed, it was why I was going. It was just what he'd promised, that I'd get to see the greatest band in the world, my Achilles heel. Lords of Oblivion. Marcus had turned me on to them. Month by month he'd drip-fed a store of mythology—there was plenty of it, at least in Columbus—that said that Nic Devine, the band's singer, was a giant: Iggy Pop, Jim Morrison and Mick Jagger in one man. We were stranded in the mid-eighties, surrounded by posture in every direction, cheap hooks and pancake makeup and fishnet stockings, bands that couldn't be troubled to break a sweat on stage or barter their souls, worshipping instead at the High Church of the European Cigarette. Lords of Oblivion were different. You could hear it in their records, the way the singer shrieked, bargained, pled and howled, the way the band commanded your speakers until you were ready to beg for mercy yourself. Their shows were said to be Passion Plays, outriggers and enactments of the Apocalypse. Your head rang for days afterwards, and—if the accounts of witnesses were to be believed—Nic Devine did everything but resurrect the dead. The records couldn't approach the reality of the performances, I'd been told over and over and, given this, it was simple. I would see the band play or die trying. The rest, Marcus's gassing on about how Columbus was a bohemian paradise, a sort of Paris Commune for misfit kids, was secondary. You could live without food or cheap rent or sex even, but music? Lords of Oblivion were the key.

"You all ready to order?"

Our waitress came back. And as I stared into her face, I saw it there too: youth, mystery, life in its uncut form. That thing for which we were all always searching, a newness perhaps, a sense that we were the first people to whom anything interesting ever happened. She stopped and she sighed in her orthopedic shoes. Her face was a cumulus of Middle American moods. Only Marcus and Lena were tripping, yet her brassy beehive seemed to sparkle with gnats of electricity. Her eyes were a lucid Cadillac-black beneath them. She squinted at my mangy quiff.

"Did you lose a fight with a weed-whacker, hon?"

Marcus and Lena burst out laughing. To them, this place—this part of the country we were just entering, no longer New England nor affixed to either coast—was home. To me it was unfathomable, irresistible, true. And even this woman, whose name tag read Joyce, was a part of it, a part of the New World indivisible from the Old, a tiny wilting slice of eternity. I'd never met a woman called "Joyce" before, the name so old-fashioned it could as well have been from the future. I watched her pour out our coffee, flexing her marzipan wrists, shaking her head at whatever was so funny.

"What can I get you?"

Everything, I wanted to say, anything. Just give me one of all you've got.

****

We'd be there in the morning. I'd find out what was true and what wasn't. In the backseat Lena took the cap off a video camera and began fiddling with it. Invisible Dan drove, and I lay my head against the window and thought still about our waitress. Could I capture whatever this was about the country—wherever we were now, and were going—and our lives? Could Lena? She aimed her camera out the window, shot footage of fields glazed with moonlight. She was making a movie, shooting much of it, *Wisconsin Death Trip*-style, inside the three insane asylums that crouched on the outskirts of our New England town. The mist of the Gothic that clung to her seemed to cling equally to Columbus itself. I'd heard the story about the Olentangy Bridge, where a couple on a blind date had parked and then the guy gotten out of the car to walk for gas. They were seventeen, and the girl had waited alone in the dark until she began to hear a scraping noise on the roof of the car. It was petrifying. She waited and waited, finally leapt out of the car to find her date had hung himself from the bridge overhead. The scraping sound was his feet. These urban legends were nearly believable, even if half-original. I knew they had probably happened elsewhere, everywhere and nowhere, but when Marcus told them I believed all the same. When he described his friends Marcus quoted William Carlos Williams, *The pure products of America go crazy*. If this were true—there was no reason to doubt this at least, given the soft-spoken intensity he and Lena seemed to share, the batshit consumption of every drug they could find hiding under yes, ma'am, no, ma'am politeness—I was ready to go nuts too, although hopefully not before I'd had a chance to see the sights. The Village Thrift Emporium! Perry's Bar! Nick's Nook! Marcus had instilled in me a reverence for these places I'd heard so much about, a feeling that was one part patriotism and another part nostalgia for something I'd never encountered, a homesickness for someone else's home. It was easy enough for me to feel then, this longing I didn't yet have to pay for.

"OH—"

Dan hollered as a truck whisked into view, its lights filling the cab. I tucked my head between my legs. At the last second it swerved and blew its horn. Marcus and Lena seizured with laughter, as the car shook, rocked violently in its slipstream. *Close call!*

"Jesus," Lena muttered. "You two guys are so uptight!"

She yawned. Dan turned the key in the ignition, edged his way back into traffic. The pure products of America go crazy. Fine. That was the song in fact that was playing on the mix-and-match tape Lena had made for our journey: James Brown's "I'll Go Crazy." It swung softly from the speakers as we red-lined along I-80 at long last, trucks passing and honking while Dan struggled to get the car into third. Soon enough it would be morning. What were those cruciform shapes out there in the fields? Scarecrows? Poor Dan hunched over the wheel, as freaked as if we'd wired him to a bomb.

"You'll take over again when we get out of Pennsylvania, right?" He nudged me. "Right?"

"Sure, Dan."

He and I were the only ones now left awake.

Also on Lena's tape: the Count Five, Tommy James & The Shondells, Hüsker Dü. This mixture of rehabilitated retro-cool with Middle American hardcore and AM radio cheese was exactly the thing I envied in my friends, being esoteric and accessible at the same time. What did Dan or I know about this? To me, California had begun to seem so dowdy, so common. Its glamour didn't hold any surprises. Like our invisible driver I yearned to be seen, to explode against the bright clean lines of the world behind me. These Midwestern kids owned certain things, a pop tradition they didn't need to step away from. A Grand Funk Railroad song kicked in, whether ironically or otherwise. This was just the sort of hairy business I'd been taught to abhor in high school, when I'd turned my back against the heavy metal thunder of my youth. "We," the creeping punk rock sophisticates; "They," the hesher cheeseballs. Not that I even knew any hesher cheeseballs, which breed had died out in my part of Los Angeles no later than 1982. But Marcus and his friends didn't even have to bother to reject this stuff, since it had rejected them since birth. Somehow, that only made them cooler. That they loved it too—a culture they could simultaneously despise—was my lesson in living in ambivalence.

I'd collect more about that, maybe. For now I was just going to nod my head and look out the window and hum, where the songs had hooks to hum to, and try to sleep. Dan's shift at the wheel would last until he killed us, or until we got close enough to need someone who could actually navigate the gearbox. Whichever came first.

****

"Hey, I see it!"

I opened my eyes. Marcus was reaching forward between the seats, tapping me on the shoulder as he pointed out towards the windshield. I flinched against the light.

"What—"

"We're here!"

Had I slept? My mouth tasted of last night's coffee. An acrid tang. Where we were now looked exactly like Pennsylvania—or Iowa or Idaho, they were all the same to me, these States. Just hill-less unbending highway, the same place we'd been all night except for the sunlight that now shattered the grimy plane of the windshield and my own demi-sleep. Lena's deck played Tim Buckley, "I Must've Been Blind." Everything seemed backwards. Shouldn't the sun have been behind us, if we were headed west? Dan was still driving, if that was an apt description of his excruciated stapling-to-the-wheel. The expression on his face was that of a cadaver flipped over in a horror movie. Marcus had just informed him he would need to find an off-ramp.

"Now?! You want me to do that right now?!"

"Yes, now," Marcus said, calm as ever while Dan jerked the car into the right lane. "How did we get turned around?" He stretched and shook his head. "Never trust a Trotskyite to do the driving."

Dan was too busy to retort—he was aiming for an overpass, a turnaround
he might be able to navigate without downshifting—and yet Marcus had his
number.

"Just use that overpass up ahead. You'll be fine, there."

Dan grunted. He was indeed a Trotskyite, just as Marcus was a
Leninite member of the Communist Workers Party. The two of them bickered
constantly. In the mid-eighties it was still possible to be a Communist in
America. Marcus was an aggressive recruiter, flew to conferences in Boston,
Seattle and Atlanta. At fourteen he'd founded Animal Suffrage, Columbus's
first vegetarian socialist straight-edge band. He'd been ideologically active
now for six years. At that age, I myself had been no more active ideologically
or otherwise than my fascination with marijuana, surfing magazines and
pornography permitted. I'd been a Zeppelinite, a metallurge, owner of both a
skateboard and a twenty-sided die: the first album I bought was not by Wire
or the Sex Pistols or Brian Eno, it was—horror of horrors—Aerosmith's *Get
Your Wings*. Marcus on the other hand had read Hegel's *Philosophy of History*
in its entirety and practiced after school with his own socialist hardcore
band, the kind of music that was barely even a rumor to me in 1980. He was
a competitive chess player and spoke three languages. It seemed like he'd
been born vegan. Everything was worked out, systematized, defensible. He
arrived at Harper College with his possessions packed in a steamer trunk, fresh
off a year-long expatriation to Geneva. I still had a pair of OP shorts in my
wardrobe somewhere. Hidden like a shameful secret in our dorm room.

"Where are we?" Somehow, Dan managed to turn us around without
banking off the overpass walls. I gestured out at the green stalks I presumed
were corn. Wheat would've been yellow, right? "What exactly am I supposed
to be seeing?"

"Look. Open your eyes."

I yawned. "This looks exactly like Pennsylvania to me."

"Shows what you know. We've crossed the border," Marcus crowed.
"We're in Ohio! Can't you *smell* it?"

Beside him, Lena offered an indulgent smile. She sat in a Z-shape,
her legs pulled up alongside. There was something leonine—it was too subtle
and grave to be merely feline, kittenish—about her. She had the perfect last

name. *Royal.*

"Not so much," I said. "I can't smell anything."

"Aw, honey." Lena patted my cheek. "You'll learn."

"That Ohio air," Marcus said. *Uh-hi-uh.* Every now and then he'd punch a word like that to let me know he meant it, that the Midwestern fascination wasn't just—though it was also—an affectation. "Smell that?"

He wore a gray cardigan and Hush Puppies: the muted uniform of a retired schoolteacher. His dark eyes were enormous, beneath black bangs that grew like vegetative tendrils, almost all the way to his chin. His pale face had the worried cast of an East European Jew's, his forehead creased with early lines.

"What am I smelling?"

Marcus rolled down the windows further, lit a Chesterfield with shaking hands. He had the palsied, uncertain body language of an octogenarian, what happened when your diet was mostly coffee and LSD.

I stuck my nose into the air and sniffed like a hound. The wind whipping past my face was warm, humid, dirty, touched vaguely with diesel fumes and fertilizer. The generic highway air of Middle America. There was no salt in it, as in L.A.; there was not the piney, resinous depth I'd come to love while I was in New England.

"That Ohio air!"

Marcus laughed. An aggrieved Dan ground the gearbox as he attempted to downshift. The car shuddered and swerved.

"Shit!"

It was midmorning now, and there was traffic everywhere. Highway 80—I'd been so disappointed to discover we couldn't possibly have taken 61, or Route 66—was awake now. Trucks rocketed by, carrying beds full of tomatoes, trailers full of fiberglass pipes. We fishtailed crazily in their wakes.

"OH!" Dan yelled, as we spun once again, two-hundred-seventy degrees towards the shoulder. "Little help?"

We spun in circles, like a Roman Candle, spraying dirt and gravel everywhere while Marcus cackled. Lena just sat with her hands in her lap. Finally, we rattled to a stop.

"Jesus!"

Invisible Dan let go of the wheel. Brought his head down for a second against it. His shirt-sleeves were soaked through.

"Why don't I take over?" Marcus said. He stepped out of the car. LSD or no LSD, I'd feel a lot safer with him in the driver's seat.

Lena's tape had ended and we idled for a moment in silence. Now that we were not moving I could feel just how hot it was. The air so still it was practically a solid. Wherever we were, it was exactly where we'd been five minutes or five hours ago: flat green fields untroubled by hills and bisected by a thread of highway that might have gone on forever.

This was where we were headed? The Ohio I'd heard so much about?

2

Bell Bottom Blues

"Hey, is that the Outerbelt?"

I knew Marcus's city better than he did. By now I understood
Columbus the way I did few things, as we crossed under a sign for Interstate
270.

"That is, right?" I pointed towards the interchange, out there in the
hazy distance. "It's the Outerbelt! Cool!"

If I'd wanted to I could have embarrassed myself by disclosing all I'd
retained, everything I knew about a city most people chose to avoid. That
the Outerbelt was a circular highway, built in the 1960s to link a series of
suburbs—Worthington, Westerville, Grove City, Gahanna—to Columbus
proper, and to connect them all to the city's airport, for instance. That it was
exactly 54.97 miles in diameter, and that at night it opened up to hot-rodders
and muscle-car drivers, people who wanted maximum throttle on their V8
engines. Between two and five AM, the Outerbelt hummed, it roared with
automobiles drifting across its eight lanes like NASCAR racers. I knew this,
and tons more besides, about a place I'd never set eyes on. Yet as we reached it,
as the city's small and turbid skyline flickered into view, I suddenly understood
I was entering another world, and that Marcus's myth-making had in a sense
undersold the strangeness of where we were going. The deeply American
ordinariness that could, to someone from the coast where exoticism dulled
our palates, seem paradoxically gargantuan, overwhelming in its utilitarian
function.

"Look!" Marcus pointed towards a squat, gray ten-story office
building. A little green office park spread around it, flecked with white bits of
corporate sculpture. "It's the Weberman Medical Supply Center!"

"Oh, God," Lena said. "Remember?"

Marcus shook his head. "That was so fun."

"So fun! Remember?"

"I'll never forget it."

Lena sighed. "One of our best nights!" She looked at me and added. "We're home. Marcus and I never feel we're home until we've watched the sun come up over the medical supply center."

"Preferably on acid."

It might have been the Taj Mahal they were discussing, the cathedral at Chartres. I said nothing. We were entering some Gnostic zone of experience, where I would be forced to sit and stare into the void of my own ignorance. The sun made a bitter red eye ahead of us, piercing the strata of pollution over the minor skyline. As this was no different than every other city in America that wasn't New York or Los Angeles, it was like no place I'd ever seen. I felt at once enlarged and diminished by it.

"What should we do first?" Lena said. "Go VTEing?"

"No," Marcus said. "Let's Kroger."

"Kroger? Isn't it a little soon for Krogering?"

Marcus nodded at me. "I want to give our friend here the full experience."

"Let's go to Graceland!" she said.

"No, no—Bob Evans!"

Invisible Dan looked up from his book now. It was the same Marxist tome he was always dragging around with him, a set of essays by Louis Althusser. He was no more in step with whatever Marcus and Lena were talking about than I was.

"Did you know Althusser never learned to masturbate until he was twenty-seven?" he said.

"Is that right?"

"He felt just terrible about it." Dan shook his head.

"Yeah, I would too," I smirked. "If it took me as long to figure something like that out." Scholasticism without masturbation seemed to me dry and unhealthy, like fries without ketchup, hamburgers without Russian dressing. "Was he a smoker? What on earth did he do with his hands?"

Lena had rotated into the front passenger seat. She fiddled with the cassette deck while Marcus drove, turning up the volume on the Flamin' Groovies' "Him or Me (What's it Gonna Be?)" One of those tinny, ambivalent AM-radio ultimatums that Xeroxed the Beatles' influence into infinity.

"He killed his wife, y'know."

"I do know that," I said. "Louis Althusser took an ax/gave his wifey forty whacks."

Lena stiffened. Marcus turned around with a look of unlikely concern.

"Actually he strangled her."

"I know." Dan sighed, as though he'd known the deceased wife personally. "Poor Hélène."

We rode on a moment in silence. Marcus lifted the subject away from ax-murdering by asking Dan whether he thought it was true Marx had opened up the "continent" of history. I watched the trucks around us, kicking up Styrofoam cups, gum-wrappers, tinsel-bright litter so fine it seemed consubstantial with the air. Rolling along 270, I wondered—since none of these buildings were actual landmarks, all of them may have been—that there was no more hope of apprehending America than of sketching a whale from the inside. Amorphous as my own home city was it couldn't touch this one for its sense of being infinitely extendable and repeatable, encircled over and again by other identical cities, just as it was by its own Outerbelt.

****

I stepped out of a dressing room in the Village Thrift Emporium. This was the "VTE" they'd been discussing in the car, a room the size of a city block filled with vintage clothes and second-hand bric-a-brac. That dead-skin sweetness of grandparents and libraries.

"Whaddya think of *these*?" I said. Gesturing to the slacks that hung off me, wide legs swaying like a grass skirt. They'd looked cool on the rack. Marcus put his hand to his chin and considered.

"Hmm."

This was the place where his unspectacularly faded half-shtetl half-psychedelic wardrobe had its origin. For as long as I'd known him I'd envied the outré paisley shirts and geriatric slacks, the forest-green cardigans that looked wooly and mean as hair-shirts yet somehow proved themselves as soft as kittens, reeking of mothballs and patchouli. *Ya like it?* Marcus would puff up proudly. *I got it for thirty cents at the VTE!* I stared out now at a hectic aggregation of shirts, furniture, pulp paperbacks and LPs, the scuffed, pale coronas of their worn sleeves over there on the racks. I saw bowling clocks and lava lamps, old Jim Thompson and Charles Willeford novels that would soon be worth a fortune, lost psychedelic records that would someday fetch hundreds of dollars yet for us were just twenty-five cent objects of derision waiting to become Frisbees, coasters and wall hangings.

"What d'you think?" I repeated, while Marcus looked me up and down.

In a few minutes we'd be off to Lena's house—she seemed in no hurry to get there—but had pulled over briefly for this little shopping orgy. Invisible Dan browsed the used book section, while in my shopping cart already I had a scratchy tweed overcoat, a Mechanical Man alarm clock and a beat-up copy of Stevie Wonder's *Talking Book.* Marcus grinned. The pants were a silvery, striped poly/wool blend, slightly unctuous in their silky texture. They were cool, unless—

"Oh, very nice." he snickered. "If your name happens to be Isaac, or Barry."

"Wait—"

"Yes! Very nice!" Oh no! Marcus sing-songed, "Diamonds in the back/sunroof top/diggin' the scene in your—"

"Bullshit!"

"Yes! Those trousers are great, if you happen to be a pimp! If you're a—"

"Shut up!"

"—wife-beating, menthol-smoking, disco-biscuit-gobbling—"

"Oh, please—stop!"

I covered my face with my hands. Marcus was beckoning Lena over. These pants were hopeless, I saw now. Hatched with a subtle herringbone pattern that brought them closer to inner city Detroit than Episcopal Iowa, that midcentury plainness for which I hadn't yet developed my eye.

"Ha!" Lena tilted her head back for a better look. I dodged away as she fumbled for her video camera. "Oh, those are great!"

"No."

"They are." She stepped forward, squeezed my arm. "They're fabulous."

Her sarcasm was tender, where Marcus's was ruthless. He wanted me to feel like a rube. She instead just dripped gentle condescension. I was adorable, like a little boy playing dress-up.

"They're great. You can lead us all into the urban wilderness."

She turned and plucked an olive-green jacket from the rack next to us. It had some sort of brocade pattern on it, but she didn't even need to check for quality or fit, just tossed it into her cart.

"I'm getting near the ten-dollar limit," she sniffed. Off she went. I looked at Marcus.

"I'm buying these."

"Suit yourself."

I waited until Lena had passed safely across the room. "Why doesn't she want me to see her house?"

Marcus looked at the floor. "Did she say that?"

"No, but I can tell."

Whatever it was Lena wasn't saying, Marcus wasn't either. I'd overheard them talking once about the general extravagance of what they called the "Royal Manor," mocking her father's peculiarity, but they were being awfully tight-lipped now. All through the drive, Lena hadn't said word one about her family. Her dad owned a chain of low-budget legal clinics that operated on behalf of the city's ghetto poor. I gathered this had made him a very rich man—he was in the papers constantly—and if this seemed a little backwards or crass, it was hardly a crime. Their house was rumored to be the biggest in Ohio, and since he came from immigrant stock and his own parents had owned and operated a beloved local bakery, the columns loved to play up this angle as well. *The Caked Crusader*, they called him. But I didn't think Lena was simply ashamed of all this. Her evasion seemed to rest on something else.

"Don't worry about it," Marcus said. "Why don't you go pick out a leisure suit to go with those trousers? You can wear it tonight to The Second Hand."

"The Second Hand? Are we gonna go?"

"You were the one who wanted to see the sights."

The Second Hand was the ultimate musical mecca, the dive bar of my dreams. The Replacements had played there. Sonic Youth, Big Black, the Embarrassment, Big Dipper. How many nights had Marcus and his friends spent there, how many epochal rock 'n' roll experiences had I already missed? The Second Hand was also allegedly one of the few venues in which Lords of Oblivion were welcome anymore, one of the few that would book Nic Devine at all.

"We'll try The Second Hand," Marcus said, then lifted an eyebrow. "You never know."

"D'you think? Really?"

At this point the band's sets were mostly guerilla actions, underpromoted even when they were announced at all. The story was that Nic Devine had been kicked out of and/or banned from nearly every venue in Columbus for his reckless behavior, the fighting with bandmates and trashing of venues that seemed to me to be every real band's right. A detailed anecdote involving duct tape, fire extinguishers and underage cocktail waitresses had been sketched in the last issue of a local magazine called *The Attack*. But maybe Nic just needed someone to help him direct all this energy properly.

"Could be."

"Could be?" I snapped. "What does that mean, 'Could be?'"

Marcus shrugged. "You'll have to find out."

"Oh, give me a break."

"You think I'm kidding?"

"I think you're full of shit, yes. How do I know this band even exists anymore?"

He smirked. "Oh ye of little faith."

"Yes. Little faith. Why don't we just camp out in front of The Second Hand and wait?"

"OK. Those pants'll do nicely for a tent."

I laughed. But it was bitter and I was sick of him yanking my chain.

What if Nic Devine was just the middling-capable singer in some average
bar band, which my impressionable ears took too seriously? What kind of a
legend could you be, if all of four hundred people knew your name? If a singer
freaked out in a club and there was no one there to see it, was that rock 'n' roll
insanity or just a tantrum on a medium scale? For Marcus and I to love this
band all by ourselves suggested two alternatives. Either they sucked, or we did
but we just didn't see it. Nic, I thought. It wasn't like Marcus knew the guy
either, but together we affected the first-name familiarity of Tiger Beat readers,
hysterical pre-adolescent girls. At best it was juvenile, too silly. Whether
or not Nic was special, and even though the records—just two measly little
independent 45s—were fantastic. When I first heard them they'd changed my
life.

Marcus stroked his chin. He nodded down at my pants.

"So are you going to buy those? We've got places to get to."

3

Letter to A Fanzine

Here's how it started: I was walking down the hall in my freshman dorm and heard a racket. A real racket, not just the spacecake hippie jams that emanated from half the rooms on the hall I'd just transferred away from, nor the rubbery New Wave tedium that rang from the other half. This sound was furious, keen and exuberant. The singer sounded like he was being beaten to death. As I drew closer, the "song" dissolved into a psychedelic puddle, raw energy collapsing towards chaos. No synthesizers, no solos. It was music out of time.

"What's going on?" I asked one of the several people who were pushing down the hall away from it. Everyone except me. "What is that?"

"Two-seventeen," the guy said. A rat-faced kid from DC with his hat jammed low on his forehead. "Sucks."

"What, the room does?" I looked at the scrap of paper from the housing office. "Hey, two-seventeen—that's my room."

"Lucky you, dude. Maybe you can ask him to turn it down."

"Why don't you do it?"

He laughed. I recognized him from my cognitive science lab, and from the night he'd passed out in the quad and woke up mummified in paper towels. "Nah. It's that guy."

"Which guy?"

"The cat with the suits."

"I see."

I went down the hall. I knew who he meant, he meant that guy—that one guy—whose politeness struck others as intimidating. Here on a campus full of spiky punks and bully boys, maniacs who stripped naked or attempted suicide on the campus's closed-circuit television network, there wasn't really another way to interpret him. Good manners were a form of aggression. I pushed open the door.

"Hello—"

Hey! Hey! Hey! Let's go take ourselves a real long walk!
Your eyes are like axes, my head's on the block—

He was sitting on the gray-carpeted floor, hunched over a crappy plastic turntable, the kind that came in a suitcase, wired to an equally crappy pair of speakers. A spray of Dylanesque verbiage, hardly intelligible, exploded through these courtesy of the slender little 45 he was playing over and over again. The record ended in a shower of shrieking HEYs and backwards-tracked vocals, a refrain along the lines of I WANNA SEE YOU CRAWL! CRAWL! CRAWL! It was so cheaply pressed the needle slid from mid-chorus toward the label before the last note had ended, at which point he picked it up and placed it back at the beginning once more.

"Hey—"

HEY! HEY! HEY!

I had to wait for it to play through, two minutes and change before he looked up and saw me. At this point he grinned—he had a particular, toothy smile that seemed both inclusive and stand-offish, a sort of cross between a Cheshire Cat's and an ax murderer's—and shook his head before dropping the needle yet again.

HEY! HEY!

"What is this?" I yelled.

Because it really wasn't like the music I was already into. It was more primitive than the Ramones, yet more sophisticated than the Stooges; it was unselfconscious, noisy and thrilling, with one foot in the Delta past and another lodged deep in the future. It was wholly American, as raw as any Sun Records rockabilly 45 yet as catchy and immediate as the Beatles. It involved a Vox organ, lots of shouting, some basic guitar and drums that had been mic'd too softly or else too loud: the whole thing vibrated and echoed in a way that suggested there was no gentler volume at which to play it. It was all or nothing. A record made by people who loved life and hated women, unless it was the other way around.

"Lords Of Oblivion," he shouted. "Don't ya love it?"

"Yeah!" I yelled. Even if this wasn't true, yet. "Who are you?"

He wouldn't speak, until the record finished again.

"Shouldn't I be asking you that?"

"I'm your new roommate. Reassigned this morning."

"Yeah?"

"Yeah. I was Willie Hartnell's."

"Oh. Gosh." He nodded. "You weren't there when it happened?"

"No. I was at the Commons."

"Good. He'll be alright. He shouldn't have eaten that stuff."

"I'll say. The tube says 'for topical use only' so I can't imagine what he was thinking. Anyway, I was reassigned."

"Hmm." He stuck out his hand. "I'm Marcus."

"I know." I nodded towards the record-player. My ears were still ringing. "So...who are Lords of Oblivion?"

"You don't know?"

"I'm afraid not, no."

"Gosh." He sniffed. "That's a pity."

"Is it?"

"Yeah. I suppose you've never read *The Attack* either."

"Um, no. You'd better enlighten me."

He looked me up and down. "Where are yuh from?" he said. Distinctly, he said "yuh."

"L.A.," I said. "What about you?"

"Clumbus," he said—again, distinctly skipping the "o." "Clumbus, Uh-hi."

"Uh—" It sounded like Ojai, almost, but I wasn't that much of a rube. I knew what he meant. "Ohio, right. Near Michigan, sort of."

He looked me over again.

"Clumbus," he said, "is the pharmaceutical capital of the Midwest."

"Oh, there are—you mean they manufacture—"

"We have the best drugs." He beamed. "My dad's a pharmacologist, in fact. He's a professor at OSU."

"Oh."

"We have the most beautiful people."

"Yeah?"

"And the best rock 'n' roll bands in the world. The best scene."

"I see."

He shook a Chesterfield free from its pack. The room was empty except for the turntable, a steamer trunk, and some dorm furniture. It reeked of cigarette smoke, the fusty, old man's brand he was smoking. There was an electronic chess game, too. It bleeped, indicating it had just made a move against him. He reached over and moved his own piece, then looked back at me.

"The Hangman's Gang. Plains States. Dark Matter. You don't know those bands?"

"Nope."

In point of fact he'd hooked me with the drugs and girls. I'd had better luck, thus far, with music and books, but I was more hopeful—in a way—about the other two points of this sacred constellation. He tossed me the sleeve of the single he'd been holding: four dudes in retro-looking sixties clobber, standing around a nun, or just a girl in a nun costume. They glowered like troglodytes, in a black-and-white tableau that seemed to want to suggest some sort of scene or story, but didn't. They were just four guys in old-fashioned clothes, loitering on an ordinary staircase. The girl appeared to have been imported from somewhere else, perhaps a Catholic school in Elmira, where she'd been the prettiest girl in her elocution class. Together they looked like mismatched figures in a wax museum. One guy especially had blunt-cut bangs and a goofy turtleneck and wide lapels on his pinstriped suit, like he'd missed being in the Beatles by about nine years and twice as many fired bass players, not to mention fifty IQ points.

"Hmph," I said. I'd never seen a sleeve that looked as cheap, either. The lettering was all lopsided, the ink smudgy. "How many cereal box-tops exactly did you spend on this?"

I tossed the record back to Marcus. Noticing before I did the flipside was a song called "The Backstage Door," which would turn out to sound exactly like the other.

"It doesn't quite suck though." I nodded my head, warming to it. "Play it again, would ya?"

This was how Marcus and I met. Of all the dorm rooms in all the hallways of Harper College I walked into his, drawn by two minutes and ten seconds of alienated hollering and catchy handclaps. The beginning of our beautiful friendship, as we obsessed over that record together, and over reports gathered from *The Attack* (which proved to be a local but influential fanzine, the nexus and bullhorn of Columbus's thriving Indie rock scene, curated by a mysterious man we knew only as "Tim") that Nic Devine, head troglodyte and pinstriped fifth-Beatle understudy, might actually be getting ready to make another.

"What does it say?"

"It says—" Marcus snatched his copy of the mimeographed fanzine, mailed to him by his still more precocious younger sister, or else by his friend Aaron Fratelli, founding member of Animal Suffrage as everyone who read *The Attack* surely knew—"Lords of Oblivion opened, and were cut short after ten minutes when a fight broke out onstage—"

"Ooh!"

"—between singer Nic Devine and his drummer Billy Williamson, who left with a black eye and a concussion—"

"Cool."

"—but not before they'd managed to alienate a roomful of heads with their grandiose melding of sixties psychedelia and seventies proto-punk. Unreleased opener 'I Always Carry A Lightbulb' came on like The Small Faces dry-humping 'Rocket From The Tombs,' while their inability to get through a second song suggests the rest of you will never find out exactly what that sounds like. For fans of Suicide, Sparks, Uriah Heep and the Flamin' Groovies only—"

"Wow!"

We lay together on the floor of our dorm room, beneath a low-hanging cirrus of Chesterfield smoke. I wasn't a fan of any of those bands, yet I knew exactly what it sounded like: like my wildest dreams and nightmares conflated. I had to see that band, absolutely had to, before I died. It would be like the witness of a miracle, something I could see in order to believe. Then, maybe, I could tell other people. Yet—who knew if I would ever be able to?

"You oughta come to Clumbus sometime."

"Ya think?"

We passed our fanzines back and forth, copies of *The Attack* and *Forced Exposure* we kept in glassine baggies as if they were invaluable issues of *Action Comics or Amazing Fantasy #15, introducing Spiderman.* I suppose they were, in a sense, these frail testaments to the impossible.

"Yep."

Outside it was bitter New England winter, but in here—in our hearts, warmed by the kindling of Lords of Oblivion 45s both real and imagined—it was at once Christmas and forever Spring. Marcus tapped his Hush Puppied foot, and bare branches stirred outside our window, which was cobwebbed with frost. I wore a pair of ash-gray slacks and one of Marcus's borrowed cardigans. In these, I was about as cool as Mr. Rodgers. I'd become a Columbus groupie, as impassioned about the city as I was about the band. I knew the names of the bars and the locations of the thrift stores, I spoke of Marcus's high school friends as though they were already my own. I met Lena when she transferred mid-semester from RISD, and her art-school beauty offered further proof the place was ineffable. All paled before the mystery of Nic Devine, the rock star no one else had ever heard of, whose prowling, catlike cool was my obsession. I'd missed it at first, the fact his dull scowl was in fact a face of the One True Punk, as iconic as Iggy Pop's or Roky Erickson's. Why weren't there statues, record deals, magazine covers? Why wasn't he more widely—or even at all—loved? Inside Columbus he antagonized people. *The Attack* wrote of him first with bemused tolerance and then with contempt, which he fed back by spray-painting F.T.A.—'Fuck The Attack,' allegedly— across one of his speaker cabinets. Outside Columbus they were unheard of, except in Sweden where a visionary man named Anders Baeklund, owner of a label called Glitterwig, licensed the record and managed to push it briefly into the national independent charts, where it peaked at number thirty-eight. Whatever a hit in Sweden was worth. Still, Today Sweden, Tomorrow The World, I reasoned. Someday people would know! It was the sound that told the story beneath the cheap production, the song's monstrous, irresistible hook. Even if here you still had to write to a P.O. Box in Columbus to obtain a copy. I did so and for this trouble received—o priceless treasure—a handwritten note from the man himself. It was barely legible.

Hey Man! It began. And lapsed immediately into something that mightn't have been intelligible even if I could've read it, some sort of scoobly-oobly Motor City babble that was its own form of charged-though-not-quite-politicized discourse, a real yank-'em-crank-'em-eat-me-beat-me screed. There was a frenzied pencil sketch of a pyramid, and a brief disquisition about (I think) the health benefits of amino acids, a rant about the Federal Reserve and something else about "the third eye." Either way, it signed off—from someone I'd never met—*Yr pal, Nic.*

Hmm. Well I gained with it a copy of the band's brand spanking new single, which was called "Caveman Stomp" and which was even more arrogant, more frenzied and punitive than the first. In the intervening months, Nic—I really did feel free now to call him by his first name only with us being pals and all (and what the hell kind of name was that, anyway? It had to be a stage name)—had grown out his hair and with it his sound, producing a freaked out and freewheeling, almost free-jazz skronk, a crazed theatrical yammering that added cat-calls, war whoops, jungle-drums and saxophones to that trebly madness that had been so not-nearly-successful the first time. The guitar-heavy production, credited again to one "Donovan's Brain," sounded once more like shit, which is to say fantastic in its own subversive way.

I'm so anti-social, I got a disastrous attitude
(Something something someone—I could never work this part out) *—was my kinda dude!*
I'm proper primitive, true caveman, Neanderthal!
I'll scramble your brains for breakfast, leave paintings on your walls!

I doubted I could've said it any better myself, what it was like to be alive and confused, so happy I could kill someone and so angry I could laugh. I played it for Marcus. He agreed.

"I wish I'd written that." He scratched his beard. The inability to really grow one made him look like a piece of moldy fruit, but this too would pass. It was part of a Kris Kristofferson phase that would be over by Monday. "It's so—"

"Abusive!" I stood over by the window, and what was now our crappy turntable hooked to those same shitty speakers. "Like he's trying to push us all away!"

He'd succeeded, once more, insofar as the hall outside was empty. Someone thumped three times on our door, in passing, as if to say *Fuck you, too.*

"It's perfect. That riff is totally stolen though."

"Yeah, but who cares? He makes it new!"

This was the knock on Nic, leveled again and again in the pages of *The Attack* and elsewhere: that he and his band were unoriginal, overdependent on sounds from the past. Were bands, or artists, supposed to be original, I wondered? Or was everything carried over from somewhere else? In any case I'd never heard records that sounded like Nic's, not really. He sang like he was walking across hot coals, his whole body vibrating with private belief: I wanted to live in the woods with him, so long as I could have a battery-powered turntable on which to play his records, desperately wanted to meet whoever it was he was calling out as his "kinda dude" in the song's third verse. Who was it? I could never tell, but whoever it was, that person couldn't possibly match Nic's sincerity, his intensity. The balls of my feet itched whenever I listened. I wanted to steal a car, get into a fistfight, hit the road and head to Mexico: do all the rock 'n' roll things I might otherwise never have dreamed. For three minutes I was immortal. If I played that record once, I played it a thousand times. Marcus and I both did.

"Whatcha doin' this summer?"

At last, it was spring. We walked together across the campus's muddy quad, the last snow still melting, puddling through my oversized wingtips.

"Not sure. Probably working as an intern somewhere, serving the whims of the famous. Why?"

"You should come to Columbus. We'll hook you up with an apartment. You can get one for like a hundred bucks a month."

We passed underneath some barely-blossoming apple trees, their greening sprigs the truest sign of life there was. I brushed back the hair I was growing long, myself, in tribute. My cheek stung in the lingering cold as though someone had slapped it. I rubbed the other.

"Yeah. The living's easy," he said. "You should come."

Did I believe him? All that stuff about how the merchants scarcely charged you for anything, how you could stay up all night and sleep all day and dig the pennies out of your pocket for drinks tickets, chocolate bars, mix tapes and beer. It seemed to me there were holes in his stories, but weren't there in any story that was worth telling? Weren't there even in Ohio itself? ("Round at the ends and 'hi' in the middle," as the saying went.) The startling acoustic strains of Nic's last B side, "Flower Power" (*Every minute, every hour!* went the refrain) ran through my head, while under my arm there was the mimeographed Coleridge poem I'd spent the morning discussing in my Romantic Lit seminar. "This Lime Tree Bower My Prison." I thought of my father, running amok with his silver Porsche and his gold earring, his eagerness to drink me under the table like some demented teenager in a fifty-three year old's body. My mother was in rehab, struggling to stay clean; my sisters were out running up credit card debt, binging on vodka and squid ink ravioli. My family exhausted me. It was such a fight when I went home to see and be seen clearly. I felt invisible there, drained. Only elsewhere it seemed could I be understood. From that perspective too, Columbus was as good a place as any.

"Sure."

It was a whim. Even if none of the things Marcus told me were true, how bad could a summer—just one—in Columbus, Ohio really be?

"Yeah, alright." We ducked back into our dorm. "I'd love to know just how much lipstick you've been putting on that pig, anyway. You talk about that place like it's the Emerald City."

"It is the Emerald City." Marcus flashed that angelic-maniacal smile I'd grown to love, if not to trust. "When you take the right drugs."

"I'm sure."

I could feign all the skepticism I wanted. But the fact was, I was hooked. Shaking my head I added, "Hey, ho! Let's go!"

4

Farmers' Daughters

We pulled up in the long driveway of the Royal Mansion. White gravel crunched under our tires. Birds twittered in the branches of the two Japanese maples that framed the front door, thick as a fortress's. Even by the distended standards I'd observed back home this place was impressive, a monstrous chalk-colored outcropping of limestone and mortar that must've had at least ten bedrooms. Its own stature walled it off as effectively as a moat. There was no street to speak of. The house sat by itself at the end of a long avenue of maples and elms, in a quiet corner of a suburb called Wilkerton Heights. Lena stiffened as we pulled up the drive. I could see the tension in her neck, her jaw pulsing as she worked on a piece of cinnamon gum. It was obvious she didn't want to go home any more than I did. I shifted against the mountain of camphor-smelling sweaters and shirts piled beside me in the backseat, enough clothes to last me a lifetime even as I still wore my denigrated trousers. I'd rehabilitate them all by myself. Invisible Dan closed his book and stared yearningly at the house, while Lena hopped out and scurried towards the front door. I guess she wasn't going to invite any of us in.

"Take the car," she called back to Marcus. "I won't be needing it 'til later."

She slipped inside. I caught a glimpse of her dad, a bearish man with a sandy-brown beard and rose-tinted sunglasses, a barrel chest parting his silk bathrobe. He looked like a Jewish gangster. Lena ducked his embrace, and the door swung shut behind them. For a moment we sat in the silence of the long drive, the engine ticking in the morning heat. The windows of the house were like arctic water, dark and reflective. You couldn't see anything except the trees outside, the still branches outlined against the sky. Somewhere in the distance I heard rushing liquid, a creek that must've run along the margins of the property. Marcus got out and came around to take the wheel and Dan murmured, "So. This is the place, eh?"

"What place?"

His voice trembled with suppressed violence. How close love could run to hate, when it was rejected! He twisted his lips coyly. "The place where it happened. The slaughter of the bourgeois pigs."

"God, what are you, Charles Manson? It's nineteen eighty-seven, not nineteen sixty-seven!"

Marcus got back into the car.

"What happened?" I said to him. "Marcus, what happened here?"

He sighed, and looked at Dan. "Have you been spreading rumors again?"

But what had happened, he explained as we pulled away, heading back over to Wilkerton Square—how embarrassing that I might identify the city's subdivisions even, Bexley, Grove City, German Village, Campus; I felt like a stamp-collector or a model-train enthusiast in my insane devotion to this city's minutiae—was a quadruple homicide many years before. Fourteen summers ago a teenaged boy woke up one day and ate a bunch of LSD, then butchered his father, stepmother and twin sisters with a kitchen knife. It was one of those local episodes that had gained a certain tenancy in legend, embroidering itself into a ghost story. The house was haunted. In fact it had stood empty until seven years ago, when Lena and her family moved in.

"Her brother started hearing things," Marcus said.

"Wait—Lena has a brother?"

"Her brother started hearing things," he repeated. I thought I knew Lena fairly well—we'd been hallmates also; she cut my hair and kept me company whenever I fought with my own family, but now I wondered that I might know her not at all. "He started waking up at night. There were noises, voices—"

"Oh come on!"

"It's true. He freaked out, had some sort of a breakdown."

"He did?"

Marcus nodded. "He's in Central Ohio Psychiatric. He's been there a year and a half."

I didn't know whether this was true. Maybe it was just another of Marcus's extravagant fantasies. We slid past a quaint-looking cemetary, mossy headstones all askew like decaying teeth. I was beginning to suspect Marcus's fear of the truth was pathological.

"How old is Lena's brother?"

"Three years older than she is. Peter."

"So is that why she gets quiet, whenever someone mentions her family?"

"Pretty much." Marcus shrugged. "That's pretty much it."

Pretty much. Hmph. Well, I guessed if it were my brother—if I had a brother, who'd done such a thing—I mightn't mention him much either. Things were never as they appeared. Wasn't that the obvious lesson here? I rolled down my window to savor the taste of that Middle American air I'd begun to get used to, stared out at the houses that, in their Colonial plainness, were about as close to exotic as I'd yet found. But if the magic of this place was already beginning to fade—if I was a gull, a stooge, a dupe—at least I wasn't alone. Invisible Dan had fallen for it just like I had. Together we stared out of our respective windows, searching the suburban landscape perhaps for something that was not there.

****

A car whisked in front of us as we pulled into the parking lot of the Wilkerton Square Mall, a gleaming silver Porsche 914 driven by one of the most beautiful girls I'd ever seen. There were two in the front seat, both redheads. Music blared from their stereo, that proto-Gothic, cheap-drum-machine-based sound that was a mating call for our tribe—the March Violets' "The Lights Go Out"—so I sat forward and watched as they parked nearby and tumbled out, gripping each other in a tangle of long limbs and Nordic skin. They gasped in shared hilarity, then straightened up and waved to us. Oh, thank you, I breathed, to whoever it was one thanked for such things. Thank you.

"Marcus, Marcus Gerard!" one of them hollered, a tall girl whose scarlet hair fell just past her shoulders. Her face was a cluster of pale asymmetries. "Who are your friends?"

My throat tightened as she came forward and offered a winningly un-self-conscious smile. We were stopping for coffee, but I didn't need it now.

"Hi."

"Hi."

In the background Marcus and the other girl—more conventionally pretty perhaps, but less interesting to me—embraced without speaking. Invisible Dan slunk round to the trunk to retrieve his bag, then raced off towards the Ramada Inn across the lot, clean shirt in hand.

"Iceleaf," the girl said.

"What?"

"Iceleaf." She looked at me like I was stupid. I felt stupid, looking at her. Her green eyes seemed both wide-awake and drowsy. Beneath narrowed lids, they pierced me to the quick.

"I—"

I stood there a minute, my ears still ringing, head ablaze with music, wind and sleeplessness. Did they speak English, here in…Columbus?

"*I'm Felice,*" she said now, crisply, clearly. "It's customary on this planet to tell people your name, you know, when you meet them?"

Still smiling. My God, she was beautiful—hardly less so than that other girl—with eyebrows like sidelong commas, cheeks that grew hollow when she sucked them in to consider me.

"Hey Marcus, your friend here's not the sharpest tool in the shed, is he?"

"Sure he is," Marcus called back, "he's sharp as a razor. The old knife's edge."

This girl shortened my breath. It hurt to look at her.

"I'm—"

I couldn't trust myself not to maul my own name. *Mad fool. Masshole.* Finally, I just shook her hand. While she looked me up and down, taking my measure. It wasn't just that she was pretty. There was a lustiness, a liveliness that made Marcus's geriatric fetishism feel silly.

"Nice pants."

"Thanks, you like 'em?"

"Sure do. Where's your Oldsmobile?"

Marcus, meanwhile, was still over with the other girl. I recognized her now, as he'd shown me her picture in Italian *Vogue*. Her name was Kitty Shore, and she looked like a screen goddess from the 1930s. Auburn hair cascaded Veronica Lake-ishly around her high cheekbones; hazel eyes sparkled above a Platonic dream of a nose. Such lunar beauty was easiest to appreciate from a distance. I couldn't imagine this girl sneezing, or sleeping or falling down. She and Marcus had known each other since grade school, became better friends while he was living in Geneva and she modeling in Paris. I couldn't help but notice too the size of the ring she was wearing, its stone almost the size of a ping pong ball. A Diamond As Big As The Weberman Medical Center.

"Oh Marcus!" she cooed. Did all the people here sound English? Since her accent really was—Mancunian? Liverpudlian? "It's so lovely to see you!"

"It's luvvly to see yew tew, Kit!" Marcus countered with a fake Appalachian. "What's with the funny voice?"

She gave a hostess's smile. Every wrinkle, every muscle on that face seemed deliberately arranged. It was like she could see herself more clearly than we could, possibly, knew everything her expression was doing from instant to instant: that strange gift of the too frequently photographed. Then she laughed, and with another voice entirely, an accent centered a little south of here—Tennessee?—she said, "Aw, it's just a little somethin' I picked up overseas."

They both laughed, hysterically. I looked back at Felice. She was the more stunning for being less rehearsed.

"That's a nice ring she's got," I said.

"Yep. You jealous?"

"Nah. Are you?"

Kitty stomped her foot. Glittering red VTE heels. "Ah'm gittin' hitched!" she crowed, camping up the Southernness now. It was genuine, at its base.

"You is?" Marcus took her arm.

"Yup. Knobby's makin' an honest woman outta me!"

"Wow, congratulations!" Marcus said. "When?"

Slowly, we angled towards the Bob Evans restaurant across the lot. I said to Felice, "Knobby?"

"Her boyfriend," she stage whispered. "He's a rock star!"

We were together too, unfortunately not arm-in-arm, behind them. A yellow butterfly spiraled drunkenly in front of us, reeling in the heat.

"A rock star, huh? Bigger than Nic Devine?"

"Who?"

"Never mind."

It was heart-stoppingly hot, the air like wet gauze. My first sustained encounter with the Midwestern humidity. Sun stewed the asphalt underneath us to a soft texture, like an urban basketball court at high noon. It was barely nine in the morning. The details poured out as we walked. Kitty was engaged to a man, an English fellow whose band was indeed popular—not just with our kind, but beyond—whom she'd met when she was in London on a modeling assignment. It was a big deal. She'd been in the UK tabloids, was home in Columbus now to get away while her man toured America.

"The important thing," Felice said, "is that she's going back. She's leaving."

"Is that good?" I slowed down. Heat or no heat, I wanted to prolong a moment alone in this girl's company, make it last.

"That's great. I'm getting out of this burg too."

"Yeah? It's too cool for you?"

We stood for a second. Her Levis were spattered with paint and pale muck—I'd find out in time that this was clay, that she was a painter and a sculptor—and she wore a white, man's oxford shirt untucked and unironed. It was this carelessness that made her natural beauty swim to the surface. Where I came from girls seemed to work so hard, women paid to have lips that full and skin that clear. It was practically all they did, in Los Angeles, aspiring to the condition that was this girl's strictly by chance. *Those Midwest farmers' daughters*, as the song had it, Brian Wilson's music-box melody floating through my brain. Her eyes were light green, hair an exaggerated, theatrical red like a doll's. She dragged on a cigarette then picked a scrap of tobacco from its unfiltered end off her lip with her fingers. This gesture seemed sexy as hell.

Where there was smoke, there had to be fire.

"So where you gonna go?" I said.

"Trinity," she said. "There's a scholarship waiting for me there."

"Oh." I smiled. Weak as I was on geography, I was pretty sure Connecticut was still next door to Massachusetts until they moved it. "That's excellent, since—"

"Unless I go to England too. There's a potter in Southampton who wants me to be their apprentice. I'm thinking of chucking the scholarship. I might just travel for a while too. My plans are sort of...up in the air."

"Oh." My heart plummeted. We were climbing up the steps of the Bob Evans. I knew where Southampton was. It was nowhere near Massachusetts. "Are you leaving soon, or—"

"September. I have to make up my mind, though. The school keeps threatening to release my scholarship money."

We stopped on the threshold of the restaurant—half in, half out— while she shook a cigarette out of her pack and lit it.

"I see."

"So what's your excuse?" She blew smoke.

"Huh? Do I need one?"

She laughed. What a sound.

"You certainly do."

"For what?"

"For Clumpy."

"Clumpy?"

She gestured now, back towards the mall, her cigarette a schoolmarm's pointer. The others were all inside: I could see Dan scowling at the salad bar's infinite bounty, poking with tongs at a bit of wilted lettuce. Oh, let us, I thought.

"Clump-beef. This place."

"Um, I'm just here for the Summer."

"Good God man, why? Did you do something wrong? The judge wouldn't send you to Attica?"

I looked with her out at the parking lot, watched a woman trying to pack a baby-dinosaur-sized man behind the wheel of a dun-colored Toyota

Celica, literally wedging him in with both hands. I thought of fifties Fratboys stuffing a phone booth, a practice I'd only ever seen lampooned in *Mad* magazine. Felice's perfume, a muted blend of vanilla and honeysuckle essential oils, pierced both tobacco smoke and exhaust.

"You're saying I made a mistake?"

"I'd say so. Yeah."

She blew smoke, then flipped her cigarette out into the lot. It spiraled off into the damp, hot air. Just so, she dismissed me, turning and pushing the door open upon the restaurant's blessed, air-conditioned coolness. Calling, "Hey, Marcus, you've got a live one here, huh? Are they all this dense where you go to school?"

"Nah, it's a West Coast thing. He'll catch up!"

I followed her back towards the table, watching the twin crescents of white skin flash below her pants pockets, where she'd razored the seat of her jeans. She would lead, and I would follow. *Catch up*. There was nothing in this world I wanted to do more.

5

The Universal

Her surname was something like Baillard, but her family had anglicized it, dropping a vowel as they crossed the ocean to land, somehow, not just in the New World but in Columbus, Ohio. Her father was a professor at OSU, an astrophysicist who'd come over from Cambridge in the mid-1960s to work on a team that was building the world's largest telescope. Her mother lived in a mud hut, an hour south of Toledo. She was an art teacher, the freest of free spirits. Both of them were English, hippies who'd gotten divorced just after Felice was born. Nevertheless, she had dual citizenship, a fact which—she explained to me proudly—could allow her to live in England indefinitely. She'd barely been there since she was a baby yet in her mind, she insisted, England was home. For this reason she was thinking of chucking the National Merit Scholarship she'd been awarded to go work instead as a potter's apprentice.

"You're a ceramicist?"

"I throw pots, yeah." She swamped her coffee with sugar. "Mostly I just want to get out of here."

"It's really that bad, huh?"

"You know that song, 'Heaven is a place where nothing ever happens?'"

"Sure."

"It was obviously written by somebody who'd never been to Columbus."

"I see." I filched a cigarette from her pack. Not that I smoked, but I decided to start right here if it would lend my mouth commonality with hers. "I wish I'd known that before."

"Oh, Marcus likes to tell stories." She giggled. "We put up with it here because he amuses us."

Everything about her charmed me. The small spur of her wrist became a brand new reason for living. A shy, self-deprecating streak meant I didn't have to pretend around her, ever. I was rooked, hooked, ass-over-teakettle.

"I can't believe you fell for it! Jesus! This place is a tar pit, a mosquito trap! I'd rather spend a summer cleaning stables at a racetrack than be stuck here another minute."

"Really? It can't be that bad"

She squinted at me. "I don't know what Marcus told you, but really, handsome, you've been had."

She was younger than the others, and in fact had just graduated from an experimental high school called the RP, in Wilkerton Hills. Marcus had been there, and Lena too, all of these kids whose fey quirks and intellectual oddities were thrown into relief by our surroundings: a chain restaurant where our waitress could easily have pinned the bunch of us to our tabletop with one, shank-sized forearm. People stared. It was like living in a fish tank, almost like being rock stars ourselves, the degree of quizzical, if hostile, attention they offered us. I felt as if we were Lilliputians, Munchkins, little people who'd dared to enter their sprawling, doughy kingdom. Felice stood up to use the bathroom and I saw as I hadn't earlier the battered paperback copy of *Lost Illusions* shoved in her back pocket.

"You like that book?" I said when she returned. It happened I'd spent the last semester obsessing over *Père Goriot, Cousin Bette.* Balzac was my favorite novelist, at the time.

"Haven't started it yet. I liked the title."

"Oh," I said. "You're a big fan of...disappointment?"

"Nah," she said. "That's not something I go looking for, but...I've liked other books of his. Have you read *Père Goriot?*"

Together we leaned against the window, facing one another in the far end of the booth until meddlesome Marcus—curse him!—interrupted, saying, "Have you talked to Donnie?"

He meant Donnie Haas, who may have been the friend of theirs about whom I'd heard the most. He was in New York, at Columbia, and by all accounts the smartest, craziest and most glamorous person here. He'd been expelled from Harvard, for reasons that went undiscussed; in high school, he'd assayed an amateur translation of *Swann's Way* and had an affair with the head of a cosmetics corporation who later committed suicide. Not only was he a casual chemist—a Comp Lit major, he also manufactured his own LSD in the basement dorm—but he'd slept with four members of a famous English rock band versus Kitty's one: boys and girls alike. *There's really no gauge for how wild Donnie is*, Marcus had assured me, *He's off the charts*. In light of Marcus's own fits of chemical recklessness, this seemed impossible. The way Donnie was described, I pictured a cartoon Tasmanian Devil, a diminutive Timothy Leary type, touched with an evangelical fire.

"Nope. I think he's in Troy, with Jamie," she said. "I think he'll turn up."

"Sure, if he's not dead."

"Hush your mouth! My Donniella is not dead!"

"You never know." Marcus twisted his lips wryly. "With Donnie things could always be worse. But I'll betcha when he shows up, if he shows up, he brings us a little something extra."

"Ooh!" Felice rubbed her palms together—they made a chafing sound, their dry skin chapped and cracked almost like clay pots themselves— "Sanity Claus is comin' to town!"

I yawned, casting about for anything that might help me recapture this girl's drifting attention. I wanted to resume our talk about *A Sentimental Education*, romans-à-clef—I didn't care what we talked about, so long as we did—but couldn't find words.

"Did you know Louis Althusser never learned to masturbate until he was twenty-seven?"

"Is that right?" Felice licked a finger, and rubbed a bit of buttermilk dressing off my chin. God knows how long it had been there. "I guess he wasn't much smarter than your average chimpanzee, then."

Beside us, Dan just moped and stared at his coffee cup. For a moment I could feel his pain. My year in the liberal arts wilderness had left me without a girlfriend. At our school, no one seemed to bother with such things anyway: they just wrapped themselves in latex and fucked it—a boy, a girl, a cantaloupe for all I knew—if they were hungry. (I'd never done that, the cantaloupe thing: it was girls only, for me thus far.) At our school, politics were leftist, but sexuality was imperial. You simply took what you wanted. Compared to the kaleidoscopic patterning of that campus, the sexual and romantic mores here in the Midwest—that was an engagement ring Kitty wore, and none of us were yet twenty-one—looked almost achingly old-fashioned. I accepted Felice's consolation gift of a paper napkin and some Cremora with a heavy heart.

"Chimps are a little smarter than you think," I said, "y'know—"

But she was already lost to me, leaning over to pluck Marcus's sleeve, asking him again if he thought Donnie was bringing LSD. I looked at Invisible Dan, busy pouring more, still more sugar into his coffee, devising that sand-textured substance that would become the summer's official foodstuff and drink. We would christen it—*The Foom-Bah!*

"What say there, buddy? Having a good time?"

He just nodded. I'd never met a more innocuous person. At the same time, I felt obscurely, almost occultly connected to him all of a sudden. I stole another cigarette from Felice's pack, fired it up. An addiction, like a new star, was born. As I stared out the window, the only place I could find to look that wasn't directly at her.

****

"—wake up!"

A hand knocked the car window from outside. I had no recollection of how I'd gotten from Bob Evans back into Lena's Jetta and then unconscious all over again. Yet I had and now Felice, who'd come with us instead of Kitty (the latter had needed to dash to pick up her fiancé at the airport) was bidding me farewell.

"Sorry to disturb your rest there, Sleeping Beauty. But I did want to say it was nice to meet you."

I struggled to roll down the window, blinking at her face, the fringes of sunlight behind it.

"Sleeping Beaut—what?

"I, Miceleaf," she said. "You, Spaceman. Hello?"

"Oh. Right." I mopped drool off my cheek. Realized she might have had a beautiful view of my tonsils, and up my nose. "Nice to—have impressed you too," I mumbled.

"It's alright," she said, still smiling. "I'll see you later."

The car idled in front of a Georgian two-story house on the corner of a street called Apple Drive. Behind a picket fence a tire swing swayed in the hot breeze, above a lawn spotted with nasturtiums and dandelions. Standing further back in the front door was a paunchy boy with glasses, thirteen or so. His smirk was warped and mischievous, perhaps even a little worse than "mischievous." His feet were huge, I noticed even from here.

"Bye."

She turned and trotted up the front walk. The smell of summer grass seemed to rise up, as though directly from her. I stared up for a second towards what I guessed—knew somehow, intuited—was her bedroom window. Where I yearned to be.

"Harry, get the hell inside," she yelled to the boy. "Git! Go on, shoo! Get along, little doggie! Go!"

He evaporated like a smoke signal, an odor in stiff wind. *Presto!* He skittered back into the house ahead of her. His ratty plaid flannel shirt's tails flapped behind him, his pasty frame suggesting years of sedentation, of day-and-night television watching. As this street seemed the very apex and apotheosis of suburban American quiet, this Harry seemed to be the very apex and apotheosis, the *ne plus ultra* of obnoxious kid brothers. Ah well, every family had its irritant, the grain of sand necessary to produce a pearl. I sat up. Marcus put the car in gear. The radio played The Smiths, a song about how it was all "just a fairytale." Dan turned around, and I saw one of the penaes of his glasses was cracked. It looked like someone had shot him in the eye.

"Jesus! What happened to you?"

"Thick People," he said, with a certain masochistic satisfaction it seemed to me. Blood smudged his teeth. He rode shotgun while Marcus drove.

"Thick People? What are 'Thick People?'" I muttered.

But I didn't really think I needed to know. Instead, I twisted around to take one last look at Felice's house as it dwindled into the distance. Like a pinprick, I thought: a tiny heart of infinity.

6

Chartered Trips

We parked on High Street and made a mad dash for the bar. Ten o'clock on a Friday night, and the street thronged with fraternity types, beefcake boys escorting wobbly blondes who lolled unsteadily and bumped into our paths—school was out, for the summer!—looking a little too eager to show-us-their-tits. Music bumped from the storefronts as we passed, the slaughterhouse howls of AC/DC's "Hell's Bells," the syrupy synth hook of Springsteen's "Dancing In the Dark." We began running the instant we opened the car door, for reasons I couldn't quite figure. Marcus set the pace as we raced past rib joints and fast food palaces that seemed to be advertising the sale of whole cows, bone-in.

"Why are we running?" I gasped.

We'd stopped at his house earlier for a brief nap. We picked up Felice and now were on our way to meet the fabled Donnie, who may or may not have been bringing us drugs. This was all I knew. And then a beer can went whistling by my head. Not an empty one but a full, sixteen-ounce tallboy.

"FAAAGGGOOOTTSSSSS!"

The can exploded against a wall. It could've knocked me cold. It wasn't lobbed or tossed playfully; it was full-on pitched out of a speeding car by a guy who might've weighed two-hundred fifty pounds even before he sat down at BW3 Chicken to wash down a thousand chicken wings with a gallon of blue cheese dressing. I'd never seen people this big, men like skyscrapers, corn-fed elephantine boys who were offensive linemen—hell, offensive lines unto themselves—for the Ohio State Buckeyes, crew cut cops with constipation-red faces. Cruising to bruise us, only us.

"Hey! Hey faggot—"

A bottle shattered at my feet. Felice grabbed my wrist (she was a "faggot" too, apparently) and yanked me reeling along High. I understood now. Columbus was a shooting gallery and we were the ducks for the muscle boys who'd try to kill us. Thick People, thick of neck, heart, body and skull. If they'd had souls those would have been thick too, made of vulcanized rubber or neoprene, that foam stuff they used to make beer sleeves. We made it the block and a half between the car and the bar's door without further incident. Two near cripplings in sixty seconds was enough. We were inside Perry's, a DMZ the Thick People wouldn't enter because it was said to be a gay bar. It wasn't, though the rumor had been started by the bar's owners themselves in order to keep them away, restrain them from peeing in the kegorators and puking in the troughs. As soon as we were inside Marcus and Felice began laughing.

"Does that happen a lot?" I asked them, gasping for breath as we slid into a booth.

"Now and then," Felice said. "It's best not to go outside while they're afoot."

"Which is?"

"Pretty much every hour of every day except during football games. After which they usually want to kick everything that isn't nailed down."

"How can you stand it?" I asked. "Those Mongol hordes!"

"I know." She smiled. "Stay close."

Marcus waved to a straight-looking girl across the room: black band tee, blue jeans, Converse All Star sneakers. I glowed. Stay close.

"Maraharmon, Maraharmon!" Marcus yelled, as we made our way towards the girl.

I looked around. The clean, dimly-lit oasis of Perry's Bar seemed an improbable setting in which to score drugs. It was as if we'd decided to go find them at a supermarket, some sunny, commercial outlet where they would indeed know our names long after we ourselves were too stoned to remember them. Little brass-necked reading lamps hovered over every table. The walls were exposed brick, the booths padded and comfortable. In many ways it was more like a library than a neighborhood watering hole, though it had a great jukebox stocked with indie and sixties 45s and—what truly distinguished it from other High Street bars like Gepetto's and Buffalo Bill's—it did not smell remotely like vomit. Perry's served its beer in civilized bottles, rather than in amber spheres the size of bowling balls or human heads, those strange plastic half-gallon conveyances which only completed the penal-*cum*-Viking fearsomeness of those bruisers who were out there hunting our very skulls. The very notion of taking acid on top of this seemed questionable. At the very least, I wondered, it might've been redundant. Looking at our new friend with the curious name, whose well-scrubbed and decent-looking exterior was—likewise, in light of where I'd just been, the crazed, psychedelic cradle of Marcus's family—strangely disorienting in its own right.

"Hiya, Marcus," this girl—"Maraharmon," apparently—said. "Where you been, boy?"

****

As he pulled Lena's Jetta into the driveway of his own house that morning, Marcus had turned to me.

"I should warn you," he said. "About my family."

We were alone. Dan was sleeping at Lena's. Marcus's tone seemed funny to me. Could they be any weirder than Marcus himself? His house looked almost exactly like Felice's, tenderly suburban, and stood at the top of a development called Wilkerton Hills. A serpentine road wound round and round to get to it, corkscrewing up towards a hilltop's peak. We spiraled past block after block of clipped grass and colonial architecture, lawn jockeys and garden gnomes, arriving finally at a yellow house where a basketball hoop hung in neglected shreds above the garage. If Marcus had ever seen a basketball, let alone shot one, I'd eat my own foot.

"Warn me? What're you, my grandfather?" We climbed out of the car. "You think I don't know about eccentric families? I should remind you that mine's a little off the—"

"Marcus!" A tiny woman, all of five-three, came bounding out of the house. "Oh my goodness, we were expecting you yesterday!"

She leapt into Marcus's arms. She looked like a Buckingham Palace guard with her furry black top and pale complexion, the reddish blush spots on her cheeks.

"Are you eating? Sleeping?" She sniffed. "Oh, you've been smoking! Oh, Marcus, please stop!"

That this was his mother was incontestable. She looked just like him, only squashed, foreshortened. She was anxious, wound up just like a hypochondriac—only with all her alarm concentrating on others, as she asked me the exact same questions, taking my wrist as if she wanted to feel my pulse.

"Oh, sweetheart, we've heard so much about you! We're so happy you've come!"

Marcus blushed too, staring down at those Hush Puppies while she coddled him. She dragged us both into the living room by our wrists.

"Mawkus!" His dad bounced up from a couch that appeared as a riot of color, its horizontal corduroy wales conflicting with the zigzag lightning bolt pattern on his loud polyester shirt. It was like the one across David Bowie's face on the cover of *Aladdin Sane*. He raked a hand through his silvering, Robert Reed afro. "I'm so glad you're here!"

I scarcely knew where to look. This room and the adjacent kitchen were a clamor of drab greens, khakis, dull browns and oranges. Marcus's father's black-and-white shirt completed a messy spectrum, like that of a television on the fritz. He introduced himself to me. His accent was pure Long Island, his body tall and rangy, in contrast to Marcus's mother's and that of the younger sister—also tiny, also strikingly like Marcus—who lingered somewhere in the background.

"Say, Mawkus, I'd like to show you and your friend a little something I've been working on in the basement, if you're not busy."

"We just got here, dad. How busy can I be?"

"Great! It's a sleep aid, a soporific. I think you'll really enjoy it."

I looked at him, already scurrying over to open up the basement door, then back at Marcus. Suddenly I remembered, smiling. "Subterranean Homesick Blues" began playing on my hectic mental jukebox.

"Your dad's a pharmacologist?" I whispered.

"Yeah, why?"

"I'd like to go outside and think about the government for a second."

Marcus smirked. "Oh, don't worry about that."

His sister, Missy, came racing over then. She was twelve.

"Marcus? I borrowed your Animal Suffrage record."

"Fine."

"Also your copy of *Phenomenology of Spirit*. Plus some Adorno."

"Great. Don't overdo it. Try some Lukacs afterwards, maybe."

"Okay."

Her wide, dark eyes shone up at us pleadingly, mockingly. She was like a little baby bird, just as the father was like an auk or an emu, with that strong beak and exotic feathering. Each member of this family seemed both to contain and to expand upon the last. I realized, incredibly, that Marcus was the peacekeeper, the ordinary one: that he was this family's accommodation to the twentieth century. Since they seemed to live at once in the nineteenth and the twenty-third.

"Can you pass the sauerkraut?"

"Of course."

We'd sat down to lunch together, *en famille*. How quaint. I couldn't remember the last time my own family had done that. Nineteen sixty-nine? Someone was baking cookies in the next room. I smelled cinnamon. As we sat together at a rectangular table that was set for six, as someone else had yet to arrive. I rested my eyes from the psychedelic chaos of the den, or the rumpus room: whatever that jumble of mismatched furniture and pipe smoke next door ought properly to have been called. I had a feeling if Marcus admitted to his father he'd been up all night tripping his dad might've said, *Congratulations! Can I top you up?*

"I churned this butter myself," Marcus's mother said.

"It's fantastic."

From the kitchen, just as I was wondering if this place or this family could possibly be any weirder, there came a slapping sound. I wouldn't have been surprised to discover they butchered their own hogs—or, since they were all vegetarians, perhaps their own broccoli. Nothing would've surprised me. Except for the emergence of a tiny woman, her face like a dried currant, with a basketball tucked under one arm and a plate of fresh-baked cookies under the other. She appeared to balance herself out with these things, evenly weighted, since without them she might've been toppled by a gust of wind. She wore immaculate cream-colored sneakers and a pink knit shawl. Her eyes were Marcus's exactly: black, glistening with shrewdness. She tossed the ball and Marcus palmed it. He spun the ball on his fingertip while I stared.

"Hi, Nanny."

"Hi." Her stare was piercing. "You brought your friend."

"Yes."

"How is his hook shot?"

I would've guessed at that time Estella Groenig was a hundred-and-ten years old. In fact she was seventy-three and had survived Buchenwald with both wits and free-throw shooter's eye intact. She plunked down her cookies, which we wolfed down enthusiastically. As we did I realized something: while every family is to some extent the exaggeration of itself, this one was—still more—its own burlesque. Marcus's lonesome strangeness may have been spurred in fact by other things (I was beginning to wonder), but his exaggerations on his own city's behalf had been in fact attempts to correct the record back towards something resembling reality. I watched him, drooping there at the table in his new VTE shirt—aquamarine, with an electro-gold paisley teardrop pattern—as if this family's burdens sat on his shoulders. With one like this, all regular bets were off.

"Coffee?"

"Rugelach?"

"Sleeping pill?"

Marcus smoothed his hair, smiled shyly. This was his family after all. He was adjusted to it, even if it was by definition unfathomable, eternal in its strangeness. He drank soy milk, as all-American seeming as the other kind somehow as he tilted his long slender glass.

"I'm happy to see you, Nanny."

Later, I lay alone on the yellow couch in that nightmare living room, turning and twisting atop its pilly surface. I was supposed to sleep here? Perhaps I should get up and ask Marcus's father for a little help. I heard scraping plates in the adjacent kitchen, both parents loading up the dishwasher.

"Marcus's friend seems nice."

"Yes. Los Angeles! Can you imagine?"

No more than, I could have, them. My own family's collision of opposites—my mother the drunk and my father the ephebe, the eternal boy—had produced predictable neuroses; whereas this melding of the cerebral and the nurturing looked to have conjured something much weirder: a pair of kids with geriatric spirits, ageless, fickle and wise. I had envied Marcus everything, but did I envy him this?

"Stop!" From upstairs, his sister's voice sounded. I couldn't tell if in protest or hilarity. "Marcus, quit!"

Laughter from one or the other. I stared at the grandfather clock atop the gas-burning fireplace's mantle. A smudgy painting of Lake Erie maybe, below a cinder-strewn sky. A large pale rock, mysterious as a dinosaur egg. The clock's pendulum swung back and forth.

"Quit it! Marcus, quit it!"

****

"Why?"

The girl who asked me this had a face like a lifeline, a pure knot of Middle American reason, as she peered at me. How-many-fingers-am-I-holding-up? Her name, as it turned out I'd heard almost correctly, was Mara Harmon. She looked like a nurse, a librarian, a switchboard operator: her face was earnest, plain and chubby and sweet beneath blunt-cut brown bangs. I was so relieved to see a natural color I could've kissed her for that alone. Her T-shirt read *Soul Asylum: While You Were Out*, with a picture of an Amazonian woman breaking out of a circus tent. I'd never been so happy to see a complete stranger.

"Jesus, you came to Columbus? *Why?* Are you out of your ever-lovin' mind?"

"I guess so. Will you be my roommate?" I blurted. She'd just said she was moving out of a one-bedroom apartment upstairs above the bar to search for less expensive digs she could share.

"Sure, kid. But you still haven't told me what you're doing here."

"That becomes less and less clear to me by the hour," I admitted. As we sat together in a padded booth, sipped bracingly cold Rolling Rock. Felice was ignoring me, was deep in conversation with Marcus over at the bar.

"I'll take care of you," this Mara said, "don't worry! But you're from

Los Angeles! You have such great bands!" She named about a dozen, of which I'd never heard. Tex and The Horseheads? "You're in for a long, hot summer, boy."

"I guess." I looked around the bar, at Marcus and all of his gaily-plumed friends, the salting of VTE paisley all across the room. "Say, what's wrong with these people?"

"What d'you mean?"

I'd just watched one of them, a man about five-four (they were all so short, I wondered! Except for Marcus the guys all seemed to be tiny) dodge behind a velvet curtain that hung over one of the far brick walls, covering nothing. His feet protruded as he just stood there. There was something ass-backwards and static about it, like an ostrich's attempt to hide. His name was Krist Cooley, I knew, and he was a dancer, the first of Marcus's gay friends to come out. He'd done this apparently when he was seven. Behind me the jukebox whirred on, blasted Syd Barrett's Pink Floyd. The one about Lucifer Sam, the Siam cat—

"They're all…"

I fumbled for the word. It didn't exist. *Inverted? Switched On?* Some combination of these things. Mara took off her glasses, polished them on her T-shirt.

"I don't know what you're talking about," she said. "They're my friends."

"Right. Listen, d'you know the band Lords of Oblivion?"

"Nic's band? Sure."

"Wait, you…you know him?"

"Of course." She slugged from her beer bottle. "Everyone knows Nic. He's a great guy!"

"They do? He is?" She'd said it like Tony the Tiger, almost. Grrrrreat! "He's real?"

"Of course." She shook her head, set the beer down where it landed with a reassuring clink against the dark wooden table, scarred as an old school desk. This is real, as if to say: *Think of a table.* "What the hell's the matter with you?"

I had begun to doubt my own senses. That's what was the matter with me, and I hadn't even taken any drugs yet. Goodness, I thought, unintentionally mimicking Marc's mother. This good old Midwestern normalcy was just as mind-frying to me as its opposite. I went over to the guy behind the curtain, the little one there, in order to ground myself again in the impossible.

"Knock-knock. Hello?"

I stood there. The curtain parted and Krist Cooley stuck his face—just his face—out. He looked like someone playing an eggplant in an elementary-school play, his acne-riddled complexion peering between the purple curtains. He, too, wore round glasses, behind which he bore the wincing expression of someone offended by something unpleasant you had just said. He wouldn't ask you to repeat it. His eyes were closed.

"Ummmmmmmm—"

"Hi, um, excuse me. I'm—"

"I know who you are." He opened his eyes, now. They were gray, cat-like in their disdain when he trained them on you. "And why you've come."

"You do?" I took a slug of my own beer, skunky and cold. "Actually, I was just wondering what the hell you're doing over here, alone? The party's out here."

"So you say. I'm busy."

"I do say. And what can you possibly be busy with alone behind a velvet curtain?"

The ceiling fan turned behind us. We stood in its cooling breeze. The jukebox switched over, and started playing the Rolling Stones' "We Love You." That Vince Guaraldi-like piano line at the beginning. I guessed he was the one who'd programmed it with all this retro-psychedelia. He was wearing a Nehru jacket, electric yellow, which failed to disguise his own baseline Scandinavian blondness, hair the color of corn silk.

"Things you wouldn't understand." His voice was drawn between irony and fastidiousness. "Are you a friend of the court?"

"Like you're a friend of Dorothy," I said. "I come in peace, yes."

"Great," he said, peering both ways. "Then I can tell you." He went sotto voce of a sudden. "I'm breathing through Felice's vagina."

"You're—"

"I'm practicing," he said, while the string of tiny wooden beads around his neck—they were wrapped there like Christmas tree lights—rattled. "I've always wanted to do it, like Martha Graham says!"

"I—Martha Graham says you should breathe through your vagina?"

I looked down at his soft Capezio jazz shoes. I'd heard this somewhere in fact, this bit of advice she'd given to dancers.

"Yes." He was whispering still. "I don't have one, so I have to borrow hers."

The curtains shut as abruptly as they'd parted. Please deposit five cents for more advice.

"Are you trying to get out of here," I asked, "away from Columbus like everybody else?"

The curtains didn't move. His voice was muffled.

"I'm not in Columbus right now," was what he said. "So it doesn't really matter."

I see, said the blind man. I turned and walked back towards the bar. The ceiling fan ruffled my hair as I passed beneath it, and I watched the deformed features of everyone—myself included—elongated in the brassy fixtures. Even so, I couldn't help thinking there might have been something to this, as ridiculous as it seemed, that Krist Cooley wasn't just undergoing some sort of ironic neo-mystic epiphany. Something seemed to connect all these people, far more than just music, drugs and clothing, a shared love of the bargain textures of the VTE. Whatever it was, this nerve-net of experience, this intimacy even greater than love, I wanted to find it. It was what I'd been missing back home, and had come here to look for. Not that I might say so, as I watched Krist's feet still sticking out beneath the curtain like those of someone perched inside a stall, watched Felice, who seemed oblivious to the fact she was being occupied illegally. (What was the protocol there? I pictured a permission slip, the kind you brought with you to second grade: *Krist will be breathing through Felice's vagina today.*) Though as she stood at the bar with Marcus, leaning there on her elbow, knocking back Irish whiskey and ignoring me, I felt only despair. Everyone here was so thrillingly freaky, a circus animal with its own name, genus and species, that my own, garden-variety maladjustment was beginning to seem like timid sanity. I hated my parents? So what. Their Southern California narcissism and petty bickering were small potatoes, compared to a mother who lived in an igloo and a dad who made his own Quaaludes. The juke started playing Tim Hardin's "Red Balloon," the Small Faces version. How I loved that song, with its lyric about a "blue surprise," "pennies for my eyes." It could've been about death or drugs or anything in between. I watched the people dancing, shaking their hips and waving their arms, too shy just yet to join them as even Mara leapt up atop the bar to do the Frug, the Freddie, the Hustle and the Double Bump—

"Doniella!!!"

Felice's cry split the air above the jukebox. Everyone turned towards the door at the same time, to look at the guy who'd just come in. It was like a moment in an old Western, *Stagecoach* or *The Searchers*. He was short—of course—rubbery, with a stubbly chin and calm blue eyes and a body that seemed to hold almost no tension in it at all. He wore a fisherman's cap and an embroidered blue and white shirt that looked like he might've picked it up in Cuba, like a guayabera. He scanned the room, rubbing his blonde chin. His was the sort of empathic face you wanted looking back at you when you were in crisis: the sort who looked like he might be able to talk you off the highest ledge.

"Donniella!"

He spotted Felice. "Sweet cheeks!!"

He pounced into her arms and they whirled around the room. It was comic—Felice was five-ten—and almost sexual, almost more than sexual as they seemed to want to become one another, to get inside one another's skin: this tall girl and this tiny man, clamped together and clawing at one another, spinning like a gyroscope around the bar. Finally, they dropped into a booth and Donnie popped his fingers into his mouth and whistled.

"Listen up and gather round kiddies, step right this way, roll up, roll up for the mystery tour!" His best camp counselor voice. He clapped his hands and they all came running. "Who wants candy? I got your feelgood hits of the summer, right here!"

Hands shot up. "Oh me, me, me!!"

Everyone crowded into the booth around him. He had magnetism, I'd give him that. At once calm and galvanic, he drew people in, flocking to his particular frequency. He carried a soft leather traveler's satchel, like a man's purse. He rummaged inside it and I saw a passport, domestic and foreign currencies—that brightly-colored Dutch money—vials and keys. Donnie indeed had escaped this place, to Columbia University, two vowels and an entire universe away from here. New York City. He found what he was looking for at last. A small sheet of perforated paper, split into tiny squares.

"One for you, and two for me," he counted them around the table, "one more for you and me both, and…what about you, princess?" He looked up and took me in for the first time. "You in?"

"Yeah, sure." He held Felice's hand, which I didn't like at all. "I'm in."

I eyed him and the blotter with equal suspicion. I'd never done LSD before. Where I came from, cocaine was the hedonist's poison of choice. Ecstasy had just gained its currency there too, drugs of energy and escape, not ones of vision. I took the little square of paper he pushed across the table, which had a miniscule picture of Elvis on it. How quaint. I squinted down at my fingertip. The world in a grain of sand, was it? I didn't believe in that kind of stuff. On the juke the Chambers Brothers sang of how their "souls" had been psychedelicized. I didn't believe in any of that either. Only in music. I hesitated a moment, then popped the blotter onto my tongue. Everybody else had already done so. You only lived once, right? Only Mara, a good Catholic girl, demurred. She was sticking to beer.

"How was school?" Marcus said. "You still enrolled?"

"Think so. Last time I checked." Donnie's face had a radical, stretchy expressiveness too: it was like a Greek mask of tragedy, or comedy, depending on which effect he chose. He grinned now. "I stopped by the registrar's office last week and I wound up blowing my Comp Lit professor."

"Same one?"

"Different."

Him, I thought, relieved. He was involved with a man. Then again, did that make a difference? My college experience suggested it mightn't. Felice was giving him a neck rub. He grimaced with joy. He seemed completely dedicated to pleasure, less so to who and what offered it. All of us sat altogether in the booth for twenty minutes or so. Then Krist Cooley said,

"You'll excuse me, I think I feel my uvula getting hot."

He went off to do his own thing, Nehru coattails flapping like a little magician's. I found myself pressing my legs together self-consciously. Invisible Dan—I kept forgetting about him, he didn't do any drugs either—sat in a booth by himself, scribbling in a spiral-bound notebook. He wore a tan shirt now, and tan pants. Bland On Bland. I could hear the scratching of his pen. Were my senses becoming sharper? Lena was home with her father; Kitty, somewhere with her fiancé. Marcus would leave us soon too. Nothing, perhaps, could compete with his family on drugs, as they gathered 'round the fondue set for a cozy game of psychedelic Yahtzee. It was just Felice, Donnie and myself, heading into the black.

"Nothing's happening," I said, as I studied the bar with a mix of disappointment and relief. No swarming swans or snakes, that was still just Mara over there chatting with the bartender, clutching her long-necked green bottle.

"Just wait," Donnie said. His face alone like an amber light of warning: Happy, Sad; Happy, Sad. "Wait."

7

Lost In The Supermarket

No, wait—

"I, umm—hi," I said, having rehearsed this exchange a thousand times in the last five seconds alone. Hello. Hi. *Alka-Seltzer! Spaceman!* "May I, please—"

I stood before the counter at the A&P Mini-Mart, watching the man behind it grow a second head. He looked exactly like my high school's PE instructor, warty and middle-aged, with a throat like a bullfrog's. The first African-American person I'd seen since we entered Ohio. The air smelled of unlit tobacco, Freon from the ice machine, crumbling bits of stale Hershey's bars that were dusted along the counter. The light was a commercial halogen yellow which made it seem like I could see through things, like I was wearing those X-ray specs you could order from the back pages of old comic books. Felice stepped in.

"He'd like a pack of cigarettes." She enunciated each word perfectly. We'd discussed this situation in the parking lot. Second heads were no big deal. It was when they began breathing fire you should worry. "Camels, please."

"Filter, sir, or no filter?"

Oh, goddamnit! When you came to a fork in the road like that one, what were you supposed to do? I covered my face with my hands and began giggling, while he stood there with his meaty palms on the counter, his eyes darkening red. Was everyone here trying to kill us? And couldn't he have asked through just one set of lips?

"Unfiltered," Felice said, blinking. She knew what to do. "Thank you, sweetheart."

The guy behind the counter reached up. His skin looked iridescent, ink-dipped in the refracted, untrustworthy light of this drug. He gave us the cigarettes and we paid for them.

"Oh Bondage, Up Yours!" I squawked, as she grabbed my hand and dragged me past a potato-chip display. I knocked over a stand of Pemmican beef jerky, the clerk's hot stare on my back as we fell, shrieking into the parking lot.

"You were right about these pants," I wheezed. At last we could breathe, out here. They brushed my legs, like eels. *Electricity.* "I think they're alive!"

That poor guy! And yet, what was I pitying him for? Maybe we were the amusers, a break from the outrageous claims of the *Weekly World News* and the hum 'n' grind of the ice machine, the vacancy of the late night shift. Felice had bought a box of Quisp cereal, Red Dot potato chips she ripped into ecstatically. The whole place was full of food species I hadn't seen in years, brands that hadn't touched either coast since the mid-1970s. I could've spent weeks in there. For all I knew, I just had. Out in the street Donnie was taking a nap, laying flat on the asphalt's yellow dividing-line. Arms folded over his chest like a cadaver. *Turn Me On, Dead Man,* I thought. It was three in the morning. The likelihood of him getting run over was akin to that of being trampled by elephants. Either might happen, given the drugs we were on, yet they were equally improbable out here in the drowsy suburbs. Across the street were the shuttered fronts of a Noah's Bagels, a pet supply shop called Pawz. A shrill of crickets lifted from yards and lawns beyond.

There's no need to go on. Drugs are drugs and teenagers, teenagers, all across America. They did the things to us—and we to them—you'd expect, unspooling our thoughts and visions to one another and getting tangled in them like kittens playing with yarn. Quotidian mysticism: the things we'd figured out forever we found ourselves needing to think through, again, five minutes later. Finally I wound up alone in a car with Felice. It was morning. Donnie's mint-green VW Rabbit sat in front of his mother's house, not five blocks from Felice's. We watched as he stole his way across the lawn and crawled through a pet door.

"Why's he doing that?" I said. "Why doesn't he just go in through the front door?"

"His mother disowned him. She can't deal with the fact that he's"— she mimicked a conservative middle-aged matron's distaste—"Homo-sexual."

"I see."

We were parked under a stand of elms, the sun barely risen over the wet lawns, painting the fronts of the bone-white houses. Seed pods dropped soundlessly on the hood of our car. The cassette deck played things rackety and jagged, garbled as my heart: The Cramps' "Garbage Man"; Gang of Four's "Cheeseburger" followed by "What We All Want." Stray bits of Marxist agitpop of which I'd had enough. I moved my hand towards hers on the gear knob. She pulled hers away.

"I'm all he has in the world," Felice said. "Donnie really needs me."

"Does he?" What did this have to do with anything? What did anything—my rival—have to do with anything? "What were we talking about before? Oh yeah, the Goncourts—"

"STOP!" she shouted, lifting her arms skyward, raising them up in exasperation. "Just stop it, God, please!"

"What did I do?"

"Are you like this all the time?" she said. "So...interior?"

"What?" I stroked my chin. "What are you getting at? It's just—"

"Everything's an idea with you," she snapped. "You're so damn thinky it's making me ill. All this book talk. What next, you want to take an IQ test with me? Go audit a lecture? Stop thinking and realize there's a world out there!" She slammed her palms against the wheel. "You make me sick!"

She opened the car door and tumbled outside. My face burned, my eyes stung. The cassette ended with an abrupt click, leaving only silence. Sunlight fell through the windshield, warming my forearms. A boy swished by on a bicycle. What was wrong with me, I wondered? As she straightened up and brushed herself off. I smelled cut grass again, the breath of summer lawns. The trees along the street—maples, oaks, elms—were so, so green, their leaves nearly sheer in the morning sun. This wasn't a hallucination. This was real.

"You're, like, the *thinkiest* person I've ever met," Felice said, leaning in for a parting shot. "That's nowhere near the same thing as the smartest."

Clearly not. I sat there mortified, flaming with shame. I didn't remember a moment throughout the entire solitary corridor of my adolescence that was as lonely or painful as this one. I'd been called out. Birds sang, branches waved in the slight morning breeze all along the street. *Goodbye, goodbye.* I couldn't stand it. And what could I say that hadn't already been said elsewhere? This girl had brought me to the limits of my vocabulary. I was in love, I realized right then. In love.

"Don't think," Felice said. Before she slammed the door shut. "*Feel!*"

The door banged shut. I sat there, in the claustrophobic quiet of the car, its antiseptic, space-shuttle silence. Watching her tramp across the buttery green lawn, the ground beneath it seeded with fertilizer. *Don't think, feel!* The Beatles had gone all the way to India to hear that bit of wisdom, while I'd had to go no further than Columbus, Ohio and the deep well of my own loneliness. God! I pressed my forehead against the wheel, rolled it against the heat-cracked leather. While Felice walked across the lawn with a box of Quisp cereal under one arm, sun slashing across her dyed hair and her silk robe to make them both seem molten, a shimmering ruby-red that was the last aftertrail of my acid experience. I pressed my forehead there, feeling the wheel's braille nubs. Their unforgiving burn against my skin.

8

Sand

"You wanna get out of here?"

We were at a party the next night when she asked me. A ramshackle house downtown, belonging to one or another of Marcus's friends—apartments here too seemed a form of communal property, big tenement spaces in which the number of available bedrooms and of current occupants never exactly matched—where we stood and watched people throng through rooms without furniture or definite function, filled with ear-splitting music. A stray terrier slept at the foot of a bare mantle with its nose in a puddle of beer, oblivious to a sound that was like that of machines gone berserk, a ferocious clanging of metal on metal. We'd just endured an entire side by a band called Peach of Immortality—the sleeve read *Talking Heads '77*, but that was the sardonically appropriated name of the album itself, quotation piled atop quotation—and were now being assaulted by an outfit called SPK, which stood for Surgical Penis Klinik.

"God, yeah!" I shouted, ducking my head as if we stood in a shower of shrapnel. "Maybe someplace quieter, like an auto plant?"

It was Saturday night. I'd barely slept at all since we set out from Massachusetts. We'd come home from our acid trip and I sat in the living room of Marcus's house with Missy, wide awake at 9 A.M. and watching The Dating Game. I was still tripping, but I couldn't imagine anyone in that house would notice. Outside, Nanny was practicing her free throws. I listened to the ball's semi-regular smack on the pavement. The set was a pixilated Technicolor jumble. I was heartbroken too, but who would notice that either? Not Missy, sharing her plate of breakfast rugelach with me, studying her social philosophers. I'd managed to doze for an hour, but now here I was with Felice again, equally besieged by lust and sleeplessness. Lena's boyfriend, Terry Wheat, a moody, pretty, James Dean-ish figure in khaki pants and a wife-beater undershirt, knelt down in a corner by the stereo, smiling as he dialed up the volume. I knew one thing about Terry, he was stone fucking crazy and loved confrontation. Felice grabbed my wrist, "C'mon!"

Out we went into the humid night, which simmered with insects, away from all that industrial shrieking and banging. Lena sat on the porch rail, drinking warm beer from a plastic cup. She reached out and patted my cheek as we passed.

"You havin' a good time, honey?"

"Yeah." I sipped from her cup, while Felice held my wrist. I'd let that last, too. "Where's your shadow?"

She laughed. "Dan's having dinner with my dad."

"Really? Isn't that kind of old-fashioned? Is he grilling him about his labor practices?"

She wrinkled her nose. She really was adorable, no less. Once upon a time I might've been in trouble. "Nah. Dan's gonna intern with him this summer. My dad needed someone good with numbers."

"Is that right? Dan's gonna use his bookkeeping skills?"

That figured. In addition to being a big fat zero himself, Dan was a math major. No one did that at our school, they studied African literature or the aerodynamics of Frisbee, the quasar-like trajectory of Jerry Garcia's guitar solos. Nothing so straight as economics or accounting. In fact I remembered Lena advertising this internship—it required little more than petty-cash competence—and coming up empty. Yet Dan would have mucked out the stables for her if she'd asked.

"What a drip!" My sympathy fell away as Felice yanked my hand and we stepped off the porch, leaving its moth-swirling quietude behind. Lena wiggled her fingers.

"Bye, lovebirds!"

Oh, how I wished! The night's warm, soft air was a palm, cupping us in its semi-tolerable damp. Bugs the size of hummingbirds attacked the street lamps. Stars glittered toyishly above. Telephone poles were scarred with fliers for bands, beer blasts, missing children.

"Where are we going?"

"Anywhere," Felice said. "Nowhere—that's the trouble with this place."

We'd raced away from the party in a hurry, now stumbled to a stop on High Street, reduced to an aimless shuffle as she let go of my hand. Moved away as if she thought better of it, or less of me.

"It's the trouble with any place," I said. "Los Angeles isn't that exciting."

"That would be relative."

I nodded across the street, towards a food joint's neon sign. "What's that?"

"What d'you mean 'what's that?' How can you not know what a White Castle is?"

"Sorry. Those don't exist."

"Oh they do, I'm sorry to say. How can you never have eaten a slider?"

"A which?"

"Allow me to introduce you to the Midwest's least edible foodstuff. Which is saying something."

We crossed the street, trotting against non-existent traffic. She opened the door and we swam into the muggy interior. A close reek of hamburger grease and canola oil. The brick-brown floor tiles kissed my feet, adhesive.

"See?"

"What?" She'd handed me a couple of grayish-brown pucks, biscuit-sized hamburgers, now gestured towards them as if they explained everything. "Uh-uh. I don't."

She sighed. "It isn't you. I have to get out of here."

I ate one. "It isn't bad."

"It isn't good."

I lifted an eyebrow. "Isn't that a matter of opinion?"

Whatever sat between us, this difference of culture or else of temperament. We wheeled back towards the door and past a large—"large" even by Columbus standards, well over three hundred pounds—woman who sat alone before a pyramid of these White Castle burgers. She leered at me, tongue nosing sluglike between gray teeth. Whether she was homeless, insane or just an ordinary citizen was impossible for me to tell.

"Ooh," she murmured. I caught a whiff of kerosene, or grain alcohol.

She was dressed like a Bedouin, in graying rags. Her face darkened with sun
and dirt. "Yer a pretty l'il thing, aintcha?"

We burst out into the parking lot. I couldn't help laughing.

"It's nice to see what a diet of those does for the local populace."

"See? I told you this place was demented."

"I love it."

"You're out of your mind."

She hooked my elbow now, but I knew she didn't mean anything by it,
was just humoring me. She steered us back out to the sidewalk.

"That girl said I was pretty."

She smiled. "Isn't that a matter of opinion?"

"I'd say."

"Don't let it go to your head or anything. You do realize the average
man here has bigger tits than I do, right?"

We walked arm-in-arm. I looked up at Polaris, Venus, the scattering
of stars which would've been invisible in L.A. My mouth tasted of graying
meat and biscuit batter; the outside air smelled of motor oil, uncollected trash
and vanilla. Felice's palm pressed mine. I wanted to stay forever.

"Can I borrow your toothbrush," she said, once we were back at the
house, where the party was dispersing.

"Sure."

I don't recall why I had it with me but I did, in my pocket. I fumbled
for it, handed it over. The rooms had cleared—a few stray revelers were
out in the yard—and the stereo now played something related but infinitely
gentler. *Another Side of Surgical Penis Klinik.* A man ventured to sing an
actual melody, his German-accented voice humming an English lyric over a
bronzed, mechanical purr. The mangy dog napped on, oblivious. Felice came
back, and we lay on the floor together by the couch, huddling closely, almost
nose to nose. Nothing was going to keep me from sleep, not decibel count
or indigestion or lovelornness, nor the tormenting presence of this girl who
seemed at war with herself, if not with me.

"Hmm," I said while we lay there, drowsing side by side on the dirty
tan carpet, "who does this song? I like it."

"Me too," she murmured.

It was dark. The only light came from the outer hall, where people were saying goodnight. Lena and Terry went clomping together upstairs. Marcus, my ride, had left me again. I wanted to discover this city alone anyway, these people who would be my friends if they were anyone's. I smelled the toothpaste, heard Felice's tongue sweeping across her clean teeth. And the song with which Terry had left us, huddled together under my light suede bomber jacket, shivering for something other than cold.

> *Young woman, share your fire with me.*
> *My heart is cold, my soul is free*
> *I am a stranger in your land*
> *A wandering man, call me sand*

"Einsturzende Neubauten," Felice murmured. Her breath was a soft gust of mint, of gin and cigarettes. "Kitty put it on a tape for me."

"What's it called?"

"'Sand.'" We were dropping off together to sleep. "The original's by Lee Hazlewood and Nancy Sinatra."

Ah, I thought. This song would be ours too. Einsturzende Neubauten. If I wasn't so tired I might've leaned across to—

9

I Don't Wanna Walk Around With You

We woke at the same time. Felice rolled over, away as we were awakened by a blast of music—"music"—from Terry's turntable. He crouched there silent, sifting records in and out of their sleeves. Laibach, Swans, Whitehouse. More grinding factory blues.

"Good morning children." Terry smirked under that perfect blonde pompadour, indestructible to both wind and bedding. Man, he was handsome—for a sociopath. "I made pancakes."

We scrambled out of the house, feeling shy. Stood conspicuously apart on the lawn like strangers. Nothing had happened, but I could feel Felice thinking it: That was a mistake. Whatever it was that had almost, not-quite actually happened. We walked out into the warm morning in our unwashed clothes, moving across the lawns that were brittle with neglect. The buildings down here were mostly brick tenements, their rectangles of browning grass just afterthoughts. Somewhere nearby a dog barked viciously. I could hear the rage at its confinement, could feel the choke chain almost as surely as though it pressed against my own neck. We were beyond Campus, in a neighborhood called the Short North. We'd have to get back to Wilkerton on our own. I covered my mouth to shield morning breath.

"Are you alright?" I said.

"No."

"No?"

She looked at me. "I can't do this. I'm going away."

"Does that matter? So am I after a while."

She didn't say anything, just shook her head slightly. An indefinite gesture, like brushing away a bug. Together we walked to Bob Evans, ate pancakes-biscuits-French toast 'n' waffles, a four-starch special of Felice's invention. I couldn't believe they'd left it off the menu.

"I hate to eat anything that was ever alive," Felice said. "Really I try to stick to things you can mix in a bowl."

"Wow." Smoke clouded the booth as we sat by the window. My stomach was fit to burst already, the plates still three-quarters full with a lumpen mass of gold, brown, tan. "You are English, aren't you?"

We hitchhiked back to Wilkerton. In the backseat I sat apart from her too, angled towards the window. What could I say to bring her around? The woman who'd picked us up watched me in the mirror, her pale brow clouding in sympathy or contempt, I couldn't tell. Felice hopped out first.

"I'll see you," she said.

"Yeah, tonight at Mara's."

I watched her wander off down Apple Drive, losing herself in that suburban maze she hated. Was it just that, or was it me she detested too? I might never have guessed what was on her mind. The driver let me off at the base of Wilkerton Hills and I returned to Marcus's house alone. Bats seemed to fly out of the rafters when I stepped inside, like sparks from an anvil. Every time I went in there I was tripping all over again.

"Ooh," Missy said clairvoyantly, eyeing me from across the couch. "You *like* someone."

Her knees were up, she was drinking a mug of coffee-spiked Ovaltine. How could a little girl look so much like a little boy, I wondered, staring at the black bristle-brush of her hair?

"I do." No way would I have admitted this to Marcus, who'd have mocked my weakness. His girlfriend lived in Norway, sent him letters scented with sandalwood incense and chill jealousy. "I like someone."

"Ooh! Who? Who? Who d'you like?" she demanded, with the same rooting ferocity she'd just trained on the TV to crow, *Bachelor Number two, do it, do it, pick him!* "Who is it? Is it Lena?"

I shook my head. "Felice."

She sighed, and looked at me with a distant pity. She slurped from her mug, which read *World's Greatest Pet Owner*. Twelve years old, her strange gravity made her more like the aged courtesan figure in a French movie, the madam in a genteel whorehouse. Shaking her head.

"Poor you," she said.

"What? Why?" I said. What did she know that I didn't, at her tender-if-shriveled-seeming age? "Poor me, why?"

She slurped again. The ends of her fingers were bitten to the quick, like Marcus's, ragged little stubs protruding from the rolled and re-rolled sleeves of one of her brother's gray cardigans.

"Young hearts are made to be broken," she sighed.

I stood up. "What the hell do you know? You're ten."

"Twelve. I know that much."

"Forget it," I said. "When I was your age I only knew the four-sided die was the pointy one."

"Like your head," she said. "Felice will break your heart."

Ah, what did she know? Perhaps everything. Her words had the ring of prophecy. I felt sick thinking about it, my stomach twisting in knots. That night we went down to Mara's apartment above Perry's. A bunch of people were there: Marcus, Lena, Kitty, Krist. Invisible Dan, taking a break from his mathematical labors, pencil tucked behind his sweat-reddened ear. We sat around drinking beer—even the preferred brand, Rolling Rock, carried that ring of Sisyphean hopelessness, that sense that no one here might ever succeed in their dream of escape—in long green bottles. All of Mara's belongings were in boxes; she and I had found a place together that afternoon. A ghetto palace on the student side of High Street.

"Where's Doniella?" Felice said.

"I saw him earlier," Marcus said. "I think he's down at Terry's."

"Oh."

I couldn't gauge her tone, how natural her acceptance was. I didn't care, was happy just to sit next to her, my fingertips fanned within inches of hers. She could've been anyone, in a sense. In another, because she was a girl— the pure flower of this place which I loved, needed to love as the alternative to home—she was everybody, everything. Even if I hardly knew her at all, had exchanged few words that weren't scrambled by acid or another, earlier misunderstanding.

"I'll take one of those." I reached over and shook a cigarette from her pack. "You want?"

"Sure."

I lit two, then handed her one.

"You don't know what you're getting into," she said.

"I don't?" I wasn't sure if she meant cigarettes, the city, or just herself. We sat side by side in a far corner of Mara's living room, while Krist read tarot cards for Marcus and Lena, and our hostess's turntable—the last thing she'd pack up—played Big Star's *Third*.

"No."

Our hands were so close, our arms almost touching. The air hummed with violins, badly-tuned piano, the reckless Memphis muddle of that record I'd love the rest of my life. Thank you, Friends! We sat there for I don't know how long. I watched her face, there in the lamplight. She didn't lean closer, yet wouldn't pull away.

"Hey!!"

Mara's keys landed, jangling on the hardwood beside my leg. I looked over and realized everybody else had left. They were making a decision for us. Mara stared over from the doorway, her face a ruddy bulb of disgust.

"We're going down to Perry's. Lock up, and play safe."

She turned. Mara was a virgin, but was just as eye-rollingly repulsed as everyone else, I suddenly realized. The fact Felice and I were coming on to each other, the fact *she* was interested in me, had been plain to everybody. I'd missed it. The door swung shut and Felice looked at me finally.

"I can't do this."

"Why not?"

The record spun, side two of the PVC pressing on repeat. "Jesus Christ" was the song now. *We're gonna get born*, the singer slurred.

"You just like playing hard to get?"

She shook her head, laughed. Maybe she didn't know her reasons, didn't have to. Her best friend was getting married; her own entire life was spent in this place, this "tar pit," as she'd called it. Was it so awful to want to escape, to fear any sort of entrapment?

"No."

For a long moment we watched each other, the shadow pattern falling across her face like a strange continent. Then she launched herself at me, wrapping her hand around my neck to grab my hair. We clawed each other, kissing at last as she pressed me towards the floor. I could feel her resistance even as she weighed me down, as the air filled with that raucous Christmas hymn that would follow us, this too, all summer long.

10

Searchin'

Mara and I lugged boxes up the stairs, my hands chafing raw
on cardboard as we angled through the narrow front door. This was our
apartment, a tan-carpeted bunker with room upon room upon room—doors
just kept opening onto new ones—and black bars on the windows and no
air-conditioning. Paint peeled off the ceilings and there were waterspots and
mildew on the walls, bare fixtures that might've been burgled by previous
tenants. It could easily have slept eleven. Sills rattled in their frames when we
spoke, our voices echoing through the emptiness.

"Wanna put a pool table in here?" I said, confronting yet another
blank space we didn't know how to deal with, would have to be a screening
room or a roller rink. Sunlight swam through windows at its far end but it was
cool and shadowy where we stood. "Look! Someone left us a TV."

"Yeah," Mara said. "All we've gotta do is find a baseball bat and we'll
know what to do with it."

She nudged the television—decrepit, cracked—over with her foot.
"I'll take this room, I think."

"Great. I'll take the one at the far end of the hall." I nodded towards
Mara's bicycle, just outside the room. "Mind if I take that? I think I need a
ride, to get there."

So it was. My room had a fireplace with a tarnished rectangular
mirror hanging over it, a private bathroom with powder-pink tiles. I owned
nothing but a few books, a futon and a typewriter, but the air was all mine.
The carpet was inky, vaguely piss-smelling and checked with cigarette burns.
I lay on my bed, smoking, dreaming of Felice who continued to insist we
couldn't get involved. After we'd slept together that night she'd retreated. *I
can't, no!* Was it because she was leaving, because London called? Or was
there some other reason? She declined to say. I invited her over, played her
both Lords of Oblivion singles back to back. I thought somehow this would
win her, convince her that I was on to something. I crouched alongside Mara's

turntable in the common room, set the needle down and then stepped back so I could gauge her response.

"Christ!" It was not as I'd hoped. "What is this? It's awful!"

"No," I insisted. She sat at a folding card-table just off the kitchenette, which was Mara's and my primary social station. The table was marbled, silver-edged, the color of cut salmon, and I tried there to reason with Felice while Nic wailed in the background. "Don't you see? It's fantastic!"

"I don't know if I can see but I can hear! It's horrible," she said, pouring herself another cup of coffee. "It's not music at all, it's just…sound. Do they know a third chord? Does the drummer only have one arm?" She narrowed her eyes. "What did you say this band was called?"

"Lords of Oblivion." I passed her the sleeve. Feeling embarrassed, hurt in that way you are when someone you love attacks something else you do. She squinted at it a moment, turning it around so the picture was right way up.

"Oh."

"What?"

"My brother knows these guys."

"What? Your brother knows Nic Devine?"

"Yeah. I think so, it was a while ago."

"Your little brother? That kid I saw?"

"No, my older brother, Archie. His friend played bass in this band for a while, I think."

"Really?" I couldn't believe it. Now here was an intimate, third-hand brush with greatness. I'd slept with a girl whose brother's friend used to play bass with Nic Devine! I was practically royalty by association. "Can I meet him?"

"Who, my brother?"

"Yeah. No, the bassist."

"You don't want to do that." She blinked. "They're not really friends anymore, anyway. But I'll introduce you to my brother. You guys have similar tastes."

The record had ended, "Caveman Stomp" giving way to the less abrasive hiss 'n' pop of a needle stuck in the run-out groove.

"You really don't like it?"

Insects buzzed in the sunlight above the sink, where Mara kept plants in a window box. A Venus Flytrap nodded on its tender stalk. The silence was suddenly oppressive.

"You really do?"

"Yeah," I said. "'Like' doesn't really even begin to get at it, in fact."

What did? This band wasn't just a taste or a phase or a fad, to me. *Lords of Oblivion, c'est moi*, I thought. If she couldn't hear it, we were going to have a problem.

"Don't take it personally," she said, watching me sulk. "It's just music."

"It isn't."

I couldn't explain it though, what the band meant to me. I'd have sounded like an idiot, or a hippie. (Was anything "just" anything, besides? Didn't music connect things—people, places, experiences—until they were woven into some hitherto unexpected design? Like I said...) Well, her parents were hippies, so maybe she'd have understood.

"What do you like?" I asked her.

"Elvis Costello."

"*Him?*" There were few people in music I so actively despised. Buddy Holly's glasses welded onto a chicken-legged Englishman; all that irritating wordplay, those homonyms and puns. Rock 'n' roll wasn't supposed to be about detectives looking for clues, it was supposed to be a gesture towards the ineffable, raucous and primitive and exciting and dumb. Everything about him was a ripoff, from the name on down. "Figures."

She tried though, just as I had. Kneeling on the carpet, she sifted through Mara's record collection—a DJ at WOSU, Mara seemed to have every record ever made—until she found a bootleg recording called "Imagination (Is A Powerful Deceiver)." She forced me to listen to it.

"Tripe," I said, when it was finished. "Unadulterated crap."

She blinked, again. More beautiful than ever as she knelt beside me on the living room floor. I mightn't have understood her tastes, but her pale skin painted by sunlight, her hair and eyes! I watched the pocket of shadow at the base of her throat, her simple grace as she shook a cigarette from her pack and lit it. She didn't care what I thought, after all.

"You're deaf, boy."

"What? All I hear is words."

"Yeah?"

"Yes. They get in the way."

"Funny thing for *you* to say." Smoke curled around us both, as she laughed. "You're beyond help. There's nothing I can do for you."

"You can introduce me to your brother," I said. Maybe the deaf could lead the deaf, after all. "Start with that."

****

I took the bus out to Wilkerton, a good forty-five minute ride from where I lived near Campus. It happened Felice's brother was in town just then, visiting from New York. The mystery of her family might unveil itself to me yet, although when I got there, to the house on Apple Drive that had so beguiled me the first time, all I found was Felice and her brother reclining on the living room couch, in a roomful of colonial furniture and suburban bric-a-brac. As without, so within, I thought: a more normal-seeming house was difficult to imagine. I'd sulked a bit on the bus ride out—Felice had finally admitted to having had a tiny crush, long ago, on her brother's bass-playing friend—but forgot all about it the moment I knocked on the door and she flung it open to embrace me.

"Hey Archie," she shouted with her arms around my neck, "this is the boy I was telling you about!"

"Oh." He was taller than she was—six-four—gaunt, Byronic almost, with his thatched hair and sunken cheeks. Yet they looked uncannily alike, malnourished and English and sweet. "You're the one who's into Lords of Oblivion, huh?"

I felt better already, knowing Felice had talked about me, knowing the band had an actual witness in the form of this older brother, indisputably cooler as older brothers tended to be. He wore a camel-colored 13th Floor Elevators T-shirt, an orange sun rising above the words *Easter Everywhere*, along with tattered jeans and shredded high-top sneakers. That was his vintage Mustang convertible resting out in the drive, and he knew everything about all that mattered, from Japanese monster movies to the most occult rock 'n' roll bands. He lived in New York, had already realized Felice's dream of escape. She idolized him, as I would've too if he were my brother. She had to respect his opinion, which after all was the same as mine.

"Best band I ever saw, bar none." He lifted his eyebrows. Beside him, Felice did the same in a different spirit. Together they looked like echoes, quotations of a single face: two bands covering the same song, differently. "They were incredible. Transcendent. It was like every tune you ever loved, playing at the same time."

Wow, I thought. Transcendent. "You saw them? As in, actually perform a whole set, live? They didn't just fistfight?"

"Many times. I saw them many times."

We sat in a room filled with a grand piano; a fireplace; photographs of Felice and her various siblings in silver frames. The silence in the house was somehow dense, opulent. A flute, a metronome, a record player atop a cabinet filled with scratched LPs: these things waited to disturb it. I saw evidence of the kid brother in a pack of M-80s, left carelessly in open view. Everyone else was out, however.

"You did? This was when your friend played bass?"

He shook his head. "Tom was only in the band six weeks or so. I saw them a bunch of times though, in '83 and '84."

I tugged at my ear for a second, mopped it with a knuckle: something had gone wrong with my hearing. I wanted to ask him more about Tom—I thought he'd said "Tom"—but he added, "Nic Devine is the greatest rock 'n' roll singer of all time, I think... It's just a pity you won't be able to see for yourself."

"What? Why?"

I'd drifted off a moment in the silence, amidst all that wooden furniture as dark and rickety as kindling. I rarely went places where there wasn't music playing, so I'd plunged into reverie. About Felice, her brother, family, drugs, time—all the other things that were on my mind—and these words snapped me out of it. He and I were alone on the couch. Felice had gotten up to fetch something to drink.

"What are you talking about?" I asked.

"Nic's retired," Archie said. "The band's broken up for good."

"What?!! That's impossible!"

"How is it impossible? Bands break up all the time."

"Not this band."

I looked around the room at the brass utensils by the fireplace; the ash-free mantle; the thumb-smudged piano stacked with sheet music. These things were meaningless all of a sudden, free from even their ordinary functions. I couldn't figure out what any of them were for.

"How d'you know?" I repeated. "Was it a formal announcement?"

Felice came in carrying beer in frosted glasses, a box of crackers. I thought of David Bowie, proclaiming Ziggy Stardust's retirement to a shocked audience. *Not only is this the last show of the tour...but it's the last show we'll ever do!* Tears. Hysteria. Pandemonium inside Hammersmith Odeon. Nic might retire unmourned.

"Did I miss something?" Felice said.

"No," Archie said, nodding at me. "He did."

It seemed I had. But he added, "It's just what I hear. That he can't keep a band together, and so isn't really playing out anymore. Sorry to be the bearer of the news."

"Yeah."

I shifted on the couch, its crazy red brocade pattern the one splash of color in this otherwise dark room. Outside, beyond the drawn blinds, I heard a distant sound—beyond the mowers, the near-silence of the suburbs—like gulls, the anguishing cry of my desire in flight. What was it? How could I have come this far to find disappointment?

"Sorry," Felice said, laying her palm for a moment on my neck. "I'll introduce you to my younger brother. He's even worse than that band. You should hear him play piano."

She laughed, and Archie said, "How is the monster, anyway?"

"The same."

I didn't care. How could I have come all this distance for naught, I wondered? And what was it about Nic Devine? What made him so difficult to work for, or with?

"Did they change his medication? Is he calmer?"

"A little," Felice said. "He's on Ritalin now, but it doesn't seem to make any difference."

Later, Felice would tell me all about the younger brother—how he had real behavioral and psychological issues that the family was trying to take care of—but I didn't believe her. Didn't everyone's little brother have problems? Didn't I? Eleven and a half weeks remained in my summer, that wished-for eternity. But it felt as though it was already over, crippled before it began.

****

"FIIII—IIIRREE!"

The band onstage was called the Hangman's Gang, and they were the worst I'd ever seen. Crisp, energetic and competent, they were nevertheless fey, campy: every note they played was undermined by irony, so there was no sense they might be able to deliver anything else. Instead, they offered nu-wave cabaret, mincing through an Ohio Players cover to end a set I'd just watched in a Lebanese-American bar called Brother's Keeper's. Incredibly, this place was packed, and—even more so—the band had just signed a deal with RCA. This was what people wanted, apparently. It wasn't that they were bad players—objectively speaking, they may have been better than Lords of Oblivion—but there was an absence of conviction. Wasn't a band supposed to mean it? Instead, here was the singer dressed in a feather boa and sparkly black bikini briefs; a guitarist who'd just swapped his instrument for an ukulele. And there was the bassist, chiming in with a strangulated harmony vocal in his high-water golf pants and suspenders, taped-together horn-rims sliding down the bridge of his nose. *The way you push, push—*

He looked ridiculous. They all did, pogoing away like spastic weasels. That this was the guy who'd played bass in Nic Devine's band astounded me. He was tall and skinny, with a glottal voice and the foreshortened face of a thyroid victim, a greasy black konk of hair flopping over his glasses. The idea that Felice—or anyone—could've had a crush on him was ridiculous, and if I were Nic I'd have fired him for stylistic reasons alone, watching him antz across the stage, slapping and popping his bass with his eyes bugging. I stood at the rear of the room while people went nuts. Finally, the band wrapped up the song and the set, so I pushed my way forward through the throng. The air smelled of sweat and lamb, grease from the nearby kitchen. I elbowed over to the bassist, who stood on the lip of the six-inch high "stage," the short riser on which most local outfits had played at one time or another.

"Hey"—I reached out and snagged his sleeve—"Didn't you used to play in Lords of Oblivion? Nic Devine's band?"

He looked over at me and sneered. He didn't seem to have another expression, the way his face scrunched up behind the glasses.

"Huh? Maybe, man, why? I mean, who wants to know?"

"I'm Felice's friend…you know, Archie Ballard's kid sister?"

"Oh, right." His face shifted gears now, he lifted an eyebrow. "How is Felice?"

"Never mind. Look, what was it like, playing with Nic Devine? Why can't that guy keep a band together?"

He snorted. Was it such a stupid question? The guitar player behind him was busy untangling his instrument, sorting it free of a bunch of electrical wires. Above us the stage lights blazed. I could feel their heat across my back. The ceiling was only nine feet high, the whole room painted black like a camera obscura.

"Who are you?" he said again, while feedback shrilled around us. I didn't know his name either, didn't want to know given his attitude. I'd just come out here on my own once Archie told me this guy played bass now for the infamous Hangman's Gang. I leaned forward, shouting into his ear to be heard.

"I just want to know why you don't play with Nic anymore? Why you gave it up for this?"

He wagged his head. "Dude's an asshole, that's why. He treated us like we were minions, man, like we were Santa's little helpers or whatever. I wanna be in a band, I wanna be in a band, not serve some autocrat's vision."

He said these words contemptuously, like he'd just learned them at school and they weren't worth considering besides. *Vision.* The house lights came on now, and the PA, playing Television's "See No Evil."

"Besides," he said, "Nic's talented, but it's not like he's commercial. He's lazy too…guy needs to write more of his own songs."

I watched him as he reached over and fished an Old Gold from his pack atop the amplifier. Little squiggles were drawn across his shirt, in what looked like a parody of Charlie Brown's sweater. This guy was a loser. If he wanted "commercial" shouldn't he have been working in institutional sales, gone and sold out to an investment bank or something? (Yeah, he was that rock 'n' roll.) And hadn't his band just ended its own set with a cover? He shrugged and blew smoke.

"Give my regards to Felice," he said. And then he turned away.

I wanted to ask him more, but just then the drummer beckoned him over to help dismantle his kit. That was all I'd get. Asshole, lazy. The words with which he'd just tarred Nic rang in my mind, as it seemed they might've described him better. After all he'd just acted like sixty seconds of his time was a huge donation, like Nic was an idiot for not pandering the way his own band did to the crowd. "Demanding." Was that a bad thing? We were well past the time when musicians could be saviors, of "Eric Clapton was God" and all that hippie silliness. Even I recognized it was too late for this. But if Nic asked a lot, of his band, of his audience or of himself, wasn't this something to aspire towards instead? It seemed to me most bands now asked too little, and that we—being the ironic generation, the one who'd missed everything and now had little to offer back except sarcasm—went all too willingly along with them. If Archie and I were wrong, if Lords of Oblivion really did suck (in the end the records were inconclusive, and it was easy to imagine in person they might collapse a rickety line between greatness and bombast, excitement and chaos), the fact remained that at least they meant it. Better to suck honestly than to hide behind irony, wasn't it? Was it?

I went back out to High Street, where people milled around in a cheerful stupor, plotting their next move.

"That was greeeaat," someone drawled. Meaning it without meaning it, like skill was the best we could hope for.

****

I tore through the phonebook the next morning in our kitchen,

scrabbling frantically through the pages. Lo and behold, there was a listing!
An *A. Nicolas DeVine*, on 13th Street. An unlucky number, but who cared?
The unforeseen initial and capitalized "V" threw me a little also, yet there
wasn't another listing close. It was him! It had to be! I picked up the rotary
phone in the kitchen and then—raced off, leaving the receiver bouncing
against the wall. Why bother with half-measures at this point? It was 9 A.M.
A little early, by our summertime standards, but I'd wait on his doorstep all
morning if I had to. I'd been in Columbus less than a week. The soles of my
sneakers skidded and slapped against the pavement as I ran through the hazy
morning, so muggy and oppressive. Thunder rumbled above.

The address I was looking for proved to be close, just on the other
side of Indianola. A drafty-looking Edwardian, painted a drab black. The
whole structure seemed to sag, leaning-tower style, with age and casual
neglect. Mosquito screens peeled from the exterior windows, and last autumn's
decaying leaves lay piled up still on the lawn. A rain gutter dangled from the
porch eave. It was set back from the street, the whole massive house—three
stories—resting on a double lot. The place was big enough for a rock star, who
had oceans of space and time at his disposal. At the same time it didn't appear
that anyone lived here at all. A white plaster lion, the kind you see in front of
libraries and museums, crouched atop the front steps. An air of decrepitude
prevailed. Only as I came near did I see the porch had lately been repainted.
Its boards shone gray, and there were neatly-kept flowerpots filled with
marigolds. I heard music inside now too, cranked up to excruciating levels
behind the thick oak door with its brass knocker. I recognized it as Big Star's
"Feel," the singer wailing about how he felt like he was dying, was never going
to live again. The song had that early-seventies John Lennon quality, where
every word felt like it was torn from deep inside its author's guts. I lifted my
hand to the knocker, took a deep breath.

What would I say to Nic if he answered? You changed my life? I
worship your band? Both were true—I had never loved a band the way I loved
his—but I was embarrassed. Even Marcus's attention seemed to have waned
the past few weeks. I barely saw him at all now that we were both here, and he
was working some weird warehouse job—prole to the core—with long hours.
But he was on to newer thrills, uncovering some passion for the fat Elvis after

he'd discovered a copy of the *Blue Hawaii* soundtrack in the bargain bins of the VTE. Without him I was alone in my obsession. I took another deep breath. My heart was hammering. I lifted the knocker.

And then dropped it. I turned and ran, bolting up the street. My passion overwhelmed me, making me speechless with terror. I skittered up the uneven sidewalk while the first fat raindrops fell, past defiant frat boys grilling on their lawns—it was never too early for them to get started—beer guts jiggling in the early June heat. When I was a kid I'd once tried to trick-or-treat a house people told me was haunted, and that's exactly what I felt now, that same rising sense of irrational, pant-pissing panic, my guts twisting up towards my throat. According to *The Attack*, Nic Devine was a psycho. If he punched out his own drummer, how would he treat a fan? I booked it all the way home. Mara found me there, leaning against the kitchen table and gasping.

"What's with you? Marathon training?"

"No…just tried…to visit Nic Devine."

"And? He kicked you out of the house for some reason?"

"No." I recovered myself, straightened up finally. "I chickened out."

"You did? Why?" Mara laughed. She ran a glass of water from the tap. Her hair was a rat's nest, she'd just woken up. "Nic's a total pussycat. Why don't you go see him at work? That way you won't be disturbing him or any… visitors he might have. He works at the Kroger's down near German Village."

"Wait, he works at—he works at a grocery store?"

"Sure." She turned and set the glass on the sink beside her. Stood there in overalls, hands in her pockets. I don't know why I hadn't thought to ask her sooner, since she seemed well acquainted with everyone on the local scene. "He works the graveyard shift, midnight to six."

I stared. Outside, the rain spattered and washed, sizzling on the roof and against the windows. My first real thundershower. Gray light shifted, kaleidoscopic, behind her.

"The world's greatest rock 'n' roll singer works in a grocery store? How is that possible?"

"I dunno." She laughed. "You thought those singles made him rich? Hey, Otis Redding worked in a gas station," she added. "Life's not entirely fair."

So it wasn't. But surely this couldn't be it? Surely Nic's life wasn't all boxes, cash registers and cans?

"DeVine? Try produce." A man in a butcher's apron looked at me from a face that was creased with worry lines, the color of cocoa butter. He looked like he'd been hit in the nose repeatedly, like experience had somehow flattened out the features he'd been born with.

"Hey Bill?" Another fellow, in coveralls, with a red and white gingham-checked shirt on underneath them, skinny and pale: a scarecrow. "Nic quit last weekend."

"What?"

"Yeah." The second man sauntered over to us, looked me up and down skeptically. "Management bought him out."

"No kidding? I didn't know about that."

I stood between them, with no idea what they were talking about, perched in the eternal twilight of the supermarket after dark. Lunch meats, pickled vegetables, boxes and boxes of cereal stretching away in what seemed infinite lines. Never the twain shall meet. The second man rubbed his balding head.

"Sell out."

"What?" I had no idea what they were saying, but this was too much for me. "He's not a sellout! Nic's the opposite of a sellout! He's a hero—"

"DeVine?" The butcher laughed.

"Yeah. He's a musician. He's a star—"

This cracked them both up. While I stood in the Freon chill of the meat department, my palm leaving its print against a glass cabinet filled with innards, liver, steak.

"A star? Yeah, boy sure could stack them cans! Go, Johnny go!"

They reeled. Laughing and laughing.

"You're sure we're talking about the same guy, kid?"

"Yep."

I turned away. Nothing depressed me more than the thought of Nic at the mercy of these—philistines, slaving away in this place where the sun never shined, or it always shined, and an arctic wind blew through the aisles. He'd quit! Good for him!

"Give our regards to Broadway, kid!"

"Yeah! 'Stairway to Heaven!' Alright!"

I reeled into the parking lot, clutching a cabbage of all things—like the very head of John the Baptist, it seemed—under my arm. Drooping under the weight of such ridicule. He'd quit. Thank goodness for small favors. The pavement smoked after another recent thundershower, the moon showing through scudding clouds above. A full moon, vampire weather. And I wondered if I would ever find Nic Devine, or if he would simply remain apocryphal, pitched somewhere between sarcasm and superstition: those twin signals of a civilization in collapse.

11

Vampire Blues

"So...are you working?"

My father and I sat in Sunset Plaza, having lunch on the terrace of an Italian restaurant, picking at plates of spaghetti alla checca, under brown umbrellas sheltering us from the sun. He ate and I sat there sedated—I'd flown home for two days to have my wisdom teeth removed—under the influence of liquid Valium. He drank espresso. My tongue and jaw felt clotted, heavy, even as my skull floated like a helium balloon. I sounded like a *Peanuts* character's parent when I talked, my jaw not cooperating fully with my intention.

"Not really."

"Why not?"

I couldn't explain. This was the way I felt all the time when I went home—not about work, of course, but this disjunction between my thoughts and feelings, words and deeds. This seemed to happen whether or not I was on drugs or in pain.

"I dunno...I've only been there a week."

"A week's a lifetime, if you're a fly." He spread his arms with an almost prosecutory zeal. "What've you been up to?"

In a sense, my relation to my father was the normal parent-child dynamic, inverted. I prevaricated while he asked the forever unanswerable, *Why?* I could've said, chasing a band, chasing a girl, chasing a dream: these things would've been equally misunderstood. Light flew off the pale sidewalk where we sat, struck the mirrored faces of the shops and office towers across the street. A whooshing parade of drop-topped Porsches and 450 SLs in bronzed mid-eighties colors. This was the Sunset Strip, where everyone and their aunt seemed to want to be, everyone except me. I couldn't see this place clearly, either. I wandered through it like a blind man, dazed by heat, by sunlight, by uncertain feeling. My father smiled at our waitress—barely my age, brunette—as she came by to clear our plates and refresh my iced tea. Wind kicked across the patio.

"You're having fun?" he said. Leaning back in his chair, arching his chest in a black T-shirt. My father wasn't a monster or even a disciplinarian. In a sense it would have been easier if he'd been either of these things. Instead he was a hedonist and egotist, a playboy at age fifty-three. "Eating lots of potatoes?"

"Dad, that's Idaho."

"Oh."

What could I say or do, in this situation? Confronted with his blend of nostalgia and misunderstanding, his unaccountable belief that it was all about him? Maybe it was, maybe I knew nothing after all. Watching him stare out across Sunset Boulevard a moment, his noble profile: weak chin and strong nose. He wore big, dark aviator glasses that made his gaze faintly skeletal, a look of hollow sockets.

"Have fun," he sighed. While the wind stirred his still-thick, silvering hair, while he stared at our waitress's ass as she bent across another table. "When I was your age, I thought I was going to live forever."

I smirked. "'When I was your age?'"

So it went. I couldn't relate to any of it. Blood trickled between my teeth as my father fixed me with that paralyzing Gorgon's stare. What we had here, I thought, was a failure to communicate. Nothing new in that. But I did think if I was ever going to understand my own hometown and my profound aversion to it, I'd have to do so through Columbus. Did everyone long to leave the place they were from? Did everyone eventually return? How many songs had been written about that, about "going home?" My father grew up in Beverly Hills. Sun seemed to beat from his face, the coppery skin, burnished bronze of an L.A. native. I'd go blind if I lived here. And all of this—have fun; I thought I'd live forever—wasn't this, too, the sort of vapid West Coast hedonism my friends on the other coast made fun of? Justly, I thought. But like the song, like John Doe and Exene said: I had to leave.

****

"Wake up!" Mara shook me, where I lay on my futon. "Time to get up!"

"What?" It was nighttime, ten-thirty on a Friday. I splayed, face down like a drowned swimmer. I'd taken a painkiller earlier—my jaw still ached—and passed out. Now I lifted my head. "Huh—"

"Get up. Knobby's here."

"What—here, in the apartment?"

"No, in town. We're going out to meet him."

Outside, heat lightning flickered dimly on the horizon, with no rain to go with it. 'Knobby' was Kitty's fiancé, the Goth king. I rolled over, sighed. Eyes adjusting to the dim, gummy air in the room. That old carpet smell.

"Why do I care about some pop star from England?" I muttered. "I'd rather sleep."

"Because Felice'll be there," Mara said, reaching over and turning on the bedside lamp. "Get up."

"Unh—Okay" I shielded my eyes from the sudden eruption off the bulb. "That'll do it."

"I figured." She watched while I scrambled to my feet. "Don't *over*do it, loverboy."

I fished on the floor for suitable duds. Mara was already dressed, glammed up in VTE black. I suppose I was curious about 'Knobby,' since it wasn't every day a bona fide rock 'n' roll star came to Columbus. His nickname, for instance: why did people call him that? I found black motorcycle boots, black jeans, a shirt that smelled enough like patchouli to pass for clean. I hadn't seen Felice in over a week, not since that afternoon I'd sat with her brother and she'd ridiculed both of our tastes. Maybe I'd have better luck this time, maybe, maybe—"Where are we going?" I called down the hall, where Mara was brushing her teeth. "Brother's?"

"Lady's"

"Lady's?" I listened while she spat and ran the tap, checked my own reflection—I still struggled to adapt to the light, my eyes burning with the afterimage of a bulb—in the mirror. "That place'll be a mob scene. It's practically an altar to Knobby as it stands."

"Yeah." We met in the hallway, on our way towards the door. "We've gotta go pick up Lena first, too. Her car's in the shop."

We rode out to Wilkerton in Mara's decaying AMC Gremlin. For various reasons, I'd come to remember the date as a historic one: June 13. On our way, we listened to a tape of Knobby's first band. Named after an architectural school, they were the progenitors of the Goth movement, had inspired a generation of people in England to wear black lipstick and fishnet stockings; his current one had scraped the American Top Forty once already and would soon score an honest-to-goodness Top Five hit. Even the Thick People here would've heard of him; fliers proliferated on High Street that summer, occasional pieces of fan graffiti. *We Love You, Knobby*. To the kids in Columbus—and even to someone from outside it, like me—he seemed from another planet. The likelihood of seeing him in a dingy nightclub on High Street was akin to that of finding the Pope in a Rax Roast Beef. The first song he ever recorded, all rackety rimshots and echo-soaked vocals—a paean to the original Dracula—filled the car as we pulled up Lena's long, gravel-paved driveway. *Undead, undead.*

"Is Felice here?"

"She said she'd meet us." Mara winked at me. "Be patient, sport."

I'd been curious to see the inside of Lena's house, yet its ground floor turned out to be most ordinary, if large. A regular red-tiled suburban kitchen with sleek modern fixtures: a Krups espresso maker over by the sink, a stainless-steel fridge the size of a meat locker. Wealth may have enhanced the scale of a thing indefinitely, but never changed its nature. Eight bedrooms remained simply bedrooms. Invisible Dan, who was bivouacked here for the summer, mooched around in his robe and slippers. He had a cold, was not going out. He may as well have been in another county, for all he got to see of Lena anyway. So near and yet so far! Her father, a mountainous six-three, hovered nearby. He rubbed his palms together anxiously, to Lena's extreme embarrassment.

"What're you guys doing?" We sat in her kitchen doing vodka shots, waiting 'til closer to midnight to leave. "You're going out?"

"*Yes*, dad." She sighed. "Going out."

He had an Old Testament face: craggy, bearded, mountain-like behind those rose-tinted glasses. Leon, was his name. The beard was cut square like

Abraham Lincoln's, but otherwise he looked like someone who'd arrived late or soon to the Studio 54 party, gold ropes jingling around his neck and wrists. Chest hair a little too clearly in evidence. I could see where Lena's discomfort came from. As if the more he aged, the greater became a hunger for the trivial.

"I'll tag along," he enthused. "It'll be fun."

"I don't think so," Lena said, squirming. "Dad, *please.*"

He looked injured as Lena flipped her tea—she'd made it too strong—into the sink. We were leaving. She had to go over and give him a hug, explain almost as you would to a puppy or a sick toddler.

"Dad, I'm sorry," I heard her murmur. "It's for kids only. It's a club."

"But I *am* a kid," he protested. "I'm not old."

"You are, dad. You're forty-seven."

He reminded me of my own father this way. Mara and I stepped out through the porch door and into the drive, kicking white pebbles with our heavy shoes. Would we be like that when we were older? I didn't know whether to hope so or not, whether the purpose of age was to accrete wisdom or retain vitality. Perhaps neither, or both. Lena came out a minute later, shaking her head.

"Sorry."

"For what?" I said.

"He's embarrassing."

"*All* families are embarrassing," I hugged her. You should see mine. "Where d'you think embarrassment comes from?"

We piled back into our car. Dan had shot the transmission on hers with all that gear-grinding.

"How are things working out between your dad and your secret admirer, anyway?" I asked. "Are they having pizza parties together at lunch? Playing canasta on those lonely bachelor evenings at home?"

Maybe I mocked Dan to distance myself from my own feelings: after all, the things I wanted didn't seem any more within reach. He'd hardly said a word to any of us just then, but simmered and seethed. He'd looked at Lena with an injured, almost resentful expression when she'd told him we were leaving. But she just laughed. "My dad loves him. He's the only guy in the office who can decipher my dad's handwriting. They have a special kind of bond."

"Huh," I said. Her parents were divorced. The Columbus *Dispatch* had referred to her dad as Columbus's Most Illegible Bachelor on account of his famously obscure jottings, the legal pads nobody could read. "Maybe I should give him my note from Nic."

We rode downtown rocking Knobby's band at top volume, all of us lost in whatever hopeful thought consumed us. Mine was for Felice to notice me again and bend my way. We parked and sauntered along High—there were too many of us to worry about Thick People—to where a crowd had gathered outside Crazy Lady's. One girl was tugging at her raven-colored hair and crying, tears running little irrigation channels in her pancake makeup.

"Is he here?" she gasped to her kohl-eyed companion.

"I think I saw him! Oh my God!!"

We made our way past the hoi polloi, the Gothic sprites on the stairs, all aquiver as if waiting to meet the Beatles, feeling that little surge of privilege that goes with bypassing the velvet rope. The place we called "Lady's" was like every second-string nightclub in America, a windowless hot-box painted black, two rooms with a bar and a dance floor and a "VIP area" that would've been empty most nights, or just annexed to the bar. I spotted Felice—finally—in this back room, sitting beside Kitty. She lifted her arm and waved. I went weightless with relief and exhilaration. On Kitty's opposite side sat a tall, pale, pointy guy—his limbs, joints, hair, everything seemed peaked—in tattered blue jeans, a psychedelic silk shirt that looked like a sunset painting by Turner.

"Knobby, this is everyone. Everyone, Knobby."

Pale kneecaps poked through the holes in his jeans. Even his ears seemed pointy, like a Vulcan's. His sculpted silver-blonde hair was like a shuriken, a ninja's throwing star.

"So," I said, while I shook his hand. His fingers were long, delicately articulated. It was like clutching a bird's skeleton, barely a handshake at all. "Why do they call you that?"

Total silence. Kitty looked at the tabletop and blushed, and then Felice burst out laughing. Terrific. I felt like I materialized before her only in the most stupid or humiliating situations. I looked down at his hands, which were enormous.

"Forget I asked," I said. "Anyone need a drink?"

Laughter rippled around the table. "Yeh, sure, man." He peeled off a twenty and gave it to me. "Get yerself one. Oi, Crabby," he added, speaking to a pale-skinned, lanky kid with a jet-black fringe and a sleeveless Sisters of Mercy T-shirt in the next booth—I recognized him as the band's drummer— "whatcherdrinkin?"

"Lager."

"Vodka tonic," Felice said, softly. Smiling now. There was hope. "Please."

I went off to the bar in the next room. "Crabby." I knew better than to ask about that one. Over on the bare checkerboard dance floor they were playing the Ramones' "We're A Happy Family." The room reeked of clove cigarettes and essential oils, a cloying, smoky-sweetness. I bellied up to the bar, where Mara was talking to some guy with thick, auburn waist-length hair. It looked like a mourner's veil, Cousin It's mane. Who let him in here, I wondered? As Marcus had explained it, the only people in Columbus who had hair that long were the dozy rednecks from suburbs like Gahanna, the satellite towns where time slowed to a crawl and it was still 1971. People in these alternate alternate-worlds worshipped a band called the Dawgz, local one-hit wonders who'd scored their nationwide moment of fame with a song called "(Feelin' Fine) My Sweet '69." Anthemic to the brink of insanity, with mutant power-chords that called to mind the worst of such bands as Mountain, Montrose and Nitzinger—a slackadaisical, Southern-fried boogie—"(Feelin' Fine)..." might have been the worst song I'd ever heard. Thirty seconds were enough to guarantee a corresponding drop in IQ points, and its title might even have been the most subtle and elegant thing about it. It's a double-entendre, dude! I looked at Mr. Chimneysweep with all the contempt I felt for both the song and the misogynist hippie-rock culture it represented. On his arm was a trashy-looking bottle-blonde in a black leather bustier—didn't it figure?—a girl who could've stepped directly from the poster of one of those Russ Meyer movies like *Kitten With A Whip* or *Faster, Pussycat! Kill, Kill!* Her breasts seemed to have lives of their own. I watched as they crawled across the zinc top of the bar.

"A vodka tonic and a scotch 'n' soda," I said as Kate Blum, the bartender, came round and took my order. Mara grabbed my wrist and was about to say something but then someone tapped her shoulder from behind. She whirled. What was that about, I wondered? Why so excited? I asked Kate, "How's tricks?"

"Pretty good," she said. I'd met Kate last weekend. She was not just our bartender but our priestess, a Wiccan. A crucifix hung upside down around her neck, her hair was baubled with tiny glass beads. She had the sharp features and rouge-red cheeks of a marionette. "Rock star brings the big tippers."

She nodded at the dirtbag next to me. Her long blonde cornrows clicked like an abacus as she turned; several were pulled back and braided into a long silken rope, a bellpull that fell halfway down her back. I waited for my drink to arrive. Looking over at Felice, who was hemmed in between Kitty and the wall. I doubted anyone would get there before I did. The bar was lined with Columbus luminaries like Gary Hauser, the front man for Plains States. Gary may have looked like a three hundred pound junkyard dog, mangy, unshaven and all too often drunk as a lord at ten in the morning behind the till at *School Daze* records where he worked, but secretly he was an intellectual.

"You gotta understand what Proudhon was saying," Gary said, little flecks of spittle raining into Lena's ear, "he didn't mean 'Property is Theft' to suggest ownership was a crime, exactly, he meant—"

Gary seemed to epitomize yet another side of Columbus, the one where ambition was superfluous and you could be a medium-sized carp in a medium-sized pond. Neither famous nor not-famous, simply known. A six-pack dangled from his wrist, which was thick as a ham hock. I wouldn't have wanted to be on the wrong side of Gary, no matter how socialist his policies. From the next room came the sound of tinny darkwave psychedelia, Echo & The Bunnymen's "Angels and Devils," cross fading over Love's "The Red Telephone." Arthur Lee chanted his words about being normal and "wanting his freedom" as the new song faded in. I turned back to the bar and shivered. Here in the main room it was freezing, the AC dialed up to maximum effect so that everyone could wear their heavy Gothic armor. Yet the guy next to me wore only a threadbare T-shirt with a Big Daddy Roth cartoon on it, a bug-eyed, fly-halo'd scumbag above the legend *Rat Fink A Boo-Boo*.

"Jesus," I said. "It's like a meat locker in here. What's with the sub-zero temperatures?"

"A meat locker?" He snorted. "I'm vegetarian."

He seemed like contradiction itself, like anything I'd said would've provoked a similar response. Did he want to pick a fight with me? I didn't have time, needed to get Felice her drink. Beside him, the trashy blonde didn't say a word. His hair seemed both natural and uncanny, almost vine-like as it hung halfway to his waist. Beneath it I could sense a certain brightness. An edgy charisma.

"You don't think it's cold?"

"I guess," he chuckled. "I don't really notice these things."

"Oh no?"

His eyes were dark, unexpectedly intelligent. His too-emphatic smile wasn't trustworthy. It was showmanlike, touched with psychosis. He seemed like a cross between Jack Nicholson and Roadrunner, quivering with original energy.

"I only notice the important stuff," he said. "Not bullshit like the weather."

"Oh yeah? What 'important stuff' would that be, man? Kung-fu and the nearest pair of garden shears?"

He nodded. Good one. Then he swept his arm around the room.

"Nah. I was thinking more about how these people suck. How every nightclub and every band in Columbus sucks, for example. That seems to me like something that could use its dissertation."

I stared. He spoke a normal volume, but the music seemed to stop. Everyone could hear him.

"Um, you think?"

Gary Hauser looked over with a sudden interest. He had five inches and a hundred-twenty pounds on this guy. It wouldn't be pretty. I nodded over towards Knobby.

"So you're not really a fan of the Spacemen?"

"Not really, no." It seemed this roomful of nosy, partisan vampires might tear him to pieces just as easily. "In fact I think they're terrible. Bunch of flaccid Anglo posers."

He rolled his eyes, gave each word its weight before he picked up his drink, a White Russian, and drained it in one solid, wholesome-seeming swig. Mopped the milky white mustache it left away with his thumb. I half expected him to ask for a plate of cookies. Several of Knobby's minions glared at him. Their long fingernails, painted black on boys and girls alike, seemed to glisten like knife points. Was he out of his mind?

"Listen," I said, "you can't tell me *every* band in Columbus sucks. There are some pretty good ones."

"Yeah? *Who?*"

Conversation along the bar stopped. Almost every musician in Columbus was here, punk heavies like the Demon Dogs and a lesbian power trio called Skank, whose singer moonlighted in repossession. Kate Blum herself sang in a band called Dark Matter. She may have been a Good Witch, but you didn't fuck around with the occult either. Gary Hauser swiveled in his seat, cracked his knuckles and cleared his throat. A sound like the rumblings of an upset volcano, an angry god.

"Name me one band in Columbus who doesn't suck." My new friend beamed suicidally, like he was proud of the ass-kicking he was about to receive. "Just one."

"Plains States," I blurted, although they actually did suck. Hard. "Plains States are—"

"PFFFFF," my friend said. "Piddly little New Wave singalong nonsense. They. Suck."

He spat these words into Gary Hauser's face.

"They suck. Suck suck suck. I wouldn't use a Plains States records to line my cat's litter box, they suck so badly. I wouldn't want my poor baby's paws to get contaminated." He rolled his eyes. "Now who else?"

I stepped back. Expecting Gary to reach out and snap this joker's neck left-handed. Yet instead he just stood there, rubbing his scruffy beard. A wry smile played across his face. He too seemed to find this guy entertaining.

"Well look," I said, "I happen to know one band in Columbus who are great. Besides Dark Matter, who—"

"Please." He rolled those googly eyes again. "Dark Matter are literate."

"Oh right," I said. "Of course. Heaven forbid, anything should be *literate.*"

He kept his mad, overconfident smile. For a second he looked obscurely, almost occultly familiar. Who was this guy? I'd seen his face before, but couldn't place it out of context. "Rock 'n' roll should be pre-literate," he sneered. The first thing he'd said with which I almost agreed. "Really...if you can put it into words it's probably not worth saying in the first place."

"Damn straight," I said. Which one of us was humoring the other? "I'm with you, bro."

This whole time the tall woman in the bustier beside him hadn't said a word. But now she reached into his shirt pocket and pulled out something brown and dusty-looking, then fed it to him. Her lips flexed kissily. She was like a harem girl feeding an emperor a grape.

"What's that?" I said.

"Peyote. Want a button?"

"No thanks. Look," I said, gesturing out towards the whole bar, the dingy, dark Midwestern-Gothic alternative-watering-hole that was Crazy Lady's. In the next room the lights of the dance floor flashed forlornly; a disco ball rotated above, refracting them, a fly's-eye view. "You can't tell me every band here sucks. This is all we've got, this place." I may as well have said This Planet. "And there is one band in Columbus I think is amazing. Better than the Rolling Stones ever were." I took a deep breath. "They'd be bigger than Jesus, if I had a say."

"Bigger than Jesus, huh?" My companion laughed. "Enlighten me. Who is it?"

Everyone was listening. I didn't care. I emptied my lungs above the strains of a new song floating over from the next room, something that sounded like everything my best-beloved band in fact stood to oppose: campy and stiff, feeble and cheap. It was David Bowie and Bing Crosby's chalk-and-cheese duet on "The Little Drummer Boy," I realized. God knows why the DJ was choosing to spin it in June.

"Lords of Oblivion," I shouted. "Lords of Oblivion are the best rock 'n' roll band in the world and I don't care who knows it."

My new friend just cast his head back and laughed. He guffawed, actually. I'd never heard anyone do that. *Uh-haw, haw-haw.* He threw his head back, and mocked me in full.

"Um, no." He said finally, mopping away tears. "I'm afraid not. If you really think that, you're beyond help."

This guy's face nagged me. I'd seen it pictured somewhere. It had that likeness-to-an-inaccurate-likeness quality, like the square root of an imaginary number. But I had no time to figure it out as *everyone* was laughing at me, I realized. Why? Even Gary Hauser who'd just been insulted. Gary was laughing at me too.

"If you think that's a good band," he said, "I can't do anything for you. They're hopeless. Every time I hear them, I want to pluck my ears straight off the sides of my head and bury them at the bottom of the ocean. Scout's honor that they're awful. Just terrible."

I took a big slug of my drink, melted ice floes atop a distant rumor of scotch. Felice was struggling up from her booth and I thought I'd best put paid to this conversation before it was too late.

"Listen," I said. I was beginning to mistrust the evidence of my senses. Did Lords of Oblivion even exist? What if Archie had just lied? Did *anyone* hear what I heard, I wondered, as that absurd Christmas carol droned in the background? "You've seen 'em? Lords of Oblivion... exist? They're not just some hoax made up by *The Attack*?"

"I'm afraid not," he said. He shook his head and scowled at the floor like a reluctant cowboy, like John Wayne feeling bad about a slaughter he was nevertheless about to head up. "It'd be better for everyone if they'd just disappear."

"They won't though," I said. I heard the pleading in my own voice. "Will they?"

People were still snickering. I didn't blame them. I was like an adult, begging at the altar of Santa Claus. Desperate for something I should've outgrown long ago.

"No. I'm afraid they're around for the duration. But every time I've heard 'em..." Another regretful headshake. "It hasn't been pretty."

I turned back to the bar and picked up my drinks. My face was burning with embarrassment. I struggled back towards Felice, vodka tonic and Crabby's lager slopping onto my shirt and—alas—my crotch. This just got better and better.

"I love that band," I said as I waded back towards the crowd. "Their singer's a genius."

"Oh I doubt that." He crunched another peyote button. "You must have low standards."

"They're low enough that I'm wasting my time talking with you," I said. "I'm off. Thanks for the information."

"No problem."

I stepped away, leaving him to mutter something about how if Nic Devine is a genius then I'm Batman. This set off a fresh round of tittering along the bar. Mara intercepted me as I strode away.

"How'd that go?" she asked. She wore knee-high go-go boots tonight, and had done her hair up into a Dusty Springfield beehive. How people did transform around here, I thought. Everyone and their alter egos.

"How'd what go?"

I looked over her shoulder. Everybody was jammed cheek-to-jowl trying to squeeze into the back room, hoping they might catch a glimpse of the honest-to-goodness real-life rock star in our midst. Knobby crouched—I could see his hair from here—in his booth, signing autographs on napkins, slapping hands with the Goths who all wanted a piece of him. The dance floor lights flashed, a sequence like one of those memory keypad games: pink, peach, red, blue, green. I sipped my scotch and soda.

"Your conversation," Mara said. "How was that?"

"What, that guy?" Felice was coming towards us now. Maybe, just maybe, the evening could be saved. "Who was that guy? Is he a friend of yours?"

"Kinda," Mara said. "He's sort of a local eccentric we all put up with."

"Well I don't know if it was just the peyote talkin' or what, but he started in with some trash about Lords of Oblivion and how bad they were. We got into an argument."

"You did?"

"Yeah. He said they were the worst band in Columbus. You and I both know the Dawgz are the worst band in Columbus," I said. "I don't know what his problem is."

"Wow." Mara threw a sympathetic arm around my neck. "You set him straight, of course."

"I tried."

She looked me up and down. Felice arrived and of course she, too, looked straight at the stain in my crotch. She arched an eyebrow.

"Wanna dance?

"Sure."

Mara just stood there, trembling with laughter.

"What is it?" I said. "What's so goddamn funny?"

The air filled with the familiar, chugging strains of the Velvet Underground's "I'm Waiting For My Man," that hammering, one-note piano riff that kicked it off. The dance floor started to throng, people moving out of their chairs and pushing forward, following the directive of the music. Marcus crowded into the booth back there between Knobby and Kitty; Gary Hauser frowned and nodded, pontificating in the face of everyone who'd listen; Krist Cooley stood over in the corner doing James Brown splits and Temptations spins, executing every move to perfection. What a circus this place was! Yet the guy I'd been arguing with had just left. The girl in the bustier was vanishing out the door behind him, steering her tits ahead of her like turret-guns. I looked back at Mara.

"That was *him*, you dolt," Mara said. She stared at me with that same incredulous just-how-dumb-are-you look she'd fixed on me the night Felice and I finally slept together, when I'd waited about ten thousand years to make my move. "That was Nic Devine! I wanted to introduce you, but—"

My face was numb suddenly. My whole body tingled. I bolted for the door, pushing through the crowd as Mara seized Felice's arm in some mixed access of hilarity and pity.

"Oh honey," I heard her say. "I thought you liked smart boys!"

I jammed my way out the door and into the crowded stairwell, caromed off of a wall, almost tripped over the pointy end of someone's Gothic slipper as I all but fell down the stairs. I tumbled onto the street, skinning my knee and my palms as I landed on dirty concrete. I scrambled up. Fuck! He was gone! I saw the taillight of his motorcycle, the girl in the bustier's lightning-gold hair streaming away below her helmet as they zoomed off down High Street. I stood there, staring. Stunned. Until the taillight vanished, and the street was empty once more.

Fuck.

I limped back upstairs, my palms raw and burning, my embarrassment dissolving into something worse: a pure, almost suicidal, frustration.

"Hey, hon, you spilled your drink," someone said, as I trudged upstairs.

"I don't need it."

I flashed my stamped hand at the doorman and stumbled onto the dance floor. Felice, too, was gone, with Knobby and his entourage who'd slipped out the back. That figured. I needed a lobotomy, I thought. A luck transplant. Something that would let me be other than who I was: a loser, unable to seize my brightest opportunity even when it stared me right in the face.

II

Minus Zero

12

Bargain

I made my way across the lawn, striding towards the house I'd fled from once before. Summer grass crunched beneath my steps, yet there were new flowers, blood-red roses growing in all the window boxes. Blossoms the size of grapefruits. Whoever lived here—Nic Devine, I presumed—was clearly a horticulturalist of some skill. The velvet curtains remained drawn, the windows trembled faintly in their frames. I heard again the intestinal groaning of music played loud, well above the pain threshold for whoever was inside. Once more I hesitated in the shade of the portico. Then knocked. I pounded with both fists. Above the door, on the lintel, were carved the words *Donovan's Brain*: this was the name credited with producing both Lords of Oblivion 45s. I don't know why I hadn't spotted it before. I banged again.

"Yeah?"

The cat from the bar answered, sleepy eyed and barefoot, sporting a blue silk shirt with white polka dots like the one Bob Dylan wore on the cover of *Highway 61 Revisited*. It was three in the afternoon. In broad daylight he was more immediately recognizable from his sleeve photographs, Nic Devine in the flesh. His hair was a lot longer, his features not nearly so blurry as they were in the mimeographed black-and-white pictures.

"Who's Donovan's Brain?" I said.

He looked me up and down. He didn't appear to recognize me from the bar, as the guy who'd defended him against his own slander three days ago. The street was quiet in the baking oven of daylight. Against its carless silence the music fairly exploded out the door behind him. It sounded like Humble Pie, one of those hairy seventies hard rock bands I'd learned to loathe on basic punk principle yet had never actually heard. The singer sounded like he was undergoing sinister methods of interrogation.

"Who the hell are you, man?" He squinted at me. "You got me outta bed to ask me that?"

"Yeah."

"Shit." He yawned. "I can't tell you, anyway. It's a secret." He eyed me, poker-faced. "Who are you, man?"

"I'm your lawyer," I said. His boldness rubbed off on me. I felt alive. "Right now, I'm your only friend."

He grinned, finally. That high-wattage, charisma-crazed smile. "Nah, man, I recognize you. I was just puttin' you on."

"You were?"

"Sure." His head jolted up and down. "A friend of mine is a…friend of mine, or something like that! C'mon in!"

I stepped inside. The song ended and what began next—it must've been a tape, not an LP—was Elvis Presley's original 1955 version of "Mystery Train." It sounded nearly identical though, as anything would have at such timber-cracking volume. Echoing vocals fought back against hollow pockets of rumbling bass distortion.

"Lemme just turn the music down to conversation level." He dipped into the next room a second, adjusted the volume knob by a micromovement while I stood at the foot of a wide staircase. "There."

I didn't notice a difference. We still had to shout to make ourselves heard. It was like standing in an airfield, loud enough to make a person cry. Despite which, and despite the long hair, he almost reminded me of Elvis once he let his guard down. There was a certain aw-shucks hillbilly politeness—he might've been making fun of me the other night, but he might've simply been embarrassed—even an equal rough-hewn charisma. That coltish vitality was like the young King's too.

"You're not gonna tell me who Donovan's Brain is?" I said.

"Should I?" He mocked.

We stood in the hall, under a glass chandelier. The interior of the house smelled earthy, herbal: it smelled surprisingly like a garden. These rambling Campus houses more typically reeked of mold, old socks, generations of vomit and beer. The stairs tilted up to a second-floor landing, the room to the left was a living room. Disorderly as a playpen, scattered with musical instruments, vitamin bottles, and black vinyl records in and out of their sleeves. The tape ended, with an abrupt click. Our voices startled, carrying sharply into the silence.

"Alright," he said finally. "Five bucks."

"Five bucks?"

"Yeah. Donovan's Brain's a little shy."

I'd always wanted to know this, who was responsible for giving those records their thunderous mono sound, their wizardly primitivism like Little Richard or the '63 Beatles. *A Wall of Mud Production, by Donovan's Brain*, the two sleeves said. I rummaged in my pocket for a fiver and forked it over. He told me.

"The hell you say!" I squinted. I should've felt ripped off. But I was getting the hang of Nic's sense of humor. "That can't possibly be! I thought he was dead!"

"He is dead. Rumors that he's still alive are greatly exaggerated."

"I guess so!"

He tucked the bill in his pocket and chuckled serenely. "Hey, you asked."

"Can I come in?"

"Sure." He moved aside, motioned. "Want something to drink?"

"Why not? You fixing White Russians? Moscow Mules? Am I gonna get some value, for my five bucks?"

He laughed. There was so much VTE booty in the next room my eye didn't know where to light. A cardboard cutout of Jane Fonda starring as *Barbarella*; a pyramidal Crest toothpaste supermarket display; a Fender Rhodes electric piano disassembled, in pieces on the floor. What looked like a life-sized mannequin in a nurse's uniform, perched on a camel-colored mohair couch, before the cream-colored kidney-shaped coffee table. The curtain liners behind her were leopard-skin; there was a zebra-striped club chair. It was a sixties-themed psychedelic tree house, a flat Mick Jagger could've kept in Knightsbridge while "Play With Fire" climbed the British charts in March of '65. I would not have been surprised to find a Bentley out back, a liveried footman ready to serve Mandrax martinis on a silver tray.

"Say, babe? You wanna get us a couple of Training Wheels?" Nic said.

The nurse moved. Like a window-display stewardess, suddenly come to life. My God.

"Sure, Nic."

Her accent was Southern. She was as blonde and buxom as the girl in the bustier but was not, I was almost certain, the same girl. Beautiful, unless it was just the outliers of beauty, the idea of it that clung to her through mood and manners and body language. I never got a clean look at her face. She got up and came back with two huge beer steins filled with electric-blue liquid.

"Window cleaner?"

"Drink up."

I nodded after the nurse, the hostess, whatever she was. I'd never find out.

"Is that your girlfriend?"

He beamed. "She's my friendgirl."

"Is there a difference?"

He laughed. "What do you think, Sherlock?"

Then he settled back on the couch and I, his inquisitor, took the club chair. Above me an original poster for a James Bond movie, *You Only Live Twice*. Sean Connery surrounded by bathing beauties.

"So. You like the records, huh? What else can I tell ya?"

One question seemed just then to answer itself: that of why a complete unknown should be so reclusive. For all I could see, Nic Devine mightn't need to venture outside often, or ever. This room was proof against loneliness. It held absolutely everything a young man could want.

****

"Uh, wow—"

Two hours later, I was mumbling, stumbling, propping myself up against the pinball machine in the corner of the dining room. I needed to use its frame for support. As I neared the bottom of my third Training Wheel I'd forgotten everything this side of my own name. There was something important but never mind, I was with my hero. "What the hell d'you put in these things? They really sneak up on you."

Nic laughed. He moved nimbly on his feet. Float like a butterfly, sting like a bee. "Things do. Another five bucks and maybe "Donovan's Brain" can tell you what you wanna know."

The pinball machine's lights made me dizzy. Black spots swam before my eyes. Tilt! What was I forgetting? Behind us there was an enormous rectangular dining table that could've accommodated twenty people, loaded with bowls of fruit. Nic reached over and grabbed a banana, himself seemingly sober as a judge. He'd just whipped my ass five times on what was, naturally, a tribute to the Who's rock opera, a vintage 1970 *Tommy* pinball machine. See Me, Feel Me, it read across the top. Even at the VTE it must've cost a small fortune.

"When I was a kid I used to think the lyric was 'that deaf, dumb blanket...sure plays a mean pinball,'" I said. "Even if that doesn't actually make any sense."

Nic cackled. "Sense is overrated! I'd rather have a cheeseburger. Or...I would, if I wasn't vegetarian! Meaning's for suckers and school kids. You're not a student, are ya?"

I gulped the last of my Training Wheel. It tasted like lemonade, laced with agave and graveyard dirt. "Not today."

"Great! Hey, let's go listen to some records!"

Hanging out with Nic Devine, I found, was liking hanging with your older brother, if your older brother had seemingly unlimited financial resources and infinitely great taste. Every day would've been like the first of summer. We raced—he raced, and I stumbled—into the next room, filled with box upon box of dusty seven-inch singles. There were old soul records on King, Minit and San-Su; punk 45s on Hearthan and Rough Trade; girl groups on Cameo and impossibly rare garage rock or funk records that might've been pressed in editions of a few dozen copies, regional treasures that had never escaped the heartland. A first edition of Edward Abbey's *The Monkey Wrench Gang* lay over on a table beside rare and gorgeous volumes of Phillip K. Dick and Tom Wolfe, Raymond Chandler and Jim Thompson. *Counterfeit Unrealities*, read one spine; *Savage Night*, read another. Apparently the VTE had been plundered before Marcus even knew where to find it. (And where was Marcus now, now that I was hanging out with our hero? I hadn't seen him, and I doubted suddenly he would care. Now at long last it felt somehow like all of this, Nic and the band and even the city itself, all of it was on me.) The amber lampshades were art deco, silver saltshakers had the satisfying heft of brass knuckles. He blew dust off a record—"The Loser," it was called, with the artist's name scratched off the label, only the slogan, Tomorrow's Hits Today, 'Right Round The World, left legible—and sat it down gently on the turntable. I couldn't imagine Nic knew anything about losing—the guy was too clearly a winner—but the song was phenomenal. Jamaican sunshine soul harmonies, airy as a helium balloon. As always, he played it at tooth-loosening volume. I felt its sweetness ripple through my sternum, a whole shimmering summer compressed into two-minutes-fourteen-seconds. Once he filed the record, I knew I'd never hear it again.

"Don't you have neighbors?"

"Sure." He grinned, crouched over there by the stereo, at his feet different musical instruments: a Vox Starstreamer, Fender Jaguar, Burns Jazz Guitar. I had to cram this question into an interstice of silence; he was getting ready to blow my mind with another seven-inch brick of psychedelic brilliance, this one pressed on yellow vinyl. "One of 'em's upstairs."

"Don't you have neighbors…who aren't sex slaves?"

He stepped back from the turntable, having set the needle down. We moved away as if he'd just lit an M-80, scrambling for cover at the far end of the room.

"Nah. I used to, but he moved."

"Gee—" I flinched at the concussive blast—"I wonder why?"

He played songs by the Stems, the Thanes of Cawdor, the Green Telescope and the Eastern Dark, contemporary non-hits by up-to-the-minute revivalists who were themselves already being copied; played the Swamp Rats, the Illusions and the Humans, sixties bands so obscure their own families might never have heard of them; played Bob Dylan ("Outlaw Blues"), James Brown ("Forever Suffering") and the Rolling Stones ("Everything is Turning to Gold"), with the other Stone—Sly—looking down at us through star-shaped glasses from a poster that was stuck to the ceiling. Everything sounded great as I lay on the spinning floor, another Training Wheel weighting my chest while Nic told me the story of how he came to fund this extravagant little lifestyle. He'd worked the night shift at the grocery for a long time, he said, the last six years as a union employee, a stock boy, before ownership persuaded him to quit.

"They'd been trying to get me to quit forever," he said. "They wanted me out so they could go non-union. Finally they made me an offer I couldn't refuse."

"How much?"

We rested on our backs, hearing the soft pop of a record stuck in its run-out groove. Richard Hell & The Voidoids' "Blank Generation." I could see, too, the bantam wiriness of his forearms, the veiny musculature that came from stacking cans as well as playing guitar. Bony fingers like a puppeteer's.

"Ten grand."

"Seriously?" Even if in Columbus, at that time, ten grand was ample money, a year's freedom at least. "You sold cheap."

"Ahhh." He chuckled. There was a crack in the ceiling below the poster, running straight through Sly Stone's heart. "Maybe it was just a tiny bit more."

"Twenty grand?"

"Could be."

Whatever it was, there were two motorcycles in the backyard; a Traynor Reverb amp with the price tag still attached; that pinball machine. Not to mention the rent on this place, which he didn't appear to be sweating. I cleared my throat to broach the topic I'd been edging towards all afternoon.

"So now you're ready, right? Now you can devote yourself full-time to the band!"

"I can?"

"Yeah." I was sober now, but the room still seemed to spin. A paisley shirt by Nic's head had little black hypnotist's cones on it, a lopsided optical pattern like a repeating representation of infinity. Like the concentric grooves of a record. "Can't you?"

"Sure." He laughed, got up, changed the 45. Dr. Alimantado, the reggae toaster, sang "I Am The Greatest Says Muhammed Ali," a song off *The Best Dressed Chicken in Town*. Nic spread his arms, sardonically. "Come get me, world!"

"Don'cha sort of...have to?" I sat up and looked at him. I knew hardly anyone had bought the first two records, but he'd released them himself. He was what, twenty-two? I put him at just a few years older than I was. You weren't supposed to set the world alight with your first recordings, was my feeling. In fact you were supposed to fail. Almost everyone did that, from the Beatles on down. It was where soul came from. "Why wouldn't you? You're not making those records just to sell, are you?"

"What other purpose could they have?" He nodded outwards, towards the room. "I've got plenty of dishes, plenty of coasters." He snorted. But then he seemed to grow thoughtful. "I did record something recently. I thought I might put a record out in the fall."

"Yeah? You got a band?"

He looked at the ground. Even his voice seemed small and modest for a moment, like a jazz drummer's brush. Over in the corner too were worn copies of John Coltrane's *A Love Supreme*, Archie Shepp's *Fire Music*, Art Blakey & The Jazz Messengers' *A Night at Birdland*. He wasn't just a primitive, a secret sophistication lurked within.

"Nah," he said. "I just borrowed a bunch of guys from West Virginia called The Peacocks. But their guitarist's a monster, you gotta hear him!"

"Play on."

He cued up four new tunes on the tape deck. They leapt out of the speakers with a frantic intensity. They were so fierce I had to wedge myself into a far corner in order to listen, to parse the constituents of their sound. Yet each seemed detailed and incredible, and each a quantum step forward from the last. An avalanche of Fender-punishing guitar-wallop called "You Bother Me"; a contemptuous, semi-electric kiss-off to a girl called "I Can Stand It (Better Than You Can)," a field-holler of intimate disgust with a guitar riff borrowed from T. Rex; a groaning cover of an obscure sixties song—obscure even by the obscurantist standards under consideration—by the Fourth Form called "Too Far Gone;" and lastly, bestly, a murky, hunch-backed spasm of a tune called "The Art Goblin." This buried Nic's outraged shouting under so many layers of guitar squall you could barely make out a word of it, a real nervous breakdown committed to wax. All of these songs were fantastic, an immaculate amalgam of sixties psychedelic orthodoxy, punkish seventies aggression and that sullen, snotty petulance that has been rock 'n' roll's from the beginning. It was closer to art brats like Pere Ubu than it was to the Rolling Stones, yet way, way closer to the Beatles than it was to Surgical Penis Klinik. The hooks were huge, enticing, indelible no matter how strange. It was the kind of racket that seemed bound to become popular, only after it had stunned the underground. Who knew, perhaps its time would come? It seemed even then just a hair's breadth ahead of the go-go-go Eighties: laced with a galvanizing pessimism. I stood in stunned silence, pressed back against those thick, theatrical velvet-curtains.

"That was—amazing," I said finally, once I'd found my tongue. My head was clouded, ringing with the aftertrails of sound, my voice muzzy as if I had a cold. "So when are you gonna put those out? Have you sent those off to labels?"

Nic leaned back and looked at me.

"You think I should?"

"I think you will. I think you *have* to, or I'll, I'll—"

"Huff 'n' puff and blow my house down?"

I shook my head. Speechless, blinking. "I'll repossess your pinball machine. You can't live like a rock star if you're not ready to become one."

"Gee, thanks." He laughed. "I'm ready to play Buckeye Stadium whenever they can fill it up for me."

"Whatever," I said, though an idea was hatching in my head even as I babbled. "You *will* put that out, right?"

"Eventually." Nic yawned. His cat, Monster, watched fatly from the arm of the sofa. Orange tail swishing. "I guess."

"You *guess*? Why not send it out to labels, see if you can get someone else to do it? Those songs should be played on every college station in the country."

He lifted his eyebrows, all sarcasm now. "You think that's what'll happen?"

I looked at him. "If you make more than eight hundred copies."

"You think people want this stuff?" He leaned back. A little seam of afternoon sunlight, the molten white of a forge, burned between the velvet curtains behind him. "There's what people want—or what they think they want, what they can handle—and what they actually *need*. I like to think I'm in the latter business but," he laughed. "You can't control demand."

"You can't? Supply is demand, it becomes demand, when what you've got's good enough."

"Who told you that? You're quite the idealist."

"I prefer to think of it as sound capitalism."

He shook his head but then smiled, and for a second I saw it. The undimmed certainty, the front man's confidence that said he knew exactly what he had. "I suppose you can always coax it. Demand's kind of like a girl. They always give in in the end."

"That's probably true," I said. "For you."

"Yep."

What was I forgetting, I wondered again? It was right there on the tip of my tongue. Whatever it was, I brushed it away. He lifted himself off the far arm of the couch.

"C'mon. I wanna show you something."

I followed him back through a kitchen cluttered with blenders, soy-milk cartons, halved apples oxidizing on the counter, picture postcards of Betty Page and old zombie movies taped to the fridge. Outside in the shadow of his garage a Triumph motorcycle rested above a Rorschach blot of grease. Inside against the far wall there were multiple boxes of his own 45s: all the copies of "Caveman Stomp" and "Crawl to Me" that never sold, and which he'd paid to press himself. Together it appeared there were dozens, perhaps even a couple hundred of them in sum.

"Tell me why I do this?" he said. As we breathed in that heady smell of virgin vinyl. "Is it for my health? Because I *know* they're great records. But if no one hears 'em…"

He tapered off. And I had no answer for this, truly.

"What happened to these guys?" I nodded down at the sleeve picture of the original troglodyte band—Dave McDonagh, Pete Neil and Billy Williamson, the drummer who'd allegedly been in prison—as I'd first seen them. "How come they're not on the stuff you just played me?"

"They're a temperamental bunch." He smirked. "Tough to work with."

"I see."

"Billy and I are in touch. But all those guys only *look* like morons. It's tough to keep a band together when you can only afford to pay anybody peanuts. I've gone through something like a dozen bass players in the last year and a half alone."

"Peanuts, huh?" I thought of the guy I'd met, that snide jackass who played now with the Hangman's Gang, stared over at the quilted mover's blanket that sat under the motorcycle outside. A barbecue, black with what I supposed was vegetable matter only, leek dust, sat further over. I could smell the carbonized memory of charcoal in the air. The scent felt antediluvian, older than humanity itself. "Nic Devine's traveling rock 'n' roll circus?"

"Yep." He shook his head. Over by the porch brightly colored VTE sheets hung on clotheslines, drying in the sun. "Fifteen bucks a week won't even feed my drummer, skinny little runt that he is. You can't live on that, even here."

"Right. So how come you don't play more gigs? So you could *make* the money to pay them more?"

He shrugged. "No one'll book us."

"Why's that?"

He smiled. Maybe the rumors were true. He wasn't going to tell me.

"I have a little trouble with my equipment sometimes. Plus they just won't. We don't draw locally, and by the time you pile everybody into a van and drive three hours to Cincinnati, then back again, it's not worth the gas. We make more working in grocery stores."

"Don't you have a manager? A promoter?"

Nic rolled his eyes. "Yeah, sure. We fired him to pay for the roadies and the masseuse."

I kicked at the rough sod by my feet, as we stood out in the yard. A large bag of fertilizer rested over on the back porch. I could smell it, too.

"What about gigs further out, where you might draw an actual crowd? New York, or L.A.? You wouldn't be the first band that had to leave home to find an audience."

He nodded. "We played New York. We actually drew okay there, the last time. Maybe if we had a manager, or a promoter..."

I thought for a second. The idea, that egg that had trembled there in the dining room, now hatched in full. It wasn't a hard choice. The ones where you're guided by your own stupid optimism never are.

"I'll do it," I said.

"You?"

"Yeah," I said. "Me. Who else? I mean, how hard can it be?"

"Harder than you think. It's not like I can pay you anything."

"That's alright. I won't ask for much," I said. "Just your soul."

Nic jammed his hands in his pockets, turned away from me. "We never really had a manager," he murmured. "It's usually just me on the phone to club owners myself."

"Right," I said. "You should be making records. I'll take care of everything else."

Never mind that I knew nothing about music or booking or club owners or promotion, nothing about business or accounting or contracts. I knew nothing about anything so far as this was concerned. Which made me so underqualified I was therefore perfect. Such backhanded logic had launched the Ramones. It was punk spirit—Buy a Clipboard, Manage a Band!—applied from above.

"Just my soul, huh? You drive a light bargain."

"Every rock 'n' roll story's got the devil in it somewhere. Sign on the dotted line and I'll make you the toast of Franklin County."

He stood for a second, then nodded finally at the mason jar in my hand, the dregs of my Training Wheel. "Why not? You don't appear to have anything better to do."

"I don't! I can start right now!"

"Great! Find me a bass player and a new guitarist." We started back towards the house. Stepped back onto his porch, the rotting gray boards soft underfoot. "Those boys in West Virginia just quit on me this morning."

"Why's that?"

"Ask a stupid question..."

We walked back inside. I stepped around a racing bicycle, an extra washer and dryer for taking care of all those vintage fabrics. I stared at the fish tank that swelled with Edison-yellow and hydroelectric-blue breeds whose names were unknown to me. I watched them drift, shift unfathomably: a kaleidoscopic pattern edging close to meaning. Nic crouched down again by the turntable.

"By the way, am I supposed to guess your name?"

I looked over, startled. That we had come this far into the afternoon without my telling him, that he hadn't even bothered to ask before handing over the keys to the band. Maybe, I thought, as the fish eddied by too, in my peripheral vision, that's how it went: you could travel miles without even moving an inch.

"Of course not," I said. "It's—

13

Around and Around

"Where were you?"

I stepped into my kitchen, head still spinning from the last Training Wheel, and was flabbergasted to find Felice sitting there smoking in the dark.

"What?"

"You forgot, didn't you?" The ember of her cigarette pulsed while she drew on it.

"Shit!" By the light spilling in from the hall I could see she wore something flapperesque, a sexy black 1920s cocktail dress. Not the sort of thing she usually wore to Lady's or Quilty's or Keeper's or any of the other bars on High Street, this was for an occasion. It came flooding back to me, what I'd forgotten while I was at Nic's. "I totally space—"

"How could you forget this?" she snapped. "It's Kitty's engagement party."

"I don't really know Kitty."

"You know me."

"That's true." I thought it was true. I wanted it to be true, at least, even truer than it was. I reached over and switched on the light. "I'm sorry. I was with Nic."

"'Nic?'" She offered the tip of her cigarette a little ontological glance. "Your little friend?"

"Yeah." Suddenly it was as if she didn't think he really existed either. "He wants me to manage his band."

"Really?" She all but patted my head. *That's nice.* "I waited for you. We're late."

"How late?"

We watched each other. In the sudden light—violent as an X-ray— Felice's anger had become something else. We'd made this plan at Crazy Lady's, three days ago, and already it had slipped my mind, been swept away by more pressing concerns. Now she stood up. Her dress clung and wrinkled around her hips, her eyes flamed ambiguously. The air bore the hint of something burning. Mara must've baked this afternoon. The room was close, hot, stifling. I stepped towards her, halving the distance between us with one stride.

"How late?"

I took her wrist. She looked away. We'd been back and forth, back and forth already. Her skin was shock white, mouth darkened—a scarlet mauve—with lipstick. I watched hesitation crease her face and then leave. Her dress glistened, covered with small scales, under the light of the electric bulb. And something ticked, the oven or the wall clock, around us. How late? And how long would this summer last, besides?

I pulled her towards me. And she flew, free hand wrapping around my neck as she pulled me back just as hard.

****

"Don't touch me!" she snapped. "Leave me alone!"

"What?" Two days later we were at it again. "What are you so upset about?"

I'd chased her out of Crazy Lady's. Now we were out on the street, arguing under a streetlamp. Was it possible the two places, where we were "together" or "apart," could be practically identical? They seemed that way.

"You don't know?"

"I have no idea." We'd been dancing. My eyes had wandered towards the bar, where there may have been a cute girl sitting next to Gary Hauser. Then, without warning, she'd raced for the door. "I have no idea what we're fighting about."

"You're a guy," she said. "That figures."

"Yeah? It does?"

The girl *was* sitting there. I wasn't blind, but I wasn't Nic Devine either. I merely looked, at her calves snaking up from pointy boots, the dark sheen of her jaw-length hair. But what were we fighting about, actually?

"What does it matter?" I said. "Even if I looked—you're jealous!"

"No."

A cop car cruised past. It was two o'clock in the morning. A pair of whey-faced Goths brushed past and snickered, their footsteps ringing flatly on the concrete. Otherwise the street was empty. It was unspeakably humid, the air aglow with dim lamplight, whining with bugs who dive-bombed my ears. It reeked of chicken wings from the BW3 across the street.

"No," she repeated. "You really haven't figured it out?"

I stared at her. I was jealous, I realized. My own jealousy had set up a feedback loop, in which I kept trying to provoke her own. At Lady's she'd bought Invisible Dan a beer, which pissed me off so I'd flirted with that girl, which in turn prompted this. Where would it end?

"No," I said. Hesitating. "But anyway—"

"Anyway, what?"

Another car passed, this one a yellow Camaro. It neared the corner and slowed, taillights glowing. Thick People. Their stereo blared Molly Hatchet's "Flirting With Disaster." They shouted something unintelligible, and then sped off. Thank God.

"What?"

"Are you going to England, or Connecticut?"

"What difference does it make?"

What difference did it make, I wondered? To me, all kinds and for whatever reason, since we were still neither dating nor not-dating. After we'd slept together again and then went on to Kitty's party, it was business as usual. Felice fled back to Wilkerton and we'd met again, tonight. Being with her was like Zeno's Paradox: no matter how many times we halved the distance we'd never truly be "together."

"If you went to Hartford, couldn't we go out? I'm barely an hour from there, after all."

She looked away again for a moment, batted at a mosquito. "Why not?" she said. "I mean, if it were only about geography."

"It isn't?"

"No." She laughed. How beautiful she was when she was happy, eyes the blasted green of beach glass. "Not really."

We turned, and started to walk along High. Our voices traveled, our reflections glossing along the shuttered shop windows.

"What, then?"

She shook a cigarette free from her pack. A frantic sound, like an insect battering against glass.

"I don't trust you," she said.

"You don't?"

I understood, I really did, although I couldn't say why. I didn't trust her either, maybe. She grinned around her cigarette, the magnesium flash of her match popping as she stopped a moment to light it.

"White man speak with forked tongue."

"Oh, come on!" She was teasing me now, I could tell. We stood in front of a Dairy Queen, its plastic tables looking waxy and abandoned in the moonlight. Brown glass glittered around their bases, the shards of shattered bottles.

"I'm serious. You don't belong here."

"Neither do you. I thought that was the point."

As was the way with us, the mood had shifted, gone from anger to accusation to something else. We walked now, jostling, flirting, heading back towards my apartment.

"I'd never cheat on you," I said, "if we went out. I'm trustworthy. I'm loyal—"

"Loyalty's not the point. People cheat all the time."

"I don't. I wouldn't, ever."

"Never say never," she said. "You may have cheated on me already and not even known about it."

"What d'you mean? I've heard of people who wake up in the middle of the night and make themselves sandwiches. Sleepwalking, sleepsnacking. But I've never heard of sleepfucking."

She laughed. We angled over on 13th, now, cutting up towards Indianola. "Joke all you want. You act all innocent, but I think you're the devil!"

"Me?" I tapped my chest, and laughed out loud now myself. "You're the second person this week who's made that mistake."

She grabbed my hand. Did we understand one another? We'd just turned off High Street. I heard the revving engine of a car, that Camaro as it looped back around towards us.

"C'mon!"

I turned and sprinted, racing across the damp lawns. She ran ahead, dragging my hand towards my apartment, whipping me along like the tail of a kite behind her.

****

"What are you doing?"

Gasping, laughing, I knelt on the rug by Mara's turntable, fumbling with the 45s in the amber lamplight. Flipping through them frantically. "What does it look like I'm doing?"

It seemed like the perfect time to be listening to the greatest rock 'n' roll band in the world. Especially since it was my band now too. I found the one I wanted.

"Mara's sleeping!"

"I know, but just listen, one time, just listen!" It was late but who cared? I needed her to listen too, needed the sound to come through loud and clear. I slid "Caveman Stomp" onto the turntable, set the needle down at the edge of the record.

"Stop! I don't want to hear it."

"Yes you do."

She was laughing though. She knelt beside me on the ground and listened, did her best once more to give the band a fair shake. Angling her head so the shadows broke across her face in ambiguous patterns, lamplight splashing her skin. We drank beer from one bottle, passing it back and forth between us.

Two minutes and thirty-eight seconds later she said, "It still sucks."

"What's wrong with you?"

"What's wrong with you boy? I like songs you can hum."

"Humming's overrated. Why hum when you can caterwaul?"

I didn't care, though. In that moment we were together, kneeling there with our heads bent towards each other, the record revolving with the needle stuck in the run-out groove. I reached over and removed it. It was late and my lips were damp with beer, my adrenalin racing. The room swelled with that holy silence that follows on the heels of a great record.

"I don't need to like them, you know."

"No?"

She leaned forward and kissed me. I kissed her back. Perhaps if I had understood her in full, things might have gone on differently between us.

"You want to hear it again?"

"No! No, no no—"

She pounced on me, battering me away from the turntable, laughing as she pressed me down—her turn—to the floor.

****

In the morning I woke up first, turning in the gray light towards the ceiling. Felice was beside me still, and we were half entwined atop my sweat-damp futon. No closer than we'd been before, if no further apart. We might go on and on, fighting and fucking and searching for a definition where it was possible none existed. Even if last night we'd been happy—rolling there on the floor amidst the living room's detritus, ashtrays and abandoned Converse sneakers and record sleeves, then racing down the hall like it was Christmas morning, sprinting to the futon where we would slither out of our too-tight jeans, chew the wrong-sided buttons off one another's twenty-five-cent pajama tops in our hunger to get to the soft skin beneath—we were right back where we started from.

Shhh! Rushing down the hall, I'd knocked Mara's door open with my elbow and Felice had cautioned me. Don't wake them!

We'd stopped a second to look in on Mara and her boyfriend Paul, asleep fully dressed atop her mattress, eyes and noses pointing towards the sky.

Paul's frizzy hair splayed out and kinked against the pillow like some peroxide-bright White Panther dreamwheel.

"Look, they're snoring in unison," Felice whispered. "Isn't that cute?"

I'd envied them their relative harmony, even as we sprinted down the hall to claim our own just and temporal reward. Now I listened as down the hall Paul made breakfast, breaking eggs and slopping orange juice, shuffling around the kitchen in his bare feet. They were sweet together. He'd spent the night but Mara, that Catholic schoolgirl, would cling to her virginity. They were our opposite in that way.

I sat up and shook one of Felice's cigarettes from a pack on the sill. Outside the heat was just beginning. It rose off the pavement in shimmering waves, clotted the sunlight into a jaundiced mist. I could smell the creosote, the street's tarry sharpness. The day assembled itself before my eyes, the faraway sign of a Rax Roast Beef appearing over the rooftops opposite, vague as a flag in the heat-hazed distance; the petty skyline and the horseshoe curve of Buckeye Stadium. It was forever early when it wasn't late, always one or the other for us. But right now it didn't matter, any more than the room's essential poverty—the peeling walls, threadbare carpet, those prison-thick bars blocking all the windows—or the disagreement Felice and I were bound to keep on having, be it erotic, philosophical or otherwise. I saw us as though from some great distance, some level of elegant remove. I smoked, then flicked my cigarette between the bars. It died in the damp air, snuffing as it fell to concrete. Behind me Felice stirred. Her eyes opened, and her face wrinkled in confusion. Here we go again, I thought. But I didn't move. Even as—in that instant, before she was fully awake and we began fighting again—for a moment we were together, and we were free.

14

Disappearer

"Come quick, come quick—"

"What is it?"

Felice called me a few days later. It was July 3, the summer marching towards its midpoint. As I'd expected she scrambled back to Wilkerton in a hurry after our last encounter, out the door before I could even fix breakfast. I was sick of it, sick of being jerked around now while I stood there in bare feet by the kitchen table. I was tempted just to hang up the phone.

"What?"

"Donnie's missing," she said. "I need you to come out here."

"Why?"

"Just come. Please?"

Reluctantly, I bused my way to her house. I sauntered out into the morning sunshine, plucking at my knee-length shorts. What was wrong with me, I wondered, that I could be played this way? I let myself into her house without knocking. There she was sitting at her kitchen table in ratty flannel pajamas and doing a crossword puzzle. She stared at the squares, gnawed at the end of her yellow pencil.

"What?" I said. "Why so alarmed? Donnie doesn't seem like the sort of guy who'd want a permission slip to disappear for a couple of days."

She flung the puzzle aside. Tears pooled in the corners of her eyes. It was a beautiful day, the kitchen a gleaming cube of newly mopped linoleum and Formica. Through the window above the sink the sky was blank, radiant. The room's smell of lemon cleanser seemed almost natural.

"You don't know Donnie," she snapped.

"I don't. I know you. I'm sick of this, these phantom hysterias and all this hand-wringing. Should I or shouldn't I, England or Trinity. Make up your mind already."

"You want me to?"

"Yes." I hesitated. "Look, I don't know Donnie but usually when a nineteen-year-old doesn't call for a few days the answer is good news. He's in love. Maybe he's fallen for some fabulous guy and is having the best sex of his—"

"Donnie's not really the hearts and flowers type," she said.

"So?"

"Knowing Donnie, disaster's a given."

A glass of orange juice sat on the table beside her. She picked it up and drank. Maybe I just wanted her to be wrong. I certainly wanted Donnie to be tied up with somebody else. Disaster seemed impossible on a day like this one, besides. Her half-brother Harry, the younger one, came clomping down the stairs. He leapfrogged the final two and landed by the table. He lifted a BB gun, aiming it straight at Felice.

"Jesus!" I yelled. "What—"

He lowered the gun and snickered. Felice just rolled her eyes. Harry's hiking boots banged on the floor as he went over and ran a glass of water. The two of them didn't look alike, apart from the pale complexion. Harry's face concentrated weariness, experience even though he was all of thirteen. His eyes—dark, intelligent—flickered from one of us to the other. He nodded at me.

"Hey."

"What's up?"

I was like him once. Less heavily armed but equally sullen and annoying to somebody.

"Get out of here," Felice snapped. "Leave us alone!"

He drained his glass. With a mucusy grunt he shoved off across the room and through the side door into the yard. Gun tucked under his arm, he looked like an amateur hunter. From a distance, with his rude frame and ginger hair, you'd have taken him for an adult.

"Donnie's not like other people," Felice said, once Harry had evaporated into the yard. "He marches to the beat of his own drummer."

"What's wrong with that?"

"It'll kill him," she said. "He doesn't get up and put his shoes on one at a time. He gets up, does a rail of crystal meth and then runs outside, waving his hard-on."

I stared at the damp floor, where Harry's footprints glowed like those left along a shore. I watched them shimmer and disappear.

"What'd you call me for?" I said. "Why not someone else?"

"You're trustworthy," she said. "What I said the other night notwithstanding, you're…believable. Which is more than can be said for a lot of people around here."

"Right. You can count on me, I'd never lie." I squinted out the window. "Is that a cherry tree I see outside?"

"Stop it. Who else was I going to call, Marcus?"

"Good point."

The summer had worn on, and still he was mostly gone too. I saw him at Perry's sometimes, pumping quarters into the jukebox to spin the old country records that were his latest obsession, George Jones. Felice had finally made clear to me at last what a liar he was, as fickle as the day was long.

"So what should we do?"

I hitched myself up onto the orange Formica countertop by the sink. Privately I knew she had a point. Donnie was nuts. His family was completely crackers, even by Columbus standards. His mother was so rigid she was practically undead, a member of the Rotary Club, the school board, the PTA, the town council. Slipcovers blanketed every inch of her home. According to Felice she'd led a drive to ban certain books—*The Great Gatsby, Silas Marner*—from the school curriculum, and refused to drink from any glass her son had touched. As though homosexuality were a disease, transmissible as cooties. Most astonishingly, she was, a Republican, which was the most exotic thing I'd discovered here yet. I'd never met one. Back home my parents' friends were nudists, Buddhists and drug dealers. Half of them were terrified of the police. Donnie compensated for his upbringing in a big way, by loosening all the strings at once. I'd seen him last Sunday. He'd come by late at night to hang with Mara, instead found me home alone.

"Mind if I take a shower?" He scratched his scalp, which he'd just cropped and dyed an electric tangerine color. His skin was inexplicably dark, as though he'd just returned from vacation.

"Knock yourself out," I said.

I barely knew where he was living. He crashed with us sometimes, other nights with Marcus or Lena, wherever there was a spare bedroom or pitying family. Even so he seemed forever clean. He was transient but not homeless, too Schroeder to be Pigpen. His clothes were fresh, his scent musky. He rolled in, rolled out, but then called from a payphone in the morning.

"Hello?"

"Hey it's Donnie." He sounded excessively alert for someone up before the crack of ten. "Didyatakeashoweryet?"

"I did." I was toweling off in the hallway as I spoke. "Why do you ask?"

"Um—didyouusethepinktowel?" His words clacked against one another like those silver, perpetual-motion desk ball sets. Chik-chak-chik-chak. A sense of collision and consequence.

"Umm—"

I looked down. My heart sank, in advance of whatever it was he was about to tell me. Pink, pink, was the towel in my hand: strawberry ice-cream colored. I'd never seen anything more so. I felt a certain tingling down below, which I reached down to scratch.

"I did as a matter of fact. Why?"

"Ihavecrabs."

Click.

A bottle of *Rid* shampoo materialized on my doorstep an hour later, alongside a lukewarm cup of coffee, a nibbled cruller and a paperback book called *On Forgiveness.* Perhaps I'd read it, once I finished scrubbing my crotch and then burning the offending towel. Felice now told me his medical history also included chlamydia twice, gonorrhea, HSV one and two. He'd been hospitalized at least once for drug consumption. So it was no great leap for her to fear the worst.

"Has anything like this ever happened before?" I asked Felice. Perched still on the edge of her kitchen counter. Outside the drone of a mower paralleled that of a plane, the languid green sounds of summer. Harry stalked across the lawn with his gun raised, muttering under his breath like Elmer Fudd. "Has he ever just disappeared for a few days?"

Felice nodded. Dabbed her nose with a paper towel. "This feels different somehow. I can't say why."

She stood beside me at the sink, looked out into the day. It was true too, I'd barely recognized Donnie that Sunday night. In place of the pilgrim serenity I'd seen at Perry's was an urban toughness, a crackling energy as he banged his feet on the metal stairs that ran up to our second-story apartment. *I didn't interrupt anybody fucking, did I?* he'd called as he barged in. A creased copy of Foucault's *Discipline and Punish* peeked from the pocket of his brown leather jacket, itself beaten stiff as a tortoise shell.

"You think he'll come home?"

Felice just mopped at her red-rimmed eyes. She tilted her head in a way that seemed to mean Yes, No, Maybe, Other. She blew her nose again.

"I took him to the clinic," she said, "last time he was tested."

"And?"

"And, they told him he was very lucky. That if he kept up all the things he'd been doing he'd be dead in a year and a half."

I nodded. Outside Harry raised his gun and lowered it, raised and then took a potshot at something. A rock, probably. *Varmint!*, he hollered, Yosemite Sam-style now. *Dance!*

Who knew what it was about this place anymore, I thought; what was likely or unlikely, true or untrue? Yet I just reached over and touched Felice's shoulder, staring out at the yard.

"He'll turn up," I said. "Really, really he will."

15

Revolver

"Hey—"

Fistfuls of gravel rattled softly against my window. A man's voice was calling me from down in the street.

"Hey, wake up, buddy! Wake up!"

Nic's voice. I scrambled out of bed, lifted the window and peered out between the bars. He was down on the lawn, bouncing on his toes, a large bottle of Mountain Dew in his hand. It was seven o'clock in the morning. Day was breaking over the apartment buildings opposite. A dirty white pick up truck idled at the curb.

"Hey, buddy! Get your shoes on, I'm putting you to work."

I rubbed my eyes. "Yeah?"

"Yeah, man. If you're gonna manage this band, you may as well know what we sound like! We've got practice!"

"'We? Who's—"

He nodded towards the truck. "My drummer, Billy. He's back with the band."

I yanked on shorts, shoes, socks and hopped towards the door. This was my chance, make or break: at last I would know what this band really sounded like. I reeled out across the lawn, which was littered with the spent ends of Roman candles and sparkler twigs. It was July 7. Nic offered me the bottle of Mountain Dew.

"No thanks."

"You good to go?"

"Yep."

The air was dense with the smell of fumes—gasoline, charcoal and lighter fluid from the neighbors' barbecue—clotting inside the humidity like napalm. We walked over to the truck. The Stooges' "Search and Destroy," Iggy Pop's hectic simian screaming, greeted me as I swung open the passenger-side door of the '66 Ford Nic had modified himself. The engine revved at conversation-killing levels even just sitting at the curb; the stereo blared still louder atop that, and a skinny white guy shifted aside to make room. The truckbed was piled high with gear behind us—Marshall amps, drum parts, guitars—strapped under a plastic tarp. I imagined the EPA could've had something to say about those acrid fumes from the twice-pipes in back, pluming into the air like smoke signals. The skinny guy looked at me.

"Huh," he said.

"'Huh' what?" I said. "What is it?"

He was greasy, tall, older, and dressed head to toe in black. Sleeveless T-shirt, jeans, motorcycle boots. Martial-looking tats covered his arms and he bore a punished, semi-neutral expression. The squiggly lips of a disappointed Charlie Brown. He seemed lithe yet wizened, with biceps as scrawny as tree branches. He could've been an old thirty, or a young forty-five. He shook his rat's nest of hair. Offered the extinguished stare of someone for whom hope might've gone long ago.

"You're the fixer?"

"Yeah," I said. "That's me."

"I'm Billy."

"*The* Billy? Billy W—

"I guess so." He ripped open a package of Hostess Ho-Ho's that sat in his lap. "I'm the drummer, in any case."

He jammed his thumb into a Ho-Ho, extracting the frosting and mopping it onto his crumb-dusted Motorhead T-shirt. Nic rolled his eyes.

"He's the drummer, alright. Better than a metronome. Although a metronome's probably smarter."

Billy just stuffed his mouth with the cupcake. This was the guy responsible for the monolithic semi-competence of those records I loved so well, his hammering beats a cross between Mo Tucker and the Troggs. So far as I was concerned, Billy Williamson was the best drummer in the world.

"It's an honor," I said.

"Mmph." He nodded at Nic who was pulling away from the curb. "Maybe you can help me get Elvis here off his high horse."

Off we went, revving into the morning. I stared at Billy, fascinated. Every syllable from his lips was like gold. They all came across as monosyllables even when they weren't. I recalled that he'd recently been in prison, and *The Attack* had referred to him caustically as "the heartbeat of a band that really shouldn't have one." The rumor was he'd pistol-whipped a convenience store clerk for eighty-one bucks, and so done eleven months in the state pen in Mansfield. Junk food wrappers drifted up around his ankles like evidentiary snow, crunching in the breeze that eddied through the floor ducts. He pulled a packet of mini donuts from his pocket now and started in on these.

"We're headed out near Coshocton," Nic said. "Billy's mom's got a house out there we sometimes practice in."

"Aw, man," Billy said, "don't start in on my mom!"

"What?" Nic looked at him. "I just said she owned a farmhouse. I should apologize for that?"

"It's the principle," he mumbled.

This guy was something else. Primitive was one thing, but he seemed scarcely functional. I was excited to go to Coshocton, though. I'd seen it on a map. Of all the satellite towns of Columbus, its name was the most fun to say.

"Coshocton, huh? You live out there, Billy? In…Coshocton?"

Williamson just nodded. Looking at him closely, I guessed he was closer to forty. The head of a corncob pipe jutted from his pocket, above the circular press of a tin of chaw. However old he was, he seemed *country* to the core, the sort of rugged semi-literate hayseed I'd only ever read about in Sherwood Anderson stories. Nic beat his palms on the wheel, with that early-twenties jitteriness he and I both had. Looking out at the road his gaze cut a laser. He had the focused intensity of a sprinter on the block, choosing his routes between cars so expertly it was like we had the highway to ourselves as we coasted atop the engine's souped-up purr.

"You guys couldn't rustle up a second guitarist?" I asked.

Williamson rolled his eyes, shook another donut from the bag.

"Man, don't ask that question. Elvis here has fired every guitar player in Columbus at least twice."

"What about a bassist?"

Another eye-roll. "Bassists are no good. They just hog all the girls and make it tougher for the rest of us. Nothing good ever came out of a bassist."

Nic flexed his mouth into a grin, ignoring him. To me he said, "Hey, wanna know how you tell when a drum riser's level? When the drool comes outta both sides of the drummer's mouth. How many drummers does it take to change a lightb—"

"Aw man, don't start!"

I snuck looks at Billy, watching him dab donut sugar—it was a poor man's disco dust, make-believe cocaine—off his upper lip with a paper napkin. I studied the faded ink along his arms, the streaky tattoo of a rock and roll Santa on his bicep, scrolled with the legend *Run, Run Rudolph*. Good Lord! If Billy Williamson had offered his soul to the devil, I honestly believe he'd have been rejected. He lolled in the middle of the cab between us, his head tossed back like a groggy boxer's. *This* was the second puzzle piece of my band? He looked like someone for whom just getting out of bed in the morning was a Frankensteinian miracle. We headed east, the city's light-industrial landscape transforming into something greener, now, exurban. Shuttered shopping mall plazas and lots fenced off for development mingled with open spaces, those same yellow-blonde fields I'd seen on my original drive out. Wind blew across the cab, humid and tinged with manure. Nic tinkered with the radio's dial.

"Not this shit," Billy snapped, as Nic honed in on something—it was the early Beatles, "Leave My Kitten Alone"—along the AM band, crackling with static. "I want the hard stuff. Alice Cooper."

Of course you do, I thought, but didn't say anything. Alice Cooper?

"Psshh," Nic said. "Listen to this, you might find out what real music's all about."

"I don't wanna know what music's all about, college boy, I want something that'll turn my brains to oatmeal. The Beatles didn't even get interesting until they were psychedelic."

I turned to Nic. "College boy?"

"He went to Berklee College of Music." Billy chuckled. "He just doesn't like to admit it."

"Is that right? Mr. Proper Primitive, rock and roll should be made by illiterates?"

"Two years." He grinned, sheepishly. "I dropped out."

I turned to Billy. "Anyway, that's bullshit, the Beatles were interesting from the beginning. It was all there up front, the first notes they ever played they were psyched—"

"Yeah, but who paid attention?" Billy said. He barely moved his lips when he spoke. "They were wild out of the gate, but no one really saw it 'til later. *Rubber Soul* was where it got good."

"*Revolver*," Nic said calmly. "That's where they got it right. That's where the mind-blowing business and the songs are balanced just perfectly. A little something for everyone."

I looked at him, there behind the wheel, wind blowing hair around his face. Was that the aim of a rock 'n' roll band: to provide "a little something for everyone?" Or were they instead to reach the few, the Happy Few who could read the depths within? Both, maybe. Nic was wearing that shirt I'd seen earlier, the white one with the strange, optical pattern—like hypnotists' cones, or like those swirling teacups at Disneyland, the Mad Hatter's Ride— which could seem to lay flat until you looked and they suddenly seemed to pop out in three dimensions. (Or four, or five, even. How many dimensions were there?) In any case, this appeared to settle the argument. To make his imbecile tub-thumper shut up—no wonder he and Nic were at one another's throats all the time; I'd never met a dumber drummer—he adjusted the dial and found, lo and behold, Alice Cooper. "School's Out."

"Now that's what I'm talkin' about!" Billy said. "Real music!"

Outside, the road had narrowed to two lanes, the air hazy and pale as the sun burned through it. I stared out at the houses we passed: rust-rotted 8-cylinder automobiles hiked up on cinderblocks, their oxidizing frames flaking in the breeze; scrawny men in undershirts staring dully ahead from crooked porches. A heavy woman with her arms scorched pink looked up and shaded her eyes towards us, crouched on the brink of her withering lawn.

"What kind of name is 'Alice Cooper?'" I said. "'Alice' is like a name from a television show, and Cooper—what's a 'cooper?'"

"A cooper's a guy who fixes barrels," Nic said. "Buckets, stuff like that."

"It's Vincent," Billy said, reaching over to crank the volume still further. "That's Alice's given name. Vincent Furnier."

"Geez, that's worse," I said, looking at Nic. (*A. Nicolas DeVine*, whatever the "A" stood for exactly.) "What a ham."

"He is that," Nic said, laughing. "A ham!"

We rode for a second, and he said, "None of these guys use their real names, though. Zimmerman, David Jones, Jim"— he meant Osterberg, of course, Iggy Pop—"they're all frauds, really. Just actors."

"Iggy's middle name is Newell," Billy muttered. "That's like a post, basically."

"Right," Nic snickered. "I guess you were payin' attention some of the time in school, weren't ya?"

"That part."

Figured, I thought: shop. Where'd you go to school, Billy? Some vocational institute, I imagined. A post, as in dumb-as-a. Yet was Nic just a fraud, just an actor too? I'd find out. We rode on a while, in the hot cross breeze. Finally Nic slowed, and moved over into the right lane. The houses here were farther apart, the fields seeming to bleach out into a greater, almost metaphysical emptiness. Billy reached over and turned the radio down. He said, "So are we gonna make an album this time, Elvis, or what?"

"An album?" Nic's voice shot up as if it had just been suggested the band go disco, test out some Latin rhythms. "I don't think so, man. Singles are the way to go!"

"No one buys singles, Elvis. They're an antiquated form."

"Antiquated," Nic mocked. "Big word!"

Outside, the landscape was now a softened yet radiant yellow: these fields were wheat. Black birds—crows, I thought—flew over them. The houses were gray, paintless or scarred with a memory of red or white. They looked burnt, practically, eroded down to essence. We turned off the main highway and cut down a smaller road, of dirt.

"I love singles," Nic said. "I'll never make an LP, ever. Two songs, the killer-diller combination. That's all you need! Sly Stone, he knew it! "Everybody is A Star," "Hot Fun in The Summertime." You won't find those songs on anyone's album. Seven-inch only." He shook his head and smiled, pleased at the very thought of it: six minutes of perfection. "Singles are all donut and no hole."

All donut and no hole. If Nic Devine had a philosophy this would be it, his creed. Life was too short to endure its absences, its lacks.

"Sly Stone!" Billy squawked. We turned now at a mailbox down an even narrower path, just a car-width channel that had been hacked through a wheat field really. "My whole family's got bigger stones than that guy, he's just a blind, ignorant—"

"Don't say it!" Nic said. "Don't you dare, I'll kick your ass all the way to Cleveland—"

"What? I was just gonna say he was an ignorant fool. That happy-clappy shit of his doesn't fly with me either."

"Oh."

We pulled up in front of a farmhouse, just a low, ranch-style structure with an old red barn about fifty yards behind it. I guessed Billy didn't even know enough to remember that Elvis Costello had allegedly called Ray Charles a "blind, ignorant nigger." So they said, I wasn't there. But it gave me another reason to hate Costello, that fraud who'd stolen his name from the true King, his shtick from Buddy Holly and his logorrhea from Bob Dylan. A rip-off artist in the worst sense.

"Sly's not blind," I said. "That's Stevie Wonder."

"Whatever. Him too. No one buys singles, ace," he said to Nic, who was throwing the car into park, the clicking of the gearshift like the soft popping of a disaligned jaw. "You wanna be remembered, we gotta make an album."

"Who said I wanna be remembered?" Nic swung open the driver's side door. Stepped out into the sunshine. "I just want to exist."

"Fine. But if you wanna eat," Billy said, "you might consider this little concession to our modern age."

"I grow my own food," Nic said, as I climbed out on the passenger's side, into the mid-morning heat that seemed to coat my skin like oil. "For your sake, skinny, I'll take it under advisement."

He reached into the truck, grabbed a baseball cap—*Harley Davidson*, it read—and jammed it on his head. He turned towards the bed to load off the truck. Suddenly he looked just as country as Billy was, with his hair held back and hidden by the cap. He reached up and undid the bungee straps, rolled back the plastic tarp and began to load down the amps.

"After all," he grunted under their weight, beckoned us both over to help him. "We gotta keep you out of prison, pal." He looked, strangely, straight at me. "The devil finds work for idle hands now, don't he?"

****

Inside the barn, there was that silence, that rangy, rural stillness that magnifies every sound. Billy's drumsticks, clacking together in his back pocket as he knelt down adjusting his floor pedal. A brittle chatter like dry twigs.

"You wanna give me a hand here?" Nic asked me, while Billy knelt around his drum kit and taped off a rectangle at the far end of the barn. He ripped the gaffer tape with his teeth. *Scrrritch.*

I helped Nic carry his amplifiers and guitars from the truck to the shady end of the barn. With his hair tucked under his cap, Nic's features were more conventionally handsome. They had the whittled delicacy of an actor's.

"You grow up around here too?"

"Nah. West Virginia." He gazed up towards the rafters after he'd set down an amp, a wistful look like he was recollecting something fond. Exposed, his cheeks were hollow, almost skeletal. "My dad used to beat me for having long hair."

"Really?" I said. "In the eighties?"

He ignored me, turning back out to the truck. Sunlight streamed through holes in the roof, up where he'd been looking. Around the other end of the barn, over by the wide-open sliding door, there was an old tartan couch that looked as if it had been through a war. Stuffing erupted from its cat-scratched upholstery; three of its four legs were missing; tea-colored, continent-shaped stains were spread across its back. It didn't look as if anyone really lived in the ranch house adjacent. A tractor rusted over in the wide driveway, and mightn't have been moved for years. The fields beyond the barn were overgrown, jumbled with head-high weeds. The windows of the house were dark and some were broken, jagged glass still clinging within the frames.

I helped Nic and Billy set up quickly, then took a place on the couch. This was all I really wanted to do: watch them. We'd brought beer and I cracked one open. Sunlight warmed my forearms, whited me out of existence to them as they got ready over on the shady side of the barn. The amps' power-lights glowed green and red out of their corner of darkness, and the air filled with a malignant hum.

"You see that line, ace, that's for you." Billy pointed at the silver tape with which he'd marked off his drum kit, then gestured at the singer with his sticks. I'm comin' for you, ace. "You cross that at your own peril."

"Do not cross that line, huh?" Nic snorted. "Remember what happened the last time? I'll crack your fuckin' skull."

"Try it," Billy muttered. He settled into his seat, simmering. "I dare ya."

Above and behind them on the wall there hung a banner, its red and blue cross bars like those of a Confederate flag. It read *Coshocton High School Cougars, State Champions, 1971.* Nic glanced at me across the room and said, "You better put those 'phones on." He nodded to a pair of ear goggles he'd handed me, thick, noise-canceling headphones that weighed at least five pounds. Billy was wearing a pair—they widened his skinny head to make him look mantis-like, preposterous—although Nic was not. "It's gonna get loud!"

I slipped them on. For a second, the world went quiet. We might've been gathered at the rim of the Arctic Circle, a dim and remote isolation. I shivered as Billy tapped his sticks together, twirling them cockily as he mouthed something I couldn't make out, but which I knew was something like, *Pleased to meetcha, we're your new favorite band—*

They slammed into the beginning of a song I'd never heard, with a vicious electric tornado of a guitar riff that was half stolen from David Bowie's "Hang Onto Yourself," half sourced elsewhere I couldn't place. I felt that adrenal surge only the best and worst things in life ever give you. Drugs, love, nightmares, sex, trips to the hospital. It was certainly loud enough even with the protectors, and it was everything I'd wanted from this band plus a little bit more besides. I'd always believed a great rock song consolidated an entire lifetime's worth of feeling into seconds or less, just like an orgasm or a sneeze. Unlike those things it went on a while—long enough to attain consciousness within its frame—and it never continued quite as far as you hoped, but that's what a great song did. It held you. And for the remainder of the morning and most of the afternoon, that's what Nic did too. He delivered. Even in rehearsal—maybe only in rehearsal, for all I knew—he was the perfect front man: prowling, agitated, vain, cruel, his voice racketing off the rafters as he threw himself completely into songs that were unfinished, without any audience besides me to egg him on. His bluish veins stood out on his hands and forearms as he shaped the chords on his guitar; his eyes rolled; his hair hung wet, looking like a veil of crepe moss, once he'd whipped off the hat. Ten minutes in, he'd sunk into a crawling, knee-battering frenzy. After one song, his black-and-white shirt was half translucent, wrung with sweat. I couldn't imagine anyone putting as much energy into a rehearsal. My own throat was raw, to hear his Little-Richard-by-way-of-Roky-Erickson scream. They played a new song, a jagged Norseman's howl called "Mind of Winter," and then another original—which Nic introduced by telling Billy he'd written it just this morning—that positively floored me. Billy's gigantic, hammer-armed drumming—he was much stronger than he looked—underwrote a tremendous, serrated guitar riff that was like the *Mission Impossible* theme turned upside down, a song that drew blood it was so urgent. They played it four or five times consecutively. Finally I whipped off my phones and shouted,

"What's that one called?"

"Doesn't have a title yet," Nic said. "You like it?"

"Yeah."

He nudged aside a coil of heavy electrical cords with his Cuban-heeled boot. Barely interested in me at all, over there, though I was the only audience the song had yet had, as much a part of its creation as if I were a member of the band myself. The song was a codex, a catalogue, a stampeding rush of exultancy and confusion and loss with the words coded into the sort of blues-based near-nonsense Nic himself had hardly invented, but it was impossible somehow to miss their meaning.

Half my life I've lived in the dark!
I hear the girls screaming but my dogs won't bark...
The tale of the tape is a big fat lie,

I've lived so long I'm never gonna die...

The song rotated around this anthemic moment, *Everything lasts as long as you let it/that one thing you want you're never gonna to get it*, and there was a harmony part I couldn't make out (Billy was singing something like, *Summer's never gonna end, never gonna end*). The sort of nimble gibberish that meant all or nothing, or both. I doubt Nic made any of it up himself—the words were probably all stolen—but the song had a radiant simplicity. I could feel the singer's confusion, his impatience and rage: these things, along with his triumph over them. Everything lasts. Maybe not, but the song would, if he could ever finish and record it properly. A tall "if," given the way he and Billy were at one another, but in its incomplete way it was as great a song as "Satisfaction" or "Blitzkrieg Bop." The bones were there.

In my lap I had a list—Nic had handed it to me before I sat down—of songs he wanted to rehearse. Some were covers, others were either originals or, given Nic's handwriting, islands of sound that were destined to stay undiscovered. "Love is An American Cult," "We Sell Soul," The Screaming Dizbusters' "This Ain't The Summer of Love" and "Alone in The Endzone," by Radio Birdman. There were some leftfield suggestions too: Jimi Hendrix's "Roomful of Mirrors," a song called "Performance" by Japan. And one Billy argued vehemently against when Nic brought it up.

"I ain't gonna play it." Billy folded his arms across his chest. "That's pandering."

"It isn't." Nic flashed that irresistible, semi-ironic smile he'd shown at the bar, the one that made it hard at times to know if he was joking or not. "It's a great song."

"Jesus, man, it's for kids!"

"Yeah," Nic said. "Lots of good things are for kids. Like Tri—"

"What song?" I called out. I couldn't read the title on my list either.

"'Kids in America,'" Nic said. "The Kim Wilde tune."

"You wanna play that?" I said. "I'm with Billy on this one. It's bubblegum."

"I'm not gonna play it," Billy said. "No way. It'll be a cold day in hell before you get me to play that song. Never."

"Man," Nic shook his head, still smiling. "Never say never."

"Never," Billy repeated. "Ya fairy."

Secretly, I yearned to hear it. What could this band have done with that cheesy, chewy, sun-bright song, smuggled over from the other, above-ground Reagan Eighties, sounding like something written for a *Partridge Family* episode? I'd never know. Billy dug in his heels. I'd have to imagine the sound of my favorite band selling out. It didn't matter. Everything they did play was electric, explosive, fantastic. I wanted to die with happiness hearing them. I wanted it all to last, as long as was possible. The afternoon ticked past, the bar of sunlight shifting from my spot on the couch across the room to where the band stood. I stayed where I was, while dust and cigarette smoke plumed through those beams that shone down through the roof like spotlights. I smelled cat shit, kitty litter although I couldn't place the source, and I took off those headphones that were clamped so uncomfortably to my head. I didn't care if I went deaf. I wanted to *hear* the band in all its glory since I might never again have the chance. The arguments between Nic and his drummer, while entertaining, told me this could be a one-shot deal.

"Man, Dylan changed everything the moment he went electric—"

"It was already like that. The world was already like that, he just pointed at it."

"Ah, you don't know what you're talkin' about, ace."

"The fork was *in* the toaster, man, Zimmerman just found the outlet—"

It almost didn't matter, who took what position. They switched off in their contrarianism.

"Shut up and play the song, time-keeper, you're getting on my tits."

"Oh I didn't realize you had those, Nic. I would've treated you differently all these years."

It was the most fun I'd had, this one afternoon in the company of two guys who seemed to hate each other, ready to tear one another limb from limb in the service of rock 'n' roll. *Odi et Amo.* This phrase drifted back to me from a high school Latin class. *I hate and I love.* What was it that kept them—and perhaps everything—from resolution?

"You enjoying yourself over there, Uncle Tom?"

"It's Colonel Tom, you idiot! Colonel Tom Parker was Elvis Presley's manager, Jesus, you can't even get that right!"

Oh, but they did get it right, from where I sat. For the moment, I was so happy on my perch. Nothing bad had happened yet, and we were all just goofing off, at play. That afternoon, Nic Devine convinced me of the existence of the soul, that such a thing could be because he had so much of it. He sang from his heels, from the bottoms of his feet as he huddled over his guitar and wrecked it, strings ringing as he sweated through his hair, his shirt, his face glossed, indefinite. They kept playing, and I lost track of the songs they rehearsed. No more originals but it didn't matter. Every song became a stranger, albeit one I knew by heart, just as the originals had been like chestnuts, unknown wonders already wedged in memory. I didn't care if the band was good, or great—though they were—just that they were Starmen, strangers in my midst. Whether they could get this quality across to others, in public, that question would have to wait. If they couldn't I'd stay stranded within my obsession, be just another Chicken Little ranting about the sky. Finally, after hours of argument—with themselves and with one another— they just stopped, dropped whatever song they were playing to the ground without completion, with a crash that was as heavy as a falling piano. *WHAM!* Williamson shattered one of his sticks on the rim of his snare and Nic just— halted, standing there by the barn door, rocking on his boot heels. It was dusk suddenly. Darkness had crept up. Nic stared down at the ground, as if at the lip of a crater of silence. He leaned back and then forward, then unslung his guitar and walked towards the door of the barn. Dragging that 1961 cherry- red Epiphone Casino he'd been playing all afternoon out towards the truck. I took off my headphones—I'd had to put them back on, whereas Nic had gone on without any—and caught up with him. He looked at me, stunned. It was almost as though he didn't recognize me at all.

"Hey!" I grabbed his arm. His muscles were trembling. How could anyone do that? How did they survive? "Hey!"

Behind us Billy stood up at his kit, knelt down and began to dismantle it.

"Ha!" Billy's words were semi-distinct, blurred too as we stood in the dusky gloom. "See man, you don't *have* a band without me, pal. I *am* your band!"

I understood this to be equally true, even if I could barely trust my own pulverized ears to register my own breathing. As I looked at Nic, and said, "You're bleeding!"

"Huh?"

Blood trickled just outside his right ear canal. A narrow drip of it seemed to come from the fleshy portion, his temple almost.

"You're bleeding!" I tapped his shoulder, gestured up carefully towards the wound. He'd changed his shirt, now wore a white bowling shirt with blue trim. It too was soaked through. We stood in the purple, moth-wild twilight by the door of the barn. "You're bleeding. I think you burst an eardrum, or something. You'll have to get that looked at."

He reached up dumbly to where my finger was pointing. I could smell the midsummer vegetation, a field sweetness of mown hay. Out there in the distance the horizon line was a fiery orange. The sky looked flat like a painting or scrim, the earth itself equally so as it raced out to meet it. Billy moved around behind us, the scraping clatter of him disassembling his kit the one true proof of dimension or distance just then. Nic couldn't hear it, I realized. He brought his fingers down from his ear and stared at their red tips. I'll never forget the look on his face then: it was the radical surprise of someone discovering that he, too, was real. He pushed his hair back and beamed like it was something to be proud of, like drawing his own blood was a crowning achievement.

"Ha," he murmured. "Well. How 'bout that?"

16

The Man Who Fell To Earth

On the way home I turned to him.

"That was incredible! If you could learn to get along with other people, y'know, this band could be huge."

The engine revved, high beams sweeping the air above the road as Billy slept with his neck snapped back, as though someone had broken it. The cab reeked of sweat. Nic twisted his head so he could hear me with his working ear.

"Rock 'n' roll's not about getting along with other people. It's about showing the world who's boss! It's about winning the argument."

"Maybe." I nodded towards Billy. He really did look like he'd just been electrocuted, mouth open. "Still, would it kill you to make nice with your drummer?"

"As a matter of fact it would."

We rode on a second in silence. I watched the road, the twilight air simmering with bugs. I said, "Why don't you make an LP? One people will actually hear. Don't tell me it's because you don't have the songs for it, because you do. And don't tell me no one likes you. Plains States have a deal and they're fucking terrible. Someone will put out a Lords of Oblivion record. You don't have to spend all that time in your garage, folding paper sleeves."

Until now I'd been shy. But something in his performance had shaken me free. When he sang he was so unselfconscious he could've been naked, but so self-aware he couldn't be touched. What I wouldn't have given, to perform like that. I watched him as he drove, one eye on the road and the other on me as he bent so he could hear, his cheek flushed with the radioactive-green light of the instrument panel. Like a playing card turned inside-out, the Three-Eyed Jack. *That deaf, dumb blind kid.*

"The songs aren't there," he said. Smiling perversely. "They're not finished."

I heard the subtle movement of the gearshift, that dreaming jaw.

The radio played barely audible country hits from the fifties. Lefty Frizzell's "Always Late (With Your Kisses)," Hank Williams' "You're Gonna Change (or I'm Gonna Leave)." The sky grew dark as we rewound the steps of our journey, made our way back to the main highway. Did he not have the songs or did he lack courage? Clearly he had the heart and the brains, the talent and soul. Even if his feet were clay, he was a wizard.

"You wanna grab me my wallet?" he said. "It's in the glove box."

We'd stopped at a drive-through to observe one of the band's unofficial rules. Mountain Dew in daylight, coffee after dark. I reached over and dug it out. The radio—which he'd retuned yet again so Billy might be happy even in sleep—played Blue Oyster Cult's "Don't Fear The Reaper." I held out the wallet but it fell to the floor and I bent to pick it up. The air-conditioner ice-kissed my ear as I did.

"Here—"

It slipped open in my hand. Maybe I just wanted to examine the license, to see what his full name was. (The license too read "A. Nicolas DeVine," exactly as the phonebook had. Was it too shameful to admit? Or was the "A" for 'alpha,' 'aleph,' maybe?) But I could read his age by the light of the cashier's window: Nic Devine was thirty-four. A full fifteen years older than I was.

"Thanks."

I said nothing. Just sat there, in shock. It's one thing to be mortal yourself (even at my age I was beginning to figure that one out) but another one altogether to find your heroes are too, to learn that they will be gone before you. Nic paid the cashier while Billy snored on. How old was he, anyway? Fifty? Drummers were like the senile uncles of the music world. Blue Oyster Cult played on, that Byrds-robbing song of theirs with stupid lyrics about Romeo and Juliet in eternity, being able to fly and all that. What a bunch of bullshit! Suddenly death was just death, not transformation or flight. I felt betrayed, staring at the smudge of dried blood below Nic's ear. The skin there was tighter than I'd seen before, ticked with lines by his temple. Crows-feet I hadn't permitted myself to notice earlier. In the crosshatching of shadow it looked almost pebbled, like a football's pigskin.

"You okay, buddy?" Settling back into his seat, he accelerated. You're quiet."

We were back within city limits, across the border of the Outerbelt. Those dumpy little medical towers poked into view, the sad scattering of a skyline. This place began to feel like home to me, with everything that implied.

"Yeah," I said. "I'm fine."

****

"How were they?" Felice asked.

I didn't know what to tell her, remanded again to the dingy prison of my apartment. The kitchen's bare bulb swung overhead above us. At night this place revealed its fundamental slumminess. And I wasn't sure which answer she wanted, confirmation or denial. She'd come over to see Mara, stuck around to talk with me afterwards. "I heard you saw your band."

"They were amazing," I said, collapsing into a chair opposite her at the kitchen table. "Not that I expect you to understand."

"No?" In this light, even her face was a question mark, her body hooked like that above the table and her eyebrows spiking towards the sky. "I might understand better than you think."

"Yeah?" My chair creaked underneath me. I couldn't tell if she was making fun of me or not. Mara had left a while ago, so she and I were alone. "How so?"

Above us the bare bulb twisted on its long string. She shrugged.

"Doesn't matter. Besides, though—" she was back to teasing me now, I thought—"You're the band's manager. It's your job to love them."

"I do."

"Then why the long face?"

I watched her. How could I explain it?

"I dunno. They were great."

"Yes?"

"I can't imagine anything better."

"Oh?" She burst out laughing. "So you've peaked, is that it? Your life is all downhill from here?"

I shook my head. Maybe that was part of it, but it wasn't all: it wasn't just *my* life, besides.

"This is what's wrong with you," she said. "You worry so much. Too much, about the future." She laughed again. "At least they were good. I'd hate to see how you'd act if they were terrible."

"It's not just the band," I said.

"What is it?"

We watched each other. It was something in the air between us, in the complicity with which we looked back and forth, exposed and yet concealed from one another at once. We'd had a plan last night and she'd blown me off this time, a reversal of my own previous fuck-up. A plate of Mara's corn muffins sat on the table. I picked one up. Firm as a puck.

"Nothing," I said. "Where were you last night?"

The red plate on the table was crooked, lopsided, like a failed aerodynamics experiment or a Frisbee stepped on by an elephant. The oven ticked, vaguely.

"What d'you care?"

"What do you mean, what do I care? I waited, waited and waited but you didn't show up. You said you were coming over."

"I did." She shrugged. "But I don't think you're as upset about that as you say you are either."

I reached over and shook one of the cigarettes from her pack. I didn't want to go through this again. My wrist brushed against a book she'd left lying there on the table in front of her. I picked it up, flipped it over. It was Borges' *Labyrinths*, the old New Directions paperback with the black-and-white plynths on the cover.

"Where'd you get this?"

She shook her head. "Don't change the subject."

"What 'subject?' There is no subject." I flung my hands into the air. "We go round and round and—"

"We don't."

"We do. Are you going to Trinity or what?. You take the scholarship?"

"I dunno."

But this was a red herring too. Everything was, whether she and I were actually "dating," if my band was more important to me. I said, "What about Donnie? Have you heard from him?"

Maybe this was a red herring too. But I still thought Felice had been somewhere else, that she might've been in love.

"No."

"No?" I stretched. "Well, it's only been five days. I'm sure he'll turn up."

"You don't care about that either," Felice snapped. Suddenly, she was raging. "You think he's just on some happy little romantic spree, but he's missing, I can feel it! And you—"

"I'm sorry."

"You're not sorry." She seethed, there in the half-darkness, the shadow cast by the refrigerator as she leaned against the wall. "You don't even like Donnie."

"I don't." I startled myself with honesty, however obvious this had been from the beginning. "You're right, I don't."

"Why not?"

The bulb swung above, shadows swaying across Felice's face. Up the street a neighbor blasted Led Zeppelin, Robert Plant belting those lyrics about "got no silver, got no gold." It struck me as hopeless, any attempt to understand her, though it seemed the only attempt worth making. I thought, you could love a thing without understanding it, but the reverse was perhaps untrue. You couldn't *really* understand a thing without loving it. This was why I wanted her to hear the band. I looked at her, at that doll-red hair which summer was bleaching out, even this, so it looked less organic yet: the color of strawberry Pop Rocks or cotton candy. I said, "Because I think you're in love with him. That's why I don't like Donnie."

"With Donnie?" She stared back at me, startled. "You don't know what you're saying! It's impossible."

"Is it?"

"He's *gay.*"

"Does that make a difference?"

She passed a hand in front of her face. Her expression was blank, baffled: I couldn't read it at all. And then, for a reason I still—because cruelty, like love, is forever blind—do not understand, she burst into tears.

"You don't understand anything," she said, quaking into her hands. "You don't know what it's like to be me."

She got up, and stormed out the door. I didn't follow. What had I said, or done? What, not said or done? I was all hole and no donut in that moment. Again I had that sense of our impossibility, as though what I loved in her—or tried to love, at any rate—was exactly that which was unstable, most mutable and least clear.

"I don't even know what we're fighting about!" I shouted. "What did I *do?*"

Silence was my only answer, a silence that seemed composed of every noise there was, just as black—or was it white?—was said to be every color in the spectrum commingled. I plunked down in the H-frame chair at Mara's end of the table. Picked up the book Felice had left behind. There was an inscription in it, blurry, masculine handwriting that was difficult to read. *I was so happy to see you again*, it began. Somewhere up the block a dog barked; there was the hissing of sprinklers, the restless demi-quiet of an ordinary summer night. I tried to make out the inscription and then tossed the book aside. Picked up the corn muffin again. I was missing something, but what was it? And—my muffin tasted dry, awful, like the unleavened bread of the desert.

17

Ball of Confusion

We made up. Didn't we always? The next night, I went with Mara to the Second Hand to hear a band from Boston, a girl trio who were out of key, charming, their voices wobbling atop one another like circus performers perched on bicycles. The very opposite, in their tentative delicacy, of Lords of Oblivion. Felice seemed to love them, came over during an encore and put her arm around me.

"Sorry."

"For what?" We barely needed to lift our voices to make ourselves heard above the band. "I was the one being unreasonable."

Forget it, Jake, it's Chinatown, I thought. I'd never get to the bottom of it, perhaps didn't have to. The band launched into a goofball Blue Oyster Cult cover, this one "Burnin' For You."

"What's funny?"

"Nothing," I said. "This band needs a better drummer."

Mara extracted herself from the space between us and the stage. We were wedged into the corner, by the monitors.

"I gotta go to work," she said. "See you."

She left. It was early, on a Friday evening—the show was a happy hour matinee, and Mara had a bartending shift at Quilty's that started at nine—so Felice and I watched her go, elbowing through the crowd, spotlights glossing her clean white shirt. Later, we left ourselves, having had a couple more beers. We lurched up 13th Street, in warm twilight. Arms linked as we banged off lampposts.

"You're not actually jealous of Donnie?"

"I am," I said. "Shouldn't I be?"

"Should you?" she teased. "Should I be jealous of your band?"

"Perhaps." We didn't need to have this fight for once. "You're a little cuter."

We headed up towards my apartment, the hour that was not quite night and yet no longer day. The buildings clustered darkly in twilight, like the painted backdrop in a play. I hummed "Gimme Shelter," which the band had played for its final encore, under my breath.

"When I was younger I thought the line was just a Shoddaway," I said. "Like maybe a 'Shoddaway' was a piano or something."

"That's a Steinway, you dope." Felice pulled my arm closer. I was wearing a leather jacket, although it was scorching, just to keep the bugs off. Her fingers, slipping across slick black cowhide.

"I know that now, but no one in my house played."

"You were deprived."

We hiked up onto the lawn, the dune-like gradient that rose up in front of my building, five feet or so above street-level. I said, "Who's 'J?'" This was the initial at the bottom of the inscription in her book; unless it was "V," an inky little smudge that looked like a flying bird, almost. I hadn't been able to decipher it either. "Is that someone I need to be—"

The wind kicked up just then, bringing with it a sound that carried from the side of the building, where the steps led up to my apartment. A little mewling sound like a kitten's, yet somehow more urgent than that.

"What's that?"

"What?" Felice said. She hadn't heard it. "He's my brother's friend. You've m—"

The sound repeated, this time distinctly. It wasn't animal, but clearly human. I almost pitched forward onto the grass, that brittle field of cigarette butts and dandelion-ends, as I grabbed Felice by the wrist and ran around to the side of our building. There, Mara was sitting at the top of the fire-escape stairs, her hands covering her face.

"Hey—"

I banged my way up the stairs, zigzagging between the brick wall and the rail. Felice was right behind me, less drunk and perhaps more attuned to what was happening. I said, "What's wrong?"

And Felice pushed past me, as she saw before I did that Mara was crying, weeping with uncontrolled force. Her whole body was shaking.

"My God, Mar?" Felice knelt in front of her. "Honey, what's wrong?"

My tongue tasted like brick dust, where I'd actually licked the rough

surface of our building in my drunken passage upstairs. My back ached. And
there were tears pluming down Mara's cheeks; her knees and arms and shins,
below her waitressing skirt, were criss-crossed with scratches. I saw blood.

"Honey?"

Felice clasped Mara's hands. I had that dread sense of unreality
again, the one that had battened upon me the day I came here: it said things
were most urgent when they seemed least "real," and perhaps vice versa. Were
things most "real" when they were airy and strange, and you couldn't quite
believe them?

"I need to go to the hospital," Mara said. "Fel, I was raped."

In the soft clairvoyance that followed us around all summer—were
these things coincidences, or was the world organized, I wondered; did
experience pave the way, or in retrospect just fit things together?—it seemed
we were always ahead of ourselves, too. We always seemed to feel what would
happen next, and yet life managed to astound us anyway. We raced Mara, at
once the most innocent and somehow the most knowing of the people I'd met,
to OSU Hospital.

"Mara, honey—"

In the backseat Felice coaxed, consoled her while I drove Mara's beat-
up Ford Pinto. The radio played Roky Erickson softly, lyrics about Stonehenge
and gargoyles, the Sphinx and the pyramids. His cracked words of prophecy
murmured, for once, over an acoustic guitar. I knew how to get to the ER,
having taken Nic the night before to have his ear looked at. The girls' voices,
the seriousness of them too, sobered me.

"What happened, sweetie? Where were you?"

"I was just—"

Haltingly she told us. She'd come home from the Second Hand in a
hurry, and decided to cut through the alley behind the house. It was quicker,
she didn't want to be late. It took maybe thirty seconds off the journey. And
some guy, who she never saw, and couldn't describe, jumped her, pulled her
behind a dumpster, and raped her. It was that simple. Her cheek was indented
by the gravel, the pebbled surface where the man had pressed her down. There
was a small cut, like the nick on the edge of a table, just above her left eyebrow,
and a fine brown dust, because the alley was so dirty, along her cheek. It

looked like rouge almost, like face paint. I observed these things—it is what is so twisted, really, so awful—almost as though they were humorous, little accents of incongruity (though what was so incongruous about it? It was just what you should expect, what the world gave you) that only made the horrible in fact more horrible.

We waited for hours at the hospital. I read and re-read yesterday's *Dispatch*, dated July 16. Felice and I sat in the waiting room while the doctors looked at Mara and two cops arrived to ask questions. Mara didn't want to talk about it.

"What did he look like?"

"I...I'm not sure. He twisted my arm behind my back and then he—"

"You have to tell us," one of the two detectives said, although kindly. He had a long, tan, plastic overcoat on (a "mac," I thought) and that rumpled look that detectives have in the movies. Bushy, black eyebrows accented a face that was otherwise rheumy and lopsided, like a basset hound's. "It would help us a lot."

"It would, huh?" Mara wised up for a second, her voice toughening. "I'm sorry, but I didn't really see him."

I wanted to shake him by those plastic lapels (even as I thought, were people born to these roles? Was it all in a name, since he *looked* so much like a detective, besides) and say, it's not her job to "help you," is it? Or was it, also? It was impossible to tell in here, where the orderlies had the broad, pugged faces of Thick People and the patients, who might've menaced us otherwise—a football player who'd decided to do a belly-slide down the rail of his house's front stairwell and wound up in a face plant, cracking his cheekbone—looked helpless, wobbling around on crutches.

We walked home. Felice and I had waited with Mara all night, and now walked back having left the car behind in the pre-dawn. Everything looked different. I couldn't say why. Steam curled off our Mini-Mart coffee, the waxy cups we held in our hands. This place, at this hour, seemed neither beautiful nor un-beautiful but somewhere in between. Just another University town neighborhood where the houses all suffered the neglect of their tenants, who lapped in and out like the tides. Flowerbeds were flecked with dying, indeterminate blossoms, their pale petals all brown around the edges. A lawn was spotted with dandelions, fragile white globes, still glistening from where it had rained earlier. Someone had hung an effigy dressed in a Michigan Wolverines uniform from a flagpole in front of their porch. It hung in the still air like a piñata, or like the worst insult we could imagine. Who, finally, could say?

****

A bunch of us went for a drive that weekend, to distract ourselves and to help Mara feel better. It was an early honeymoon for Knobby and Kitty, a world tour inside the great state of Ohio. We piled in the back of Krist Cooley's battered '68 VW bus, as many of us as could fit uncomfortably inside it, and we hit the road, screaming.

"Pass the map, willya?"

"OW—what're you trying to do with that cigarette, anyway?" A woman's voice—Lena—though it was difficult to see in the rearview mirror, to figure out which cramped and jumbled body part belonged to what person.

"Sorry." Marcus was unmistakable. "Was that your eye?"

"Not my eye! I'm wearing a skirt!"

An old, yellowed Autoclub highway map—older than the car we were in, dating at least to the fifties—made its way among us, passed hand to hand, fraying along the fold creases. For all we knew it was made by a Flat Earth Society, as many of the destinations it described, the towns themselves had been renamed or reincorporated. It hardly mattered: the journey was the destination, as we whipped around the state in crazy circles.

"Allo"— Felice had taken two years of high school Russian, the accent she was just making up on the spot as we stood in a gas station phone booth just north of Cincinnati, on with the manager of the Zimmer Nuclear Power Plant in Moscow, Ohio—"is Mysleaf, from Izvestia noospypurr...we have visiting dignityurry from Moskva wanting to inspect nuclear plant."

"Pardon?"

I watched as across the lot Terry Wheat and Knobby haggled with the station's owner. Finally Knobby bent his head, as if this would settle something. The man reached out cautiously and touched his hair, as though he were a cactus. Kitty lingered over by the garage. She smiled at an attendant who stared back, bottle-jawed. With her recently-shaven head, she too looked extraterrestrial. Everyone else was already in the car, that jigsaw-box of limbs and torsos.

"Well I don't know about inspecting it, ma'am"—the plant manager's puzzlement shrilled over the receiver—"but the plant's open to the public. Every day, from nine to two."

"Very good. Will bring own mechanisms to take readings."

All around Ohio there were towns named Parma and Paris, Cuba and Rome, Berlin and Moscow. Apparently you didn't need to leave the state to see the globe. In that cranky old bus, which had no second gear, in a changeless weather, we drove like demons. What did it mean to dream of escape, if every place was the same besides?

"Let's go to Paris!" Krist's voice rang out from the pile. Like Mara, he loved Ohio and never intended to leave it. "I've always wanted to go there in the spring."

"That *was* Paris."

"What, that? I didn't see anything!"

Kitty scrolled a window down and pointed to some electrical wires behind us, drooping from a short, derrick-like structure. "Didn't you see the tower?"

Invisible Dan was pinned underneath her somewhere. He was probably the only person in the van who'd find this situation disappointing. I'd asked him, back when we stopped for lunch, how his summer was going. He'd just shrugged.

"Hey," I said. "Why don't you just tell her how you feel? You can't get what you want—what you need—unless you ask."

We were standing in front of a café called Beard's, an abandoned looking luncheonette where you could still get lime rickeys and cherry phosphates. Dan took off his baseball cap and fanned his face with it. Our reflections hung in the bluish glass behind us.

"Why don't you?" I repeated.

He shook his head. "I dunno. She doesn't like me."

"So? At least it'll be resolved. Maybe Terry'll kill you and put you out of your misery."

I watched his face. His eyes narrowed there in the patch of shade where we stood beneath the luncheonette's quaint, swaying sign. At last he seemed to realize how hopeless the situation truly was.

"Nah," he said.

I thought I'd bring him out of it. "So what's it like working for her father?"

"Interesting." He smiled cynically.

"Interesting? What's interesting about pushing a bunch of numbers around all day? You should quit."

He just kept smiling, shook his head again. It was the longest conversation we'd had all summer, and he seemed to tremble here at the end with intensity I didn't know he had in him, a rage that lifted to the surface and then disappeared. So it seemed, at least. We ambled back to the van together and joined the others. I think the group of us traveled together a lot that summer because if we all moved at once it meant no one could leave, or, more importantly, be left behind. In three days we drained the state of Ohio of whatever exotica we could find, stopping to buy Swisher Sweets cigars at a café in Cuba, playing kickball with a parking lot pebble in Rome. And then we drove home, on a Sunday. I didn't need a map by now. I knew the roads and where they led.

"Wait! We have to go back!"

In the rear there was a commotion, which I tried my best to ignore. Felice sat up front next to me, and I let her cue up Elvis Costello's "Motel Matches" on the tape deck, a concession to her love of Mr. Wordplay himself. At least we had what Dan and Lena might never, since he was too chickenshit to ask. Behind us Krist hollered, "I left my wallet in Berlin!" This was pronounced Burlin', of course. "We have to go back!"

"I'm not going back to that place," Terry Wheat said. In the rearview mirror I watched as he clutched his stomach. "It's the worst fuckin' Mexican food I've ever eaten in my life."

"What were you expecting?"

"I was expecting—"

He bolted for a window.

"Look out, 'e's gonna blow!"

Knobby shifted aside. "Don't heave on me T-shirt, man!"

His ill-fitting I © PARMA T-shirt—white with green piping, smudged with a mustard stain from the ham sandwiches we ate there—hung on him tinily, as if on a wire hanger. It was sizes too small, its sleeves creasing over his shoulders, but it was a prize to him; he (or 'e, as 'ow we loved to imitate him, this 'umble guy) planned to wear it onstage.

Terry leaned out the van's open panel, and booted directly onto the highway.

"Ugh, Christ," someone sighed.

Before us the road extended the way it always did, corn-covered and mutant-industrial. Smokestacks rose in the distance, breaking the yellow monotony. I turned to Felice.

"When I was a kid, I thought the song was 'Sleestack Lightning.' Y'know, like those lizard men from *Land of The Lost*?"

"Get out," she said. "Even you're not that deaf."

"You're right." I chuckled. "I made that one up."

She covered my hand on the gearshift. It didn't seem to matter if we were together or not, or if—no matter how she denied it—she was in love with someone else. For the moment I didn't care. Late day sun shot through the windshield and tinted her skin a glowing, almost metallic color. She looked eternal, like a statue cast in bronze. But I couldn't shake that feeling that had stalked me ever since I saw Nic play. We could run wherever we wanted to, roam the world over like we were free. But we were caught in the shadow of the clock, those hands moving forwards and sometimes back. Soon enough, we'd disappear.

18

Are We Not Men?

The telephone rang, two days later. Felice answered, her arm fumbling along the floor by my futon like a blind sea creature's tentacle.

"'lo?"

I rolled over too, brushing sleep from my eyes. She'd been here the last two nights consecutively, the first time all summer that had happened. I looked at her jeans, puddled on the floor; her shoes—two pair—flung in the corner. At last, I thought. At last.

"Hi, sweetheart!" Donnie's voice shrilled from the receiver. We both sat up.

"Doniella! Where are you? Honey we're so worried!"

I lay back down. She was worried. I was annoyed. I lay on my side staring towards the window. The thick black bars that were there to keep thieves out.

"I'm in Troy," he said. I could hear him perfectly, even as I covered my face with a pillow. "With Jamie!"

"Great!" Felice clouted me softly. She sat up. "I'll come get you. Donnie, are you—"

"I'm fine." His voice crackled cleanly along the connection, the line from upstate New York. At least he sounded upbeat, sober. I thought, there she went again making something out of nothing, crying wolf. I'm fine. "I just wanna stay for a couple more days, since Jamie's under the weather."

"Yeah?"

I tossed my pillow aside and made an I-told-you-so face. Felice seemed to watch me and at the same time be miles away, leaning towards the window with a cloudy expression.

"Well actually a little more than that. He's not doing too great."

Jamie was a medical student at Columbia, the closest thing Donnie had to a steady boyfriend. I watched Mara's cat, an orange-and-white calico, napping on our windowsill, its tiny side going up and down, up and down.

The shadow of a tree from our lawn fell over it, making the temperature for now almost bearable. Neither of us heard what he was saying.

"Oh, well we'll just—"

"Jamie's dying." The words came out in a rush. *Ihavecrabs.* "He's got pneumocystic pneumonia."

"Oh."

Felice propped on one palm, her topless body rearing up above me in our shadowy space by the window. In the millisecond it took me to do the math, play the angles, I was quiet. Down the hall Mara was up early, getting ready for the daytime shift she now preferred to work. A bassy rumble traveled through the floor. Some song I didn't recognize about how we were all puppets.

"Oh!" Felice said.

"He's ill." I'd never heard him sound so serious, so clear. "AIDS."

I lay still. And in the instant before this fresh bomb rippled to its deepest suggestive limit—before it shook up our lives for the rest of the summer, at least—I felt any number of conflicting things. I waved away the hard-on that was not yet inappropriate, watching this girl, this dream I'd been chasing all summer hugging her knees with the receiver pressed to one ear and the same half-puzzled and half-glad expression she'd been wearing since she picked up the phone. All my longing concentrated itself where she sat. I focused on the mole, the size of a pencil eraser, on the side of her right breast. I listened to the song rumbling through the floorboards, and felt the stirring of a breeze, too weak even to be called one, before—

"Oh!" Felice leaned forward just a hair. She pressed her free hand's fingers against the bridge of her nose. "Did you use condoms?"

"No, we never used condoms."

Donnie's voice didn't dip or break. He was such a great storyteller, in life, able to ventriloquize a family member's demented ravings or the precise, harried tone of a beleaguered waitress he'd seen in New York City who, after an hour of harassment from a customer who kept snapping fingers at her to refill his cup of coffee, whirled and proclaimed to the room at large, *Honey, it takes more than two fingers to make me come!* All of these people were him—the waitress, his bigoted, Democrat-hating grandfather, his screw-tight mother—

as practically *everything* seemed to be him, after a while. So it seemed now
he might've been talking about someone else. His own self fell away: it was
another person in danger. The cat stood up and excused itself, squeezing
between bars onto the window ledge.

"We didn't, ever," he said. And now his fear burst free. "We didn't ever
and now Jim is dying. He's in the hospital, and I'm afraid! I'm afraid of what
could happen next."

I watched the cat's body strain into an hourglass shape as it vanished;
watched the space it had just vacated, the empty air. And Felice just dropped
her head and stared down. Down, down, down, as if this event—perhaps
inevitable—she'd been prepared for long ago.

****

I rode with her. A bunch of us did, as this was an emergency. We
stopped to get coffee at a truck stop in New Paltz, Marcus, Lena, Felice and
myself. An original Fantastic Four, with Donnie—would he or I have been
the Silver Surfer? The Watcher?—to make five. We'd driven all afternoon
and evening through Pennsylvania. Lena was out in the parking lot talking
on a pay phone with her father, and Marcus—he would've been Mr. Fantastic,
I thought, Reed Richards: the truth grew elastic, in his hands—occupied the
opposite side of the booth from Felice and myself. His eyes drooped. It was
the bleary hour of a difficult trip that seemed to subvert all my hopes from
the original drive out in June. The gray fringe of Akron hovered in my mind,
the rust belt edges of Cleveland and Pennsylvania as they'd seemed at twilight.
Apocalyptic, infernal, their city smokestacks belching. We drove in silence,
without talking. No music. I'd tried to play some and Marcus had reached
over and shut it off. His desiccated cigarettes, since we'd forgotten to bring our
own, tasted like old string and dust.

"More coffee?"

The waitress here didn't "hon" Marcus, just slopped the scalding
liquid onto the table past his cup's rim. She wasn't fooled by his act either.

Lo, was her name according to her tag, just like that cry of discovery, *Lo and behold!* Her hair was the silken gray of a witch in a fairytale, pulled back into a fist-sized chignon. Her face was wet with makeup.

Marcus said, "What's eating *you?*"

I couldn't tell him what I was thinking, that I felt badly fooled in my decision to come here, and that I almost—almost—wished I hadn't. It was 5:00 A.M. We sat and drank, the milk in our coffee congealing into plasticky strands. Our wrists shook along the edge of the table and the caramel colored surfaces in our cups trembled anxiously back. Then I stood up—we'd been fixing to avoid the stares 'n' glares of a whole roomful of men in western shirts and trucker caps—and I hammered the table with both fists.

"Fuck all you people!" I yelled. Erupting, knocking over coffee cups. "*You're* the fucking freaks!"

I was tired of being stared at, and at the same time remaining unseen. I was tired of having my plans upset and my hopes dashed. Marcus grabbed my wrist. He was up out of his seat even before the contents of our cups and glasses, the rivers of coffee and water I'd set in motion, made it across the table and onto the floor. He yanked me reeling across the room behind him, with the survival instinct that would've served him well growing up where and when he did, all the way out into the parking lot. I clipped my head on the glass case at the register, could hear Felice, as we passed through the door, standing up to offer "Lo" apologies. Marcus wheeled on me as soon as we were outside.

"What the hell is wrong with you?"

At times like this he could drop the act completely: he sounded like any other Midwestern kid with a chip on his shoulder as we stood outside. Lena was behind us, still speaking with her father, an insomniac just like we were, while truckstop smells hung in the air and the dawn cracked open in the distance, a yolk-like sun. For the day, early; for us, late. A truck rumbled past, its silver tank gleaming, and I rubbed my head where it had just been hit. All those white and yellow blocks of Juicy Fruit and Beaman's gum.

"Nothing. I didn't mean to insult anyone."

"No?" Marcus laughed. "What exactly *were* you trying to do then?"

"I dunno." I faltered. I'd just wanted to be seen for once, to be understood, or believed. Why was that so difficult? "Grab their attention?"

"It worked." Marcus pawed at the asphalt with a Hush Puppy, kicking a pebble. "You might find a gentler approach works wonders."

Felice came outside. I still wanted to reach over and cuff him, shake him in my frustration. Beside us Lena leaned in the booth, having taken her gum out and stuck it in her unused ear, a gray pebble-shaped blotch like a hearing-aid. Her long face was grave. She tilted it to listen.

"Of course I believe you, daddy! Of course!"

Who knew what they were discussing? But everybody had to believe somebody, I guessed. You were either buying in or buying out. Always, it seemed. I looked at her hair, then back at Marcus. Peach-colored light was breaking along the horizon. I was about to say something else, but Felice came over with a T-shirt over her arm, multiple boxes of gum stacked underneath it.

"I had to buy some things, to pacify those people," she said, glaring at me. "You learned your manners from your band there, Jungle Boy?"

I shrugged. Then Lena hung up the phone, stepped out of the booth and looked at the three of us, from one to the next.

"What is it?" she said. "Let's get going, huh?"

****

Donnie met us at the bus terminal in Troy. He looked orphaned as we pulled into the lot, his little body dwarfed by all those silver Peter Pan airships. It was raining and he lifted his hand when he spotted us. His face folded into that rubbery grimace that was half grin, half existential mask. His fingertips were a dull orange from smoking so much. Everyone ran forward to embrace him, fussing and shouting. I hesitated, and then I stepped forward and hugged him too, clawing awkwardly at the thick, worn surface of his jacket.

"Thanks for coming."

"Yeah. It's good to see you."

"Likewise."

I let him go. We eyed one another. Finally he reached into my pocket and fished out a cigarette.

"May I?"

"Knock yourself out."

I watched the pale flare of the match, the grateful torque of his expression as he inhaled. With the light rain falling under his eyelashes, on his cheekbones—it was barely more than a mist, really—he looked like a Pierrot or a mime. He tucked the matches back in his pocket. Everyone stood back from us. As if to give whatever it was—our tolerance, or antipathy—room to grow. At last he looked up.

"So. Are we gonna die standing out here, or what?"

19

Eyesight To The Blind

Jamie's apartment was an old bank tower with the face of a clock. We stood by its round picture window and stared down at the Hudson River, which flared silver at twilight. The apartment was cool and spacious, filled with books, bric-a-brac andchina. Jamie was five years older than Donnie, and until recently had been a medical student at Columbia. Around the apartment were framed antique anatomical drawings, flayed-looking bodies in pink and gray and steel-blue. We were alone here, since Jim was in the hospital. Donnie had just come back to retrieve a change of clothes.

"When did you last have sex with him?" Felice said. While I eavesdropped, kneeling by the stereo pretending to go through Jim's records. Marcus sat over on the couch, reading Terry Eagleton. *Shakespeare and Society*. Lena sat alone, listlessly, all of us scattered around the apartment like bystanders, the jumbled stones of a Druidic ruin.

"When did you, Donnie?"

"May."

"And?"

"That's it," he said. "The last test results were negative, but they wouldn't necessarily have shown. It was June, remember?"

I watched them carefully, from the corner of my eye. Had *they* slept together, besides? It seemed possible, but not likely. I shivered, still. It seemed to threaten one of us was to threaten all of us, that if Donnie got sick we could—somehow—all be. I flicked through the records, breathing that sweet, reassuring smell of decaying cardboard sleeves. Erik Satie's piano notes—Gymnopedies—tumbled through the air of the apartment, falling like ice cubes into a glass. Outside, the dusk flash-fired the river and the cityscape—old brick buildings with painted 1930s advertisements still flaking off the sides—the color of an old photograph, a momentary solarized sepia. Jim himself wouldn't be able to see it from his hospital bed. He had viral retinitis.

"Didn't you know," Felice said. "Didn't you see this coming?"

Donnie shook his head. "Jim'd been sick a couple times. He had pneumonia last Christmas, but I thought—"

"You thought what, Donnie? What the hell were you thinking?"

He didn't say anything. At the hospital I'd watched him cool his lover's forehead with ice, smoothing back the sweat-damp hair. If only he'd taken as much care of himself, I thought. He didn't appear to know how.

"I'm not sure," he said finally. Smoke twisted freely between his lips. Beyond him, outside, the light paled so I could read the signs. *Liberty Bell Museum*, read one. *Meneely Forge Ironworks*. He said,

"I'm not sure what I was thinking. I just...can't tell."

20

Shadow of A Doubt

"Wanna go to Perry's and get some beer?"

When the invitation came it did so over the phone: a man's voice was low, urgent and threatening. *I'm gonna get you*, it may have said, or *What are you wearing?* I sat at my Selectric typewriter in the bedroom, its electrical hum underscoring my dread. Donnie's reappearance had shaken something loose in me: a new series of fears. Down the hall Mara was playing the new Sonic Youth, Kim Gordon whispering over an oriental-seeming guitar figure, some lyrics about being the boy "who could enjoy invisibility." I stared at a Man Ray postcard Felice had given me, taped to the wall above my desk. Two girls not quite kissing. It was too glancingly suggestive to be erotic, and yet too erotic to be anything else.

"Wanna go to Perry's and get some beer?"

"Sure."

It took me this long to recognize Terry Wheat, since these eight words were as many as he'd ever said to me at one time. I don't know why I said yes. It was hot and I was bored, lolling around the apartment half dressed. Back from Troy just last night, Felice had driven Donnie back to Wilkerton and not called since. I doubted anything would happen between them now, but who could predict? Terry—that vicious lunatic—could be just the company I needed to jolt me from my torpor.

"Hey."

He met me at the door, or I met him. I opened it and there he was, standing up on our metallic landing. Glowering in his cholo garb, with his Montgomery Clift-ish conk of blonde hair.

"You ready to go?" I said.

He looked me up and down. "Ain't ya gonna put on pants?"

More than Donnie, Terry could have been the craziest guy in Columbus. He was certainly the most confrontational. I'd seen him break a Thick Person's nose with a headbutt, draw a machete from under the seat of his truck to threaten a guy who'd merely honked at him. A white scar on his lower lip testified to a time he'd eaten a lit cigarette on a dare. I walked up High Street alongside him now while the heat rose up off the pavement and locked us in, encasing us almost like a substance, like Lucite. Cans flew out of passing cars in lazy arcs, either as the Thick People couldn't muster the will to throw them harder or else the temperature affected their flight.

"You okay?"

"Yeah. I just...gotta rest."

Terry squinted at me sharply. "Pussy. I should break your legs."

We walked the eight blocks, a journey that was practically Homeric in this heat: we sat and rested two or three times, ducked into a Rax Roast Beef to bathe in its air-conditioning and smoke a cigarette or three. We were like hoboes in a Beckett play, puttering around in circles by the side of the road. I had begun to realize—even as we contemplated hitchhiking that final, long block—you could do nothing here without exaggeration. Maybe, just maybe, Marcus's stories had a point, beyond being outright lies. Maybe there was no story you could tell that was not one somehow, and true experience, too, was just the exaggeration of itself, a life without untruth just—slag.

"You want something?"

"Sure, Mumbles, whatever you're having."

We stood by the jukebox at Perry's. My scalp prickled and my face dripped sweat. I felt like I had the flu. The jukebox gulped my quarters and began playing our Feel Bad Hit of The Summer, The Pop Group's "Thief of Fire." A series of warped shrieks and tormented howls. *I! Accept my crime!* Feeling shaky I braced myself against the juke, one palm on the plexiglass while Terry went to the bar. Across the room, Felice's last boyfriend, Roy O'Donnell, sat alone with a pitcher of beer. He was three years older, had already dropped out of Columbus College of Art and Design to go work for his father's insurance company. He looked bloated, in Bermuda shorts and a pink T-shirt, the blonde tips of his hair fading to black along with his art school dreams. The room was speckled with losers. That sad sack bass player for Hangman's Mob sat in another booth, squinting through his horn-rimmed Costello glasses at the latest issue of *The Attack*. Roy lifted his glass tipsily, offered a two-fingered salute. Terry and I settled into a booth. For a long time we didn't say anything.

"I thought I should warn you." Finally he spoke. We'd been there forty minutes or three hours, I honestly couldn't tell, staring at one another beneath the ceiling fan's melancholy breeze. Marinating in a geriatric quiet at once strenuous and companionable.

"Yeah? Warn me about what?"

I looked at him. I barely had to move my head at all to do this. An empty bottle of Cuervo tequila sat on the table; several beer-glasses, and many limes. My stomach ached, as I watched a fly, struggling on the lip of a beer glass. Terry reached over and flicked it with his finger. *As flies are to wonton boys*, I thought. He reached into his pocket and then jammed an entire sheet, at least ten hits—ten *more* hits—of blotter acid into his mouth.

"Iy cllwrrfrr," he repeated (more or less), while I said.

"It's not polite to talk with your mouth full." I watched him. "What are you saying?"

I straightened. Watching Terry take drugs had the strange effect of sobering me up, unless it was simply hard to tell. It was hard to tell. I'd done no acid, just drinking. Terry stared back, his face glistening like a strongman's—it was as hot in here as it was outdoors—but composed, as level as if he were sober. Incredibly, he seemed more so than I. Even though he'd also had more of the bottle.

"That girl."

"Which girl?" I said. "Felice?"

He nodded. My speech was thick; his, crystalline.

"She's gonna fuck you up."

"What makes you say that?"

I looked around the room. Hearing it from Terry's mouth gave the suggestion oracular force. I had no basis on which to suspect Felice of anything—not really, beyond my paranoid jealousy of Donnie; nothing she'd actually done gave me reason to suspect her of anything besides indecision. Hardly a crime in an eighteen year old.

"Why d'you say that, Terry?" I scrutinized him. "Are you fucking my girlfriend?"

He looked back blankly. Like a card player, his face was void. I thought, you would if you had the chance. But then he broke into a crooked, almost effacing grin and said,

"Nah, man. No. I'm in love with Lena."

"Does that matter? That you are?"

Footfalls fell behind us, along the sawdusted floor. I thought, there's someone here, in case Terry and I fight. The juke had fallen quiet on a Wednesday afternoon. Wednesdays in Columbus were special, little troughs of hopelessness in which the dream of escape receded to either side. Terry took a deep swallow from his beer. I watched the eagle tattoo on his bicep—an inky, green-blue smudge—flex. Promethean, I thought. *Thief of Fire.*

"Of course, man." Terry put his beer down. "I'm just saying... women."

He scowled.

"Right," I said. "Of course."

I didn't believe him, yet I didn't disbelieve him. There was a point of suspension between those two poles also, perhaps, where you could do both at once. The air between us was humid with incomprehension. He picked his beer up again and sat with his arm cocked, halfway between the table and his mouth, as if he wanted to arm wrestle. Behind me the jukebox swallowed more quarters. My elbows rubbed the table's braille plane of initials and scars, its hard wood surface like a school desk's. Then Terry said, "Go ahead, man. It's your round."

****

"Are you insane?"

"Maybe. I'm just telling you what Terry said."

"Terry?" Felice snorted. "He's a few forks shy of a complete dinette set, wouldn't you say?"

She came over to where I was sitting. She was getting dressed, to go to work and I watched her from the ledge that ran beneath my windowsill, its inbuilt surface like a settee.

"You don't seriously think I'm seeing anyone else, do you?"

"I—"

I don't. I didn't, not really, yet I hesitated. She asked so patiently, refusing to dignify my suspicion—which was beneath me, she knew even if I didn't—with alarm. Her face held little pockets of shadow, even in the wash of sun that came through the window behind me, her eyes sparkled green.

"Sometimes I think you want the world to validate your grievances," she said. "So long as it's you and your band against everybody else—"

"Oh come on!"

"Seriously. You're paranoid. And if you stay that way, eventually you'll make your nightmares come true."

She shook her head. Then turned and picked up her apron—like everyone else besides me, her summer job was waiting tables—and made her way out the door and down the hall. We were together now, was the thing. It had happened imperceptibly. Somewhere, over the last few weeks, she'd started spending more nights here. No matter that it wasn't going to last, that a letter on pale blue stationary—from her potter friends in Southampton—lay open on the night table. *Dear Felice: We are delighted to hear you are planning to come see us in September...* She'd told Trinity the same thing, her decision wasn't final, but still. I knew she was going to England, whether or not my own paranoia screwed things up ahead of time. I listened to her walk down the hall, whistling that infernal Costello song—"Imagination (Is A Powerful Deceiver)"—as she went. What was my problem? I shifted on the wooden bench, looked down at the street where Felice appeared a few moments later. I watched her walk away, disappearing into the hot and hazy afternoon, her red hair glittering like a wayward ember as she went. I gripped the bars. What was wrong with me?

****

"*Who?*"

Not that I didn't have other difficulties, wasn't accumulating bruises of all kinds and colors while I made the rounds with Nic's new demo tape, the four songs he'd played me plus a blistering cover of The Clash's "What's My Name?" I'd cornered almost every club owner in town—since there were dozens—and forced them to listen to it. I'd been up and down High Street, to bagel basements and gyro joints and straight-ahead bars: *no one* wanted to book this band.

"Lords of Oblivion." I cleared my throat. "Nic Devine's gr—"

"Nic Devine? That guy?" The voice on the other end of the phone was sharp with contempt, scratchy as though its owner had a cold. The owner of a club called The Nineteenth Whole. "Never. No way."

"Why not? Didja listen to the tape I sent you?"

"I did."

"It's good."

He coughed, noncommittally. Like he wasn't going to dignify this with an answer. "Maybe, sure, but it's not about whether it's good or not."

"It isn't? What is it, then?"

At the kitchen table, I chomped on a grilled-cheese sandwich I'd made with Mara's iron. It tasted vaguely of starch; there was an ogive-shaped char mark on it. Store bought white bread. I ate with both hands, cradling the phone to my ear as I listened.

"The last time I booked them fourteen people came. Fourteen! They played so loud they shorted out the electrical system. There was a fire in the kitchen, my bartender quit. They're bad news."

"Bad news?" I said. The only bad news I could see was not having been there myself. "Superstition ain't the way, pal. They're incr—"

Click.

I tossed my sandwich aside in disgust. Swiss cheese, bitter and old, full of holes. Why was it so difficult to find this band a stage, a home and an audience? What use were they to anyone without these things? Mara whisked through, on her way to work. She grabbed an apple off the countertop.

"Trouble?"

"Yeah. I can't book Nic."

"That's a surprise." She wore her familiar black-and-whites, smoothed down her skirt as she tossed me her apple and then grabbed another one.

"Hold your tongue and say—"

"I know," I said, "I know. But Nic's a really nice guy!"

She chuckled. "I wasn't talking about him." She ruffled my hair as she passed, bent down and kissed my forehead. "Was I?"

Then she was gone, and I was left with the ticking of the stove clock again, the heat-dazed and shadowy vacancy of our kitchen's white linoleum cube. Perhaps this band too, I felt all over again, was just a figment. Outside the confines of my heated imagination, maybe they didn't exist at all.

****

I pounded on Nic's door. Again, harder. He opened it.

"Hey, buddy." He looked me up and down where I stood panting and sweating, breathless in the afternoon heat. It was August 1. "Where's the fire?"

"Can I come in?"

"Sure." He stood aside. "What's eating you?"

"Nothing. Everything. I'm having trouble lining up your gig."

He shook his head, offering sarcastic sympathy, and smiled. In the cool of his own vestibule, with those mellow leopard skin and zebra-striped patterns visible everywhere in the next room, my panic seemed ridiculous.

"What, it's *your* gig!"

"Hey, no one said it was gonna be easy."

I followed him into the next room, where his guitar rested upright on one end of the couch. He'd been practicing. A package of Doc's Proplugs lay open on the table, a pink rubber shield was affixed to his injured right ear. There was no music blaring today, just the hiss of his air-conditioner and the latent twang of his unamplified guitar.

"D'you even have a *band*," I said, "besides Billy? Because I'm not going to be able to book you if you don't exist."

"I have a band." He sat, picked up his guitar. Tested his low E against his A-string. "I have a guitarist, at any rate."

"You do? Who?"

He grimaced, or grinned—it was tough to tell, as he looked down at his Les Paul—while the strings moved closer to harmony. "Can't say. It's a state secret."

"I see. Is this a Donovan's Brain thing?"

"Nah." Bingo, as the strings chimed perfectly. "This guy's real."

Ever had a dream that convinced you of its reality or—conversely—a memory that grew blurry, so you were forced later on to wonder, did that actually happen? Such was this band, or at least my relation to it: they were ineffable, incredible when we were apart, but so convincing when we were together it was ridiculous to think otherwise.

"I don't believe you."

"You don't, huh?" He was already beginning to resolve those two strings into a chord, the chord into a killer song. "See for yourself."

I nodded. I practically could see, leaning into the not-quite-recognizable melody. God, what was it? Another stunner with a hypnotic, circular progression. He said, "You better not mess it up, though. This guy's special. I had to promise him extra pay."

"Really?" I stood, listening. "Who is it?"

"You'll see."

It could've been anyone—Eric Clapton, "God" himself—for all I knew, or cared just then. The song, the tinny, unamplified yet majestic twanging on Nic's guitar was all I had to go by. It was enough.

"What's that called?" He'd played for about a minute and hooked me all over again. There were words too, about living in an igloo, something about a polar zone. It's all white, went the refrain. Everything is all white!

"You like it?'" he said, glancing up. "It's not bad, huh?'"

"Yeah. Sure." It wasn't his, I remembered, it was a cover of a Screaming Tribesmen song. "D'you really have a guitarist?" I said. "How come you haven't rehearsed again?"

"Who says we didn't?"

"Seriously?"

"You don't know what we get up to after hours."

He began to play again, shaking his head like there was something funny, some joke I was missing. I stood, listening to that small sound—the metallic stringed whisper—that would have to convince me, that was all I had to light my way for now.

21

A Love Supreme

Felice needed to go see her mother. It was time.

"Come on," she said to me over the phone. "It's just for the day. We'll drive up to Toledo and be back by tomorrow morning. I want you to come with me."

I couldn't miss the subtext here, the pressure underneath her words. Summer was ending. The damp air had a subtle bite. A breeze ruffled the sun-scorched tips of our lawn. Mara's cat, Nixon, stalked across the porch and then pounced, tumbling after a leaf down below. I said, "I really shouldn't. I need to find Nic a gig."

"Come on. We'll be back tonight."

I stared down at the lawn, its dromedary curve as it dropped off towards the sidewalk. She added, "I have to give Trinity my final response tomorrow. They've been holding on to my dorm spot."

I knew what this meant. She was calling me away to break up with me, or whatever equivalent it was you did with someone you were only semi-dating, taking me outside so we could have "The Talk." Her mother, English after all, would be the last ballot cast in favor of traveling overseas. I looked through the bars and nodded. May as well take it like a man.

"Alright," I said. "I'll meet you out there, and we'll go."

I hung up, got dressed and then bused out to Wilkerton. It was early yet, and Toledo was just a couple hours north. Felice had said something about getting there for lunch, and mentioned that her mother would take us shopping. I admit I was curious too, about this mother; my own had been mostly absent from the scene when I was growing up, where Felice's doted on her and vice versa. Maybe I would understand better, maybe Felice—and in some sense, the Midwest—would come into focus through this expatriated Brit and grade-school art teacher, this hippie free spirit who'd crash landed in Columbus, Ohio in the mid-1960s. Was this city as strange to her, then, as it was to me now? Packed onto a bus, standing up, surrounded by bodies fat, short, squat and tall—there was that sense, in Columbus, of everything glimpsed as in a funhouse mirror, opposed to the surgical glamour of L.A.— breathing recirculated air I stared at the landscape of shopping plazas and exotically-named gas stations sliding by. I watched a squat octagenarian fix both hands atop her cane to walk, dragging herself down the aisle in a tripodal shuffle. No one where I was from seemed to age like this.

"Hullo."

Felice's father squinted up at me as I ambled up the front walk.

"You're here for Felice?"

"Yep."

And what must it have been like to be him, too, I wondered, this shyly urbane professor of astronomy who'd landed in the thick of American suburbia? I stuck my hand out to shake and Felice came erupting out the front door behind him.

"Bye!" she hollered to someone in the house, then stopped when she saw me. "Ready to go?"

For a moment we stood in the portico's shade, the house rising white behind us. Her father sat in a small chair, a newspaper folded across his knee. *–nic to Close, as Found—* , read the partial headline I could see, the metro section of the *Dispatch*. He rocked to and fro. One calf was crossed over his opposite knee, exposing a sliver of pale shin, a black sock scrunched above his ankle. He brushed his long, silvering hair away from his face. Jangled his loafer before Felice bent over and kissed him.

"See ya, daddy."

How lovely it all seemed, as we stepped out into the drive. Her father watched us, squinting out from one of those interrogative English faces, all nose and woodchipper teeth. The keys to Archie's Mustang rattled in Felice's hand. Her hair glowed. I never got over her beauty. The flowerbeds hummed with bees, and I kicked a pebble across the drive. Her father called out, "Will you be home for dinner, then?"

"Never." Felice flashed back a mirror—or the parody—of his anxious smile, mimicked the lilt of his accent. "We'll write to you from Canada."

"I'll let Harry move into your room."

"Fair enough." She unlocked the car door, reached over to do mine as well. "Just so long as you don't let him peel the varnish off the floor with hydrochloric acid," she added under her breath, as we slid inside. "Kid's a freaking psycho."

Felice put the car into gear and then backed into the street. Her father waved. Harry came outside and stood beside him. He lifted a hand too. His body-language was lumpen, his eyes shrewd behind those coke-bottle lenses. Felice flipped him the bird.

"What is it?" I said. At the end of the driveway she stopped to lower the power convertible top. "What's your problem with him, anyway?"

She shook her head. "You really don't see it?"

Tears had gathered in the corners of her eyes. Maybe just as it was so bright.

"No. He's a kid. He just turned, what—fourteen?"

I envied Felice her family, was the thing, its aggravated Americanized normalcy. Mine was off the charts with coastal vanity. Who could relate to it? Everyone's family here seemed as harmlessly mad as this one. Up on the porch, Harry extracted a cigarette—a Carlton—from his pocket and dangled it from his lips. He offered us a circular wave and a loopy grin, a mockery of an idiot's greeting.

"You have no idea," Felice said. "You really don't."

I didn't. I'd heard tell of how he'd snuck up on her once with Nair and how he regularly tracked dogshit across her just-mopped kitchen floor and generally interfered with her adolescent life, the way kid brothers were supposed to do, but these were just stories. With my own eyes I'd seen him waving a pellet pistol around and even—as I left that day—taking a potshot at the neighbors' dog, a senile old basset hound too gimpy to move. (He missed.) This stuff was mean, but so what? He struck a match, cupped his palm around it. Their father either ignored his smoking or didn't notice, but in any case Harry looked harmless. More like a junior associate car salesman than anything sinister. A weighty, vaguely commercial-seeming dignity clung to him in the heat. Around their heads flowers seemed to burst, yellow roses and white nasturtiums. They grew thickly along the drive and under the front windows, detonating on the air. *Beautiful.* Felice murmured, "I can't wait to get out of here."

And then we were gone, wind whipping around our heads as she revved it up Apple Drive.

****

"Dear heart!!"

A woman greeted us by leaping up and down in the parking lot where we'd just pulled off the highway and into a shopping plaza, a half-hour south of Toledo. She was huge.

"Dear heart, oh dear heart, oh—"

My ears fluttered still with wind as we slowed, as Felice piloted the car into the desolate plaza that lay just off 75, where this woman was already waiting for us with paws the size of ham hocks and a body that shook while she bounced beside her Honda Civic. She was so excited to see Felice it was palpable, hopping like a game show contestant. Felice wiggled her fingers atop the steering wheel.

"Hi mom!"

I was agog. Felice had said to me during the drive, *My mother's a big lady.* I'd said, *How big? You'll see,* she said. But now that I did see I could scarcely believe my eyes. She was an airbus of a woman, a zeppelin in jeans and canvas tennis shoes with a rugged, genderless thatch of russet hair and narrow, dark, glittering eyes. Felice leapt out of the car to greet her. I just stared.

"Dear heart! Oh!"

I watched as they embraced. Felice had pushed over a photograph too while we drove, an image of her parents taken on a beach near Dover. There, her mother's face was Felice's, compressed: eyes and nose both smaller, smile a bit wider, brows black, diagonal slashes. She looked like a figure in an ink drawing by Hokusai. Her father too was slender, dashing. The picture was in black and white, faraway in both time and space and in some other sense besides. They were in love once. I said, *She doesn't look big,* and Felice said, *Oh that was a long time ago, 1962.* And we'd driven a while in silence, with the wind buffeting our heads and the sky shifting from cloudless blue to wrinkled, cerebral-gray coils. The radio played Paul Simon, that song about days of miracle and wonder that was another one I hated and Felice loved. I felt as if even this photograph was shown to me as a valediction, a way of saying *so long!* I got out of the car now and went over to join them.

"Mom, this is—"

"Oh, I know! It's lovely to meet you, I know!"

She crushed me almost as ferociously as she had her daughter. Her arms were soft, jiggly and damp in the late summer humidity. They weren't muscular, but had a boa constrictor's lung-crushing force.

"Mom!" Felice laughed. "It's a little much! You might let him breathe."

She let go. I gasped,

"Hi." And studied them, from one to the other. They did look alike, was the thing: a resemblance both on the surface and deep within, though her mother was easily 110 pounds heavier. The same lips, and eyes.

"I'm so glad to see you mom. I need your advice about something."

I walked behind them. I might be privy to their conversation, about school or art or the future, but I might never grasp what shuttled between them. Felice rested her hand on her mother's arm. My own feelings were a dilletante's by comparison. They watched each other, accents—Felice's American, her mother's still English after all these years abroad—overlapping, chiming. A wind picked up, stirring around them both as the sun poked weakly between the clouds and then vanished.

"Of course, pet."

Thunder rumbled. We stood at the base of a pink bell tower-like structure, one of those exurban buoys that signifies commerce to the adjacent highway. This mall was filled with outlet stores, the lot littered with sad little Japanese hatchbacks and eight-cylinder Detroit sedans in metallic greens, browns and grays. It looked like a place where capitalism itself had gone to die. The temple-like front of an Odd Lots rubbed up against a shuttered Woolworth's, kitty-corner to a Stop-N-Go market. In between were grates, cracked windows plastered with brown paper, a four-screen theater showing *Tin Men* and *Used Cars*. Only the Odd Lots looked more than theoretically inhabited, with people bustling in and out of its wide, triangularly-buttressed front face.

"What now?" I said. Why had we stopped here?

The wind picked up. I could taste the ozone, the electrical charge in the air. Her mother grabbed us each by the wrist and charged towards the door of the Odd Lots. The first fat drops fell around us, spattering on the gummy asphalt while Felice and I reeled after her.

"First things first," she huffed. "First things first!"

****

"Hold on a second—"

Felice stilled me after her mother slid out of the car. She and I sat in back. The front seat was heaped with Odd Lots paraphernalia, two-pronged forks and lidless kettles, gargantuan pajama tops. There was something aboriginal, superstitious about the way her mother heaped up these needless gifts at Felice's feet.

"Hang on."

Her mother crossed the parking lot. We'd just driven Archie's car up to Windsor, Ontario for dinner. It seemed like we'd just had lunch. I knew what was coming. I'd listened to the two of them talking (*You must do what makes you happiest*, Felice's mother kept saying, *you mustn't worry about the prestige*), and more importantly not talking, just watching and being, sharing a plate of French fries in a restaurant booth like I wasn't even there. *My pet. You know what to do!* She did know, I was sure. I'd been waiting all summer for her to follow her mother's example and extract herself to a foreign country. There, she'd pass from my reach forever. At least it would be settled. I thought, let's get it over with.

"I've made up my mind."

"Yeah?"

"Yeah. It wasn't easy."

"I'm sure." I'd never been broken up with before; it was different than I'd expected, the feelings somehow more elastic. "I can imagine."

We looked across a dirt lot over Lake St. Clair, towards the Detroit skyline. This seemed both miniature and vast, the lights toyish in the humid twilight. I watched her mother close towards a restaurant whose windows were all tinted black like a limousine's. Dusk again. We never seemed to be truly awake in the daytime: all the interesting things in our lives happened at night.

"I kept going back and forth," she said. "It was really difficult."

It was that hour, that moment really, when the ground appears to breathe light, halo'd like a tennis ball held up to the sun. Seven thirty-two, according to the clock on the dash. I listened to its barely audible tickings, and to the friction of our bodies on the leather seats, damp still from when Felice had neglected to roll the top up. The air was cobalt blue. I watched her mother moving, the soft clouds of dust brushing up behind her unlaced navy sneakers.

"I'm going to Trinity."

"You are? That fig—wait. What did you just say?"

She looked at me. I looked back. A sleeve, the pink arm of a shirt that was at least six inches too long, flopped over the back of the seat in front of us. All this stuff, the Odd Lots merchandise, made little sense. In its mismanufacture it seemed created for a race of people who didn't exist, Munchkins or circus performers or dwarves. I felt the same way in this moment.

"What?"

"Trinity." She beamed. "I thought about it, and I can throw pots anywhere."

I leapt into her lap, pouncing upon her in the back seat as she began laughing.

"You," she said. "That's the reason, though. It's because—"

I kissed her. A hollowness spread throughout my chest. Outside the clouds of dust—almost white—sifted into the air and began to settle even as her mother had vanished into the restaurant. I kissed her again.

"I'm glad," I said. "I'm so glad."

"You don't seem—"

"No, it's wonderful. Really "

I watched the dust settle, the yellowy clouds as if from some great westward migration. Yet, we were heading east, the land of the rising sun! Felice said, "We'll be together."

"Yeah."

I opened the door, and we tumbled out into the lot. It was empty save for our car, and the air was cool from the earlier rain. I felt the way you did, when your wishes were so suddenly granted. Hollowed out, expansive. Perhaps a little bit numb. My teeth tingled and my arms swung freely. Across the lake the skyline sparkled, its steeples sharp in the encroaching darkness. I took what felt like my first real breath of the summer. Oughtn't I to have been crazed with elation? Instead, I was weightless, uncertain. My feet seemed to barely touch the earth.

III

The Boy With The Thorn in His Side

22

It's Gonna Take A Miracle

"That's a nice tie," Felice said.

We were in her bedroom in Wilkerton, getting ready for Kitty's rehearsal dinner.

"Thanks." I mimicked Marcus. "VTE, twenty-eight cents."

I had everything I wanted. So why did I want more? I adjusted the tie's knot. It was Spiderman-red, criss-crossed with the gesso-white lines of a Pollack painting. Against my black suit, black shirt the effect was electric, violently psychedelic as a solarized photograph.

"You ready to go?"

The room was still hers: twin beds pushed up against one another, ashtrays and teddy bears, a series of books that ran the gamut from *The Green Fairy Book* to her high school copy of *For Whom The Bell Tolls*, annotated in number-two pencil. She'd lived in this room her entire life. All its furnishings were girl-sized, pink and white. Boxes were stacked against a far wall, labeled for Hartford

"Why so glum, chum?"

I sat at her vanity table, combing my hair. My face told the whole story, that face I had never known what to do with: broad, Slavic cheekbones, California-blonde hair that fell to my shoulders; a year-round tan that felt like a blemish among the New England pale.

"You look sad."

"I am sad."

"Why?"

I couldn't answer. My band—I was a meager bassist and a venue away from the concert of my dreams, though I still hadn't met the guitarist—was coming together; my girlfriend loved me. I had everything I wanted, everything I'd come here to find. I said, "I saw Terry Wheat today."

"Terry?" She shook her head. "We're not going to go through this again, are we?"

"No."

I stood up. We turned towards the door. I wasn't sure we'd "been through" this before quite, or not entirely. She said, "Don't you trust me?"

"Of course I do."

Maybe I did, and maybe I didn't; maybe the uncertainty that washed through me again and again and again had nothing to do with her at all. It could've been myself I didn't trust. I ducked my head under the lintel as we moved out into the hall. Felice snapped off the light, so the room behind dissolved into darkness.

"How's Donnie?"

We angled side by side so we could squeeze down this narrow upstairs hall together. Sunlight entered from a window at the end, and the air was hazy with cigarette smoke. I wasn't being suspicious here: Felice had taken him to the free clinic this morning to get tested.

"Scared. Wouldn't you be?"

"Yep."

We passed Harry's room on the right, the source of all this cigarette weather. The kid huffed about three packs a day. His door was closed and I heard the low groaning of Black Sabbath's "Planet Caravan." Then a sound like the snap of a wet towel, followed by multiple boys' giggles.

"What are they doing in there?"

"I don't know," Felice said, as we turned down the stairs. "I don't want to."

Down we went. Outside it was late afternoon. A single star sparkled in the fading sky beyond the picket fence, over the low rooftops opposite. I might have wished upon it if I'd had a clue what to wish for, or knew why I was still so restless and dissatisfied.

****

The rehearsal dinner was at Perry's. Its bare wooden floors were swept clean and polished. Long tables sat in the middle, with white linens and hollyhock centerpieces. The room looked elegant, transformed from its stable-like plainness. Kitty had wanted an English wedding, but for whatever reason, Knobby wanted to do it here.

"He's a little skittish," Kitty said. Together she and I stood over by the jukebox. "He threw up three times last night."

"He did?" I looked over at him where he sat in the corner, clutching his head and nursing a glass of fizzy water. "What's wrong with him?"

"He's scared."

"He is, huh? Why?"

In my heart I knew. I watched Felice, over by the bar. What was that feeling, that need that was so often written off—in men especially—as fear of commitment but which seemed instead to be something else, perhaps a sense that our time had not yet arrived? I could see rising off Knobby there in the corner, and I could relate. Lena came in. She looked upset—in fact, she was crying—and Felice put her arms around her. What could have been the matter? It had been weeks since I'd seen her. For a moment I had that feeling I'd had before I came to Columbus in the first place, that this city and its people were a many-headed hydra, a thicket of experience and personality I'd never penetrate. Like Knobby I was, as I had always been, outside. Late sun shot along the edge of the bar a moment, coloring their faces as Felice whispered something in Lena's ear. Kitty said, "I dunno. Stage fright maybe. You should see him before he performs sometimes."

"Really?"

"Yeah. I want you to do something for me, though. A favor."

I watched Felice and Lena. The jukebox lapped over into something swoony, the Flamingos' "I Only Have Eyes For You." The light faded and their faces edged back into shadow.

"Shoot."

Pale at the bar, these women like planets. Kitty lay a hand on my shoulder.

"I want you to watch him for me."

"Who, Knobby?"

"Yeah. Tomorrow. He's so nervous, and so far from home. I just want you to look after him in the morning."

"Why me? I mean, I barely know him."

"He likes you. He says you're mellow."

"Really?" I laughed. "Is that a compliment?"

I barely knew her either. She was an orphan, was all I knew—both her parents had died young—and this gave her a certain adult opacity. She seemed older than the rest of us, and at the same time obscurely vulnerable. I looked at her hair, which she'd dyed black as it began to grow back out. The frail candescence of her skin. She tipped her head. *Will you?*

"Sure," I said. I didn't want the responsibility, but it was an honor to be asked. "Glad to."

We stood by the jukebox. Over at the other end of the room Knobby had gotten up and was beginning to organize a cadre of guys—Marcus, Krist, Donnie—into an a capella singing group like the one on the juke. It was quite a sight, all of them in their brightly colored VTE dinner-jackets, the too-high trousers and winkle picker boots. Knobby himself wore a custom made Nudie suit, the western wear designer who'd made clothes for Gram Parsons. Camel-colored, with staves and musical notations all over the jacket; embroidered marijuana leaves on the sleeves. Suddenly there was a commotion over by the door.

"What's going on?"

I looked over and saw Invisible Dan, barging his way in now or trying to. Terry Wheat held him back. He shouted something I couldn't make out—he was drunk as a lord, clearly—and then dodged his way under Terry's arm, darting over towards Lena. She turned to him with an expression of pure rage before he could get a word out, then threw her drink in his face.

"How *could* you?" she shouted. "Why did you do it you fucking ass—"

She slapped him. I could hear it even over the jukebox. She stormed away and left him to stand there, dripping. A pained, sheepish smile spread across his face as he mopped it with a napkin. He wore the same Spiderman tie I did, as there'd been a whole twisted nest of them at the VTE. Everybody went for one, they were so kitschy-cool. I left Kitty and went over to him.

"What was that about?" I said. "Doesn't seem like you were taking the most romantic approach."

He stood there, his arms crooked and spread like he was simply going to air-dry. Everyone else ignored him, not that there was anything new in that.

"She's pissed at me."

"Yeah, I see that. Why?"

He shook his head, then took off his jacket. He moved with the deliberative slowness of the freshly humiliated, trying—and failing—to save face.

"Her dad's a crook," he said finally.

"So? What does that have to do with anything?"

He draped his jacket over his arm. Stared at me out of that square face, too plain really to be handsome, too lacking in distinction. He shook his head, almost like something was funny. His cheeks were flushed and I could see the coarseness of former acne patches. For a moment, I saw him. Beneath that whittled expression like a cigar store Indian's, a depth of personality and pain.

"The I.R.S. were investigating him," Dan said. "They needed help deciphering some things in his books."

"Yeah?"

It took a moment for the penny to drop. And while it did, while I waited for my understanding to catch up with what I'd just heard, Dan passed a hand over that faded brown crew cut—already dry, since it was short as a marine's—and then just strolled away, across the room and out into the night. As if the brief effort of talking to me had sobered him completely.

"You helped?" I said.

But he was already gone, already back out the door. I turned to Kate Blum behind the bar.

"What the hell?" I said. "Dan helped the feds? Why would he do something like that?"

Kate shrugged. Wise, or clueless, like bartenders the world over. She swabbed a glass, there under the wall clock. I guess Dan came to apologize, but how did you apologize for such a thing, besides?

"How did I miss this? When did it happen?"

She cocked her head. "It's been in the papers."

She tutted, and drew me a beer which she set down in front of me. I drank it. Mopped the foam—glowing, golden—from my mouth. (I supposed

I'd seen something about it, somewhere.) She said, "Love makes people do weird stuff. It's like they're not themselves."

She shook her head again and I thought of Dan's anger, his understandable if misdirected rage. I muttered, "Or more themselves, maybe. Who knows?"

****

Later that night I angled over to Knobby's table. Maybe I should get to know him, if I was going to mind him all day tomorrow. I felt like Spanish Tony, one of the Rolling Stones' fabled hangers-on. *Wanna pour me a little more plonk there, mate?* I leaned over and obliged. A skinny, ginger-haired Englishman who sat between us picked my shirt pocket for a cigarette.

"Can't afford your own?" I studied him. He was sleek, unshaven in a pale sharkskin suit. His smile was wolfish. His incisors had gold caps. He hadn't said much while I was sitting there, but radiated a proprietary air as he sat next to Knobby. "How d'you know the groom, anyway? What's your deal?"

He flashed those gold teeth. A few others were gray, giving his mouth a strange, semi-gentrified appearance. "I don't have a deal, mate. I offer them."

"Really?" I laughed. "How so?"

"Knobby's band is on my label."

"No kidding? You're Stevo?"

"Yep."

I'd heard about him. His label was one of the bigger independents in England. He picked up a whiskey bottle from across the table and topped up both his glass and mine. He handed me a business card from the vest pocket of his dinner jacket. It was rhomboid, the edges sharp. It showed the logo for Dog's Breakfast Recordings, a puking wolf under a quarter-moon. In England they'd released not just Knobby's records but a slew of them from bands who were all over college radio in the States. Recently they'd signed their first Americans, a lesbian acid-folk trio from Boston. They had everything from Goth-metal to retro-psych, with a variety of sounds in between.

"Wow. It's great to meet you."

"Thanks."

"How'd you get the label name?"

He lit his cigarette, flames seeming to leap directly from his fingertips as he twisted the match back behind the soft pack and struck it between his thumb and forefinger. That first sharp inhalation.

"It was 'Dog's Bollocks,'" he said. "Our first few releases lost so much money I decided to change the name."

"Is that right?"

"Yeah. I don't mind, really." He knocked back his shot glass then topped us both off once more, slopping whiskey onto the tablecloth. "It's a gambler's business. I thought Knobby 'ere would wind up playing third support at the King's Arms in Bristol, but look what happened?"

He let out a hyena-pitched bark and Knobby laughed right along with him. As if they'd perpetrated some joke on the world at large; for all I knew, they had. I leaned over and spoke with the confidence of the desperate, the drunk and the lucky.

"Listen," I said, "there's a band you need to hear."

****

I woke Nic with a phone call.

"Hey," I said—it was three o'clock in the morning and I'd dialed without thinking—"There's been a miracle!"

"Yeah? What?" He was lucid, alert. There were girl noises in the background. I guess I hadn't woken him up. Did he ever sleep? "What could be so important you choose to disturb me, at this hour?"

"Label interest."

"Label interest?"

I could scarcely believe it either. I'd managed, after much badgering, and after Felice had left, to lure Stevo back to my apartment. He'd sat and listened, head cocked and eyes narrow. It happened that one of his band who'd begun as Goth pretenders were now in the States recording with Bob Ezrin, and had discovered a nascent Led Zeppelinism. Their singer, who once wore

nail polish, now dressed in Indian feathers. They'd scored an American hit
that expanded their cult following into something wider. Maybe that was what
he thought of when he finally stood up and flashed that sharp, seller's rictus of
a smile. Not bad, he'd said. If you get them a showcase, I'll come.

"Dog's Breakfast. The English label. I played 'Crawl to Me' for the
head and he loved it."

There was a silence as I crouched still in the darkness of our common
room. Nic's single still revolved on the turntable long after I'd lifted the
tone arm and brought it back to rest. I couldn't bring myself to remove it.
Suddenly, I was superstitious. I watched it spin. I heard a girl, the nurse or a
different one, say in the background, "Nic, honey, are you coming back?"

"Man, England? There hasn't been any good music from that place
since 1979."

"Maybe. But I booked your gig, too."

"Oh you did, huh?"

It so happened that sitting on the other side of the table was the
owner of the Marley Music Hall, Columbus's longest running rock 'n' roll
club. I'd never thought to approach him before—it was a fifteen hundred-seat
arena, far too big for Nic's band—yet somehow I'd prevailed upon him too.
Who's this, he'd asked Stevo, who are you needing to see showcased? He was
a big, friendly white guy with dreadlocks and freckles, a trust fund baby from
Westerville. He'd never even heard of Nic Devine, but was tight with Knobby
and Stevo. Sure, why not? We're dark that weekend. He stared at us both
with veiny eyes, while Stevo neatly reclaimed the spliff I believed—suddenly—
he'd forked over for just this purpose, to get him to bend. Book 'em Stevo.
Whatever you want.

I had no idea where Stevo'd come from, this demon who seemed to
have appeared simply to facilitate my wishes—again, every rock 'n' roll story
needed The Devil in it somewhere, right?—but I didn't care.

I said, coolly, "Yep. The Marley."

"That place?" Nic's voice skyrocketed with excitement suddenly.
"Man, I saw KISS there in 1981!"

"I—you saw KISS in 1981?"

"Of course, man, I'm from West Virginia. The 'Unmasked' tour.

Look, that's great, Derek's gonna love it—"

"Who?"

"Never mind, just tell me when?"

"Friday night. Next Friday."

"Great. I'll be there. Don't worry."

He hung up the phone. I felt I'd just shot myself into orbit—never mind what Nic had just said, as any mention of KISS without masks wasn't necessarily a good sign—but I wasn't prepared to worry about that. I'd done it! By hook or by crook—I supposed, really, a little bit of both—I'd snatched life from the jaws of danger, made something happen where nothing was before. Felice came padding down the hall, Nixon writhing in her arms.

"Come to bed," she said.

"I will in a second. I just booked Nic a gig!"

"That's great." I couldn't see her face, since all the lights were off. Her body, in a nightgown, was a neutral silhouette, and her tone was hard to read. "Come to bed. I'm holding the wrong thing."

"I will. I just want to play these records one more time."

"OK."

The cat writhed sharply, and spilled to the ground. Our voices rang strangely it seemed to me, as she turned and shuffled back down the hall.

"Congratulations."

"Thanks."

It was late, the sky already brightening outside the living room window. I cued the singles and played them both twice, with headphones on. Then straightened up and went down the hall myself, where I slid into bed and found Felice was already sleeping.

23

The Wait

"Where is he?"

"I don't know—he was just here, in the elevator behind me."

In the parking lot of the Wilkerton Square Mall—the place where it all started—we stood, Kitty, Donnie, Marcus and the rest, waiting for Knobby. Krist Cooley was the flower girl, Kate Blum the officiant. Invisible Dan had been disinvited, but everyone else was present and accounted for. It was late afternoon. Across the street loomed McDonald's arches. We sweltered in our itchy thrift store tuxedos and string ties, the clip-on bows that sat crooked atop starchy, yellowing shirts with batwing collars. Gary Hauser, in a top hat and tails, had set up a Vox organ and stood with his fingers hovering over the keys, ready to launch into a psychedelic wedding march. And not sixty seconds ago, Knobby had followed me out of the Ramada Inn's elevators. I'd thought he was following me; but I hadn't actually been looking.

"Where is he?" Felice said.

"I don't know." I gestured over my shoulder. "He was right behind me."

Four o'clock in the afternoon: 4:04, according to the bank clock at the far end of the lot. And the sun angled down as we stood on the meat-gray asphalt, crimped with spidery lines, cracked with the twin punishments of extreme heat and snow. Wedding silence hung in the air. They'd chosen this place as Knobby was anti-religion, wouldn't set foot inside a church. His parents weren't coming and so my job had been simple: to lead the one orphaned skeptic to the altar to join with another. For a second I looked at the blinding shine on Krist Cooley's patent-leather loafers—he wore the same clothes he did to his waiter's job at the Colonial Inn across the street, the same cheapjack VTE suit—and at Kitty's guileless, hopeful face, white as a sundial. Someone coughed. Then I turned and sprinted back into the hotel.

"Where is he?"

I buttonholed someone—a bellboy, I guess, since he was wearing one of those gray *Quadrophenia* outfits, an embroidered jacket like an organ-grinder's monkey's—and demanded, "Where did he go?"

"Who?"

"The guy"—I clasped his shoulders—"you can't say you didn't notice him! Five-six, but about five-fourteen, with the hair? Spiky guy?"

"Oh!" He nodded towards the bar. "That way."

Figured. I exhaled, then trotted off towards the tinkling sound of a cocktail piano, following a corridor whose bordello shades were mind-frying in the shadowy mid-afternoon. The plants all looked waxen, embalmed, the scarlet carpets like the plush lining of a coffin. No wonder Knobby stayed here. It was perfect for him. And so I spotted him, hefting a curvaceous cocktail glass—there was a slice of pineapple on the rim, a drink the color of a Hawaiian sunset—by himself in the gloomy bar.

"What the hell, man? People are waiting outside!"

He shrugged and tossed the drink back, literally slopped it towards his mouth so it spilled down his chin and onto the sparkling lapels of his turquoise jacket.

"Nah, man." I'd never seen anyone—even an Englishman—so quick with the booze. He was already signaling for another. "Can't do it."

"You can't?" I reached him, caught his arm. "Why not?"

He said nothing. I repeated, "Why not?"

I felt myself in a ridiculous position as I sat down on the stool beside him, caught him staring into the mirror behind the bar. He looked hollow-eyed and wasted, as he'd been drinking all morning against my insistence. The bartender stood at the far end, polishing a glass. My face too had that startled expression, that look with which we sometimes surprise ourselves in mirrors. Who *are* you?

"I can't, man. I just can't."

"No?"

He shook his head. "Forever," he muttered. "*Forever*, man."

I nodded. "Forever is a long long time, it's true."

Against my better instincts, I found myself slowing down now, agreeing with him. I was supposed to haul him out into the parking lot and force him to the bumper of the rented red '55 Thunderbird that was both the altar and the happy couple's intended getaway vehicle. Yet I couldn't help but wonder if I should. Knobby too was barely older than we were, twenty-three or -four.

"It is a long time," I nodded. "But it's what you promised. It's your responsibility."

He snorted. "Responsibility. I play rock 'n' roll mate, that's my responsibility."

"You don't have others?"

He shook his head, indefinitely. Not "no" exactly, but "not yet," perhaps.

"Look," I said. "Kitty's a great girl, man! Felice loves her. She's—"

I wanted to say, better than you, but I couldn't. I felt as if I were mounting an attack on my own defenses. Advancing an argument I wasn't sure I believed.

"She's perfect," I said. Although this wasn't true either; I happened to know she'd made out with Stevo—Knobby's very own label boss—one night when they'd been drinking. It happened after a gig, in Louisville. Felice told me. "Come on."

Knobby just looked at me. There was a sense of time moving very slowly and very quickly at once. I knew the others would be searching on my heels, but for a moment we were alone in the ficus-quiet of the hotel bar, that airy-fairy piano tinkling anonymously—I didn't recognize a song, couldn't even tell if the music was real or canned—behind us, in the room's shadowy depths. Kitty *was* amazing, if human; as Knobby had fucked groupies on the road, this was her revenge, that's all, a wheel of motive that turned and left them even. Yet I felt to the bottom of my being too that this was fundamentally backwards: she should've been jilting *him*, just as I should not have been babysitting a man whose band was the idol to thousands, if not millions. Why did these things keep getting turned around, inverted from how they should've been?

"Let's go. Everybody's waiting."

But he stood up, pulled a rumpled twenty from his pocket and tossed it on the bar. Then said to me, "Nah. Can't, man."

There was a fire door, the kind with a red *Exit* sign above it—what in

England would've read *Way Out*—over to the left of the bar. Who knew where it went, but not to the parking lot: we were at the rear of the building. He eyed it.

"Don't—"

"I have to, man. I'm sorry."

"You can't do this. She'll die."

"*I'*ll die, if I stand still. Sorry mate."

He stood up. How could I say I understood him? How could I say I didn't? His panic rattled in my chest too, as I could imagine anyone feeling this way. Anyone except Nic, maybe. But it was Knobby's call, his funeral, not mine. I'd spent all morning up there in his suite, drinking Foster's and rolling spliffs, hoping they might calm him down. You couldn't drug someone into marital submission, could you?

He flung a fistful of change—an additional tip—on the bar and bolted for the door. And I, I didn't move to stop him. I watched his slender figure glide along parallel to the bar, his stiff quills poking up above the pyramid of bottles to show in the mirror on the wall. I tried to imagine where he might go. Nowhere in Columbus was a Goth in an aquamarine tuxedo likely to be inconspicuous. Then he was gone, even as Felice and Marcus came racing in at last. His coins were still jingling, a nickel he'd tossed there spinning, wobbling on its side.

"What happened? Where is he?"

I sat with Knobby's empty glass, a chewed rind of pineapple, his abandoned pack of Drum *fine shag* tobacco, his lighter even—from Wisconsin, with a Harley Davidson logo engraved on it—all sitting in front of me. Incriminated.

"I—"

All of them stared at me, as Lena came in also, and Donnie. The bartender stood, no more concerned or aware than if Knobby and I had been a pair of ghosts fighting. I could smell that loamy, damp scent of unburned shag tobacco: that smell has always reminded me of death, mortality and the month of October. Harvest sequences. The piano, real or canned, had resolved into something I recognized but it took me a second to place. Words flickered to mind about pulling into Nazareth, feeling half-past dead. It was the Band's

"The Weight." I looked from one angry face to the next, all of them glaring hotly at me.

"Where did he go?"

I watched Felice. Somehow I owed my confession to her. I nodded towards the *Exit* sign and said, "That way. He went that way."

24

Tombstone Blues

"God*damn*it!" I'd never seen Felice so angry. "How could you let that happen?"

"I let it happen?" We were on our way home, from what had morphed from intended celebration to wake. We took a shortcut through a cemetery off High Street, weaving blithely through tombstones. "I didn't get engaged to the guy! It wasn't my—"

"Kitty asked you to look after him!"

"I did! I'm not a babysitter, y'know. He just took off!"

"Why didn't you chase him?"

"And do what? Tackle him? Grab him by the hair and drag him out into the parking lot of a Ramada Inn for a shotgun wedding?"

The full absurdity of the situation hit me, as we stood now facing one another amid the crooked rows of stones. Some were recent, others a few hundred years old, their names so worn they were scarcely legible. Moonlight defined our way, the halogen glow of High Street receding.

"You can't force a person to get married," I said. "It's sort of an operation of free will."

"There is no free will."

"Oh gimme a break, the sixties are over! All that instant karma crap—"

"Anyway," Felice said, "that isn't the point. You should've tried."

"I did try."

"Not hard enough."

Once more, her eyes were blurry with tears. Once more, I didn't even know what we were fighting about: as always, it was both more and less than what seemed to be on the table. In the bar at Perry's afterwards, Kitty had wept so hard it undid all of her beauty. It was the only time I'd ever seen her face that way, discomposed, contorted and raw. No one was pretty that way. I'd felt her suffering the way I did Felice's anger: as something large, larger even than the circumstance that provoked it. Both were attached to what was greatest, that dream of leaving.

"I'm sorry," I said. "I am. I wanted to stop him. I tried, but he got away."

"Tell that to Kitty."

I had. I had to. I don't know that she blamed me as much as Marcus and Donnie, who were equally protective of her, did. I rested my palm for a moment on the high, worn edge of a thin, tilted stone: it was loose, almost like a tooth. The coolness of lichen against my skin.

She shook her head. "You think this is just about her. It isn't. It's about all of us."

"I'm sorry."

"You should be." After a moment she added, "I think you should go on alone. I'll sleep in Wilkerton tonight."

"Fine."

"Really?"

I hesitated. "Yes."

She turned then, without saying anything else, and began walking in the direction we'd just come from, back towards the bus routes.

"Hey! What about Donnie? What's going on with him?"

I'd neglected to ask earlier. She didn't look back, just called, "Friday. His test result will be in then. Same day as your band's show."

"Yeah?" I had to lift my voice now. "Will I see you before?"

She didn't answer. I started after her, but then turned in disgust before I reached the gate. Maybe she had a right to be angry this time. Maybe she had all along. Or maybe we weren't even supposed to resolve these things, maybe the dispute really was philosophical. Nine o'clock on a Saturday. A cooling breeze moved across the graveyard. I watched her walk back through the iron gate and out onto High Street, where she vanished under the streetlamps.

25

Burning Down The House

"Ahh, what are you worried about?" Nic shook his head, his fingers shaping the talon of a barre chord. All he ever did now when I saw him was practice. A battered acoustic sat in his lap and we were in the musty old coffee warehouse he'd rented recently in the Short North. A rehearsal space. "She'll come round."

"You think?"

It was Tuesday, mid-afternoon. Outside, cars swished by in the knee-buckling heat. I'd heard nothing, not a word from Felice—or from anyone—since Saturday. Marcus and Lena too had turned a cold shoulder. Only Mara spoke to me, as she and Kitty weren't close. I'd left messages at Felice's house, but they'd gone unreturned.

"Of course." Nic plucked his chords softly. It was easier to accept advice, somehow, from a man with a guitar, to view his cool concentration as greater self-possession. "They always do."

"I see."

In a room above Indianola—it was dank and humid, worse than my apartment for its decay—I stood and he sat on a gray couch that ran below the street-facing windows, which were cysted with enough grime they mightn't ever have been washed. It smelled of mold, plaster. One wall was half peeled back to sheetrock. In Columbus, the rent on a place like this would've been about ten bucks. Nic needed one sucker a month to ask him who "Donovan's Brain" was. Billy's drum kit sat untouched in the far corner, the sticks crossed atop his snare, and a black-and-white television on the floor in front of it played a movie with the sound off. A young Martin Sheen was emptying his pistol into a football that sat on the ground.

"Where's your drummer?"

"Same place as your girlfriend." Nic played a new, slow sequence, an unfamiliar song he was working on, bluesy and dark. "He'll show up."

"You sure?"

I felt again that sense that I was being played, that this "band" was little more than an idea. I'd seen a drummer, once, heard the singer by himself, but of the promised guitar player and the newly-alleged bassist ("I've got a guy," was all Nic would say) I'd yet to hear note one. Nic shrugged.

"Seriously. You sure?"

"Yeah. All you gotta do with Billy is promise him cookies. You got a rider for us, on Friday?"

"Yep. It's not much of one." I'd have to stop by the A&P myself, actually. "I'm afraid the M&Ms will be all mixed together. No picking out the greens."

"Fine."

He stopped playing. In the silence—for when Nic played, even alone, I listened so intently the world outside seem to stop—I heard a bus, its hydraulic gasp as it pulled away from a stop on Indianola. Across the street was a playground, girls chanting and skipping rope. *Miss Mary Mac, Mac, Mac, All dressed in black, black, black—*

"Cheer up."

"Huh?"

I turned back to look at him. Nic said, "Things work out. They do."

"They do, huh? Them's brave words from someone who used to work in a grocery store."

He grimaced. I watched the veins on his arms stand out, like the ridges on a relief map, while he played.

"You know what your problem is? You're a skeptic."

"That's a problem?"

"It can be." He shook his head and repeated, "Things work out, when you're ready. When you're really ready."

He'd cut his hair. It hung just below his shoulders now. Black electrical cables, patch cords, coiled around his feet beside a tiny Fender practice amp. He resumed playing what he'd been earlier. I said, "What is that?"

"A new song. 'The Lion.'"

I listened. It was something new for Nic, a ballad. It was ghastly. He sang it, with words about the plaster lions on his steps, a "lion of demarcation."

I couldn't stand it. The first thing of his I'd ever hated: it sounded like a show tune, the chest-bare groanings of some pro-am Freddie Mercury imitator in an off-the-Strip Vegas musical.

"Jesus," I said. "If you play that on Friday, you're dead."

"Dead?" He lifted the guitar out of his lap. "You and what army, pal? It's a B side, anyway. It's supposed to be a little...different."

I stood at the window, those streaks of soot marbling the glass so it looked almost kaleidoscopic: rain-black tears. You and what army? I wondered if Nic himself ever needed anyone's support. I'd asked him once about the line from "Caveman Stomp" that had always eluded me, the one about "(something something someone) was my kinda dude," and he just laughed at me. *No, no, it's* "my middle finger shows my gratitude." Evidently not, he was happy to stand alone. I said, "What is it about you and cats anyway? Are you a Leo?"

"Nah." He smiled. "I'm a Libra. I just like cats."

So it was. I thought, I'd never understand Nic Devine, ever. What made him tick. I stayed a while, even as my plan—which was never so organized as to be a "plan," it was just the haphazard grabbing of accident and opportunity that life always is, I believed—seemed to unravel. Where was Felice? My friends? Where, again, were the other members of this "band" Nic swore would be joining him on Friday? At least Stevo was still coming: he'd sounded more interested than ever when I spoke to him last. I've gotta see 'em, he'd raved. I mean, you never really know about a band until you see them in the flesh.

"You're not gonna tell me who the guitarist is? Or about your phantom 'bass player?' Man, I'm this band's *manager*, you can't keep me in the dark—"

"Wanna bet? The dark's a good place for you." He shook his head. "Just promote the show, pal, put the fliers up, tell the good people at School Daze to make it rain—"

"Goddamnit," I said. "No one's ever rehearsing with you even, that I've seen. You're making this band up!"

"Nope. It's not your business what we do at night. Your job is to make the show happen."

I stood by the window. At four o'clock, the girls across the street had gone home, and this heat-dazed stretch of Indianola—a corridor of brick tenements and warehouses, a neighborhood that was neither fully residential nor commercial—stood mostly vacant. I watched an old woman totter under the weight of her grocery bag as she came out of the liquor store across the street; watched two boys walk, not-quite hand-in-hand, carrying skateboards as they bumped and jostled one another with their shoulders. Ducking their heads a little as they walked, like monks in the humidity. Ordinary life. In here it was factory-hot: a Chinese laundry. And I understood nothing, not even if this band I loved was, by any objective measure, really any good at all.

"Go home," Nic said calmly, coolly as he sat; even *that* mightn't have bothered him. "Just go. When it's Showtime at the Apollo—that's when I'll be prepared."

****

I walked home, thinking I wasn't going to miss this place. Too much had happened, and Columbus stood revealed for what it truly was, which was just what Felice had said in the beginning: a fly trap, a tar pit. As I rounded the corner onto 13th, I saw Mara coming towards me. She was on her way to work. She lifted a hand.

"Felice called."

"She did?"

"Yeah."

I exhaled. It was five-thirty in the afternoon, the air a jaundice yellow. We stood on the lawn, the short crest up in front of our building. Mara's hands were slack: she carried a book—Italo Calvino's *Invisible Cities*—and a cigarette, one in either hand by her sides. I didn't think she smoked. She added, "She sounded pissed still, said it might be a mistake, but she was calling."

"OK." I looked down. "Why are you smoking?"

She shrugged. That weary, earnest and skeptical face, fringed by short brown bangs. She looked like one of the Pop Art girls who might've been seen screaming outside Shea Stadium when the Beatles played, only calm: there was something at once dated and timeless about her. "It's one of yours. I thought I might try. Want it?"

"Sure." I took it, and the book which she handed me too for some reason. "Thanks."

"You bet. Call Felice."

I went past her, started up the metal stairs. I wasn't really a smoker either, yet that hadn't stopped me. I lifted the cigarette. Stopped.

Stopped.

Halfway up the stairs, the cigarette curled smoke towards my nose. I don't know why. Didn't they say scent was the most evocative, that it routed to memory faster, or deeper than all the other senses? I don't know why, I just stopped where I was. And then turned, vaulted down the stairs, and began racing towards High Street, towards its buses, as fast as I possibly could.

****

"What the fuck you lookin' at?"

On the bus, a guy with a thinning mullet and a patch over one eye glared at me. He looked like Lemmy from Motorhead reborn as a pirate. His mustache bent like an extra frown.

"Nothing."

Behind his head the fast-moving panel of High Street was a color strip, an action painting: that one long artery that bisected all of Columbus like some mythical endless highway. It seemed to race by, yet go nowhere. I couldn't get to Felice's house fast enough. It was like the dream you have, in which you're running, running, running. I got up, moved to the front of the bus. If I was a superhero—springing to action after some tingling, extrasensory warning—I could've used the gift of flight, right? I could've seen the ten miles that separated my Campus apartment from Wilkerton, instead of taking the bus. I only knew that something was wrong. Felice would not have called, maybe. I don't know how I knew. It was the way things could be blindingly obvious and yet—still—invisible at the same time. Which meant I could be wrong: the sleeping surface could be only the sleeping surface too. I didn't know.

I'd asked Mara once, a few days ago, how she felt about her rapist, what she thought as she went on and she'd said, *I forgive him. I try to, anyway.* Like the good Catholic girl she was. And when we were in Troy, Felice had asked Donnie what he would do, if it turned out Jim had infected him? *I'll kill him*, Donnie had said. Then smiled, turning his own murder on its ear with tender irony. It was beyond me then, how anyone could feel that way about someone responsible, or half-responsible, for their own death. These people didn't worry about themselves only. They were together. In this, Felice had been right. But as I rode the bus out—unsure what I had to forgive anybody, if anything at all—it dawned on me that this was the only way to live, and that any other way was damnation. Just as to be credibly decent, you had to be credibly dark. Irony, my old bête noire, kept that balance, if anything could.

The gasp of the doors broke my train of thought. I'd almost missed the stop. I jumped out into the parking lot of a Friendly's, four blocks from her parents' house. The restaurant was empty, with that beacon-like brightness such places had at night. A solitary waitress drifted inside, moving like a fish within its isolated light. I began running over towards Felice's street, then slowed down. A soft glow rode above the treetops. It was dusk. The sluggish absurdity of the bus ride had calmed me. I was imagining things. Wasn't I always? I'd arrive and she'd be waiting, we'd make up. Eventually we'd start the whole cycle over again. It never ended. There was that silence of the suburbs, a wind rustling through the trees. The ghostly murmur of a faraway car. I smelled something autumnal, sharp. Was someone burning leaves? I'd tried to read on the bus, Mara's *Invisible Cities*, and had gotten stuck on the chapter, Penthesilia, that described one city as *only the outskirts of itself…no matter how far you go from the city, will you only pass from one limbo to another, never managing to leave it?* No wonder everyone here loved this book. It was their condition.

I rounded the corner onto Apple Drive. It wasn't until then in fact that I truly recognized what I'd smelled as smoke, at the same time I saw it, pluming into the sky down at the end of the block. I saw too the cluster of red vehicles and amber lights massed down there. At which point, incredibly, I didn't believe it. I sauntered a good third of the way towards them before I realized: those were fire trucks. And Felice's house was burning.

****

Of course I was too late. The firemen were already in the last stages of extinguishing the blaze that had taken out almost the entire second story. Their hoses spat foam, the last embers crackled skyward. Black smoke hung thick over the front yard, but the fire was almost out. A crowd that had gathered to watch had already dispersed. It was a small house, and so a small fire. The whole thing had taken place in approximately the forty minutes it had taken to ride the bus from campus. But I ran that final block with my lungs half bursting, and with that sense, absolutely identical to nightmare, that my journey would never end. I'd keep running and the house keep burning for an eternity. I passed Donnie's Rabbit, that mint-green carriage, on the street where he'd left it some weeks ago. Its ragtop was littered with seed pods from the tree above it, body angled oddly into the street. I ran and then got there, where Lena and Marcus were among the people still standing on the outside lawn just beyond the picket fence.

"What happened?"

Marcus and Lena faced the street, away from a smell that was like that of burning hair, sweet and charred and terrible. Paramedics were helping Felice's father down the driveway towards an ambulance. No one else was there, besides the firemen.

"Where is she?"

"Wasn't home," Marcus mumbled. Incredibly, he was smoking, firing up a Chesterfield even as behind him there was a vital crack. A house burned like anything else, it turned out, only louder. A shower of embers twisted skyward, like a cloud of electrified gnats. "She was out. Think she's at Kitty's."

"Who started it?" Stupid question. "What happened?"

"Harry. Cigarette."

"Figures. Where is he?"

"Cops took him. I doubt they'll charge him." Marcus exhaled, his own sharp plume of smoke blown downwards toward the lawn. "Felice says he gets away with everything."

That figured, too. Like a kid brother to the end, except in the one way—the crucial way—Felice had warned and I'd failed to believe her. The downstairs was still intact, the firemen almost finished. No one had been home. I watched her father being shepherded into the ambulance, his begrimed and tweedy pile of a self. The last pale sparks drifted skywards, like a snowfall in reverse. The one surviving upstairs window, Felice's, was opaque now, singed black like a caul. To Marcus I said, "What's everybody so pissed at me for? I didn't screw up Kitty's wedding, really."

He looked at me sharply. *You still don't get it*, this seemed to say. Instead, though, he just shrugged.

"I know. But it's how we are," he said. "It's part of living here."

"Which? Blaming everybody else for your problems?"

"No," he said, "looking after one another. We do that."

I thought, *We*. Exclusive. I might never be a part of this place, or of whatever fantasy of it I'd had.

"I'm sorry about your dad, too. What happened there?"

She shook her head. "I don't want to talk about it."

"Is he guilty?"

She looked me up and down, enigmatic to the end. Half smiling. "Are you?"

Lena was so beautiful. It was my luck or my misfortune—both—that I'd overlooked her before meeting Felice, or that she was so remote. I watched her jaw, its determined pulse as she worked on a piece of gum. I thought, was it timing or something else that kept people apart? Though the end, I would discover, would most probably have been the same, anyway. You couldn't change your—fate, if that's what it was, your destiny. She brushed my cheek with her fingertips, in what was a little too stiff to be a caress.

"Thanks, though. I'll see you, Marcus."

She turned away now, keys jingling from her fingertips as she waved, or half-waved. That green of her VTE shirt and the orange of her hair: these too reminded me of something, evoked some yearning strain of fugitive feeling I couldn't place.

"I'll see you, boys. Marcus, you'll walk home, right?"

Mmmh, he murmured, affirming. The firemen were reeling in their hoses now, and apart from them and the cops we were alone on the lawn beyond the fence, balanced on the edge of the curb. I said, "You fucking asshole. Why did you bring me here?"

"You wanted to come."

"I did. I wanted to see a rock and roll band. Have a few laughs."

"You might."

I wanted to punch him as he smiled, a peculiar wan smile, twisted to one side. Not his eager, ax-cat grin I so remembered; rather, the look of someone lording it over me with an obscure knowledge. I was sick of it.

"You might," he said. "He who laughs—"

"Oh give me a break," I shoved him. "I don't believe you. I've had enough."

He glanced over towards the house. Smoke wafted between us. If we hadn't looked together like a pair of geriatric cross-dressers in our blousy yellow pajama tops, our ill-fitting shorts, we could've been regular suburbanites at a Labor Day barbecue.

"You don't know," he said very quietly. "You don't know yet what will happen."

He plucked at his gabardine pleats, seeming lonely, lost. His eyes were dark as puddles, enigmatic as they had ever been as we stood beneath a streetlamp.

"Maybe," I said. "You're sure Felice is OK?"

"As sure as I can be. You might want to check up on her yourself."

I turned away. He said, "Where are you going?"

"Nowhere. Home. I'll see you later."

"Right."

Behind me, he erupted into a laugh, a wheezy, asthmatic croak that was like everything else about him, prehistoric and fragile. I turned.

"What is it?"

Behind him, the firemen reeled a hose across the lawn: fat, yellow, worm-like. His eyes gleamed.

"You don't believe me."

"No." His smile was back to that confident, showman's smile (I guessed that was Missouri, wasn't it, the Show Me State?) he'd flashed from the beginning. Mocking me. "How could I do that, Marcus, at this late date?"

"You might try."

He laughed again, wheezing away at his little joke. Smoke stung my eyes. I might've believed him if he wasn't such a lunatic, or if I'd simply been a bit more generous. Yet life sometimes resembles itself too intently, is too overt sometimes to be credible. As with the fire, which—having threatened all summer—astounded me when it arrived. Hence whether I believed Marcus or not seemed to me to make no difference. Just as, when I stepped onto the neighbor's lawn on my way back towards High Street, I was shocked to find it wet. The grass was still soaking from an earlier sprinkling. Cool water seeped through my shoes, ruined my socks as I plodded back the way I came.

26

Someone's Gonna Get (Their Head Kicked In Tonite)

I trotted up the concrete steps of Nic's house, passing between the plaster lions just as a hairy guy—outrageously so even by Nic's exaggerated standards—strolled out. His graying perma-frizz hung all the way to his waist; a silver-plated biker belt cinched jeans so tight they might've been painted on. His limbs moved in a kind of syncopated, disjunctive tangle, head nodding in dudish affirmation. It was possible he hadn't changed his clothes or taken a bath since the late seventies. His faded T-shirt read *Cal Jam II*, and a Gibson Flying V was tucked under his arm. He walked right past me as I stepped up onto the porch, and Nic stuck his head out the door after him.

"Later."

I turned and watched as he strode off down the walk and then stopped in seeming confusion at the curb. He hesitated, looking first right, then left, right, left, gangly and sad as some flightless bird. Finally he just staggered off on a reckless diagonal across the street. I turned back to Nic.

"Um, who was that?" I said.

Nic reached into his pocket and tugged out a lighter, which he flicked and held aloft.

"That, my friend, was Derek Whitefield. That's the new guitarist."

"What?!" I turned and looked back after him. "Derek Whitefield? From the Dawgz??"

"The one and only." He beamed. "Man, am I lucky."

"Yeah." I sank down, over against one of the porch beams. "That's one way to put it."

Dawgz records were a nickel apiece over at the VTE. I'd been subjected to a side of their concept "masterpiece," *Natas Elcyc*, just once: a miasma of overheated screaming and turgid guitar riffs, what sounded like Black Sabbath at half speed, except with one of the Chipmunks singing. Marcus and I were on the floor laughing at it. Only—this wasn't a joke.

"No way. I won't allow it. That guy's the worst guitar player I've ever heard," I said. "Does he even know how to take a solo that's less than ten minutes long?"

"We'll find out," Nic chuckled. "And 'worst' is strictly a matter of opinion. I love the Dawgz."

"Jesus."

"No, he wasn't available. Derek Whitefield's the best I can do."

He lowered his lighter finally. Shook his stinging hand. We stood for a moment.

"What's with you?"

"Nothing. Can I use your phone?"

"Sure."

I went in, dialed Kitty's apartment again from Nic's living room. This was where Felice slept, I knew, when she was pissed at her family and everyone else. No answer. The night of the fire I'd gone over there and waited, but she never showed. I went back outside.

"C'mon," Nic said. "Let's go get something to eat."

We moved off down the front walk. I said, "You heard from Billy?"

"Nope. I think he went to Switzerland to have a little operation."

"Really?"

"No. Man, you're gullible." He snickered. "Billy likes being a guy, I think."

Off we went, across the lawn. The air—not the temperature, but the air—had an autumnal edge to it, the leaves yellowing in the end-of-August heat. The sidewalk buckled and heaved with age. Someone had chalked a hopscotch grid in pale blue. I said, "What about your bassist? D'you really have somebody?"

"I do. You worry too much."

A girl came towards us, as we headed up Blake. She was five-ten, blonde, and had soft-combed hair like the mane of an animal. Wholesomeness itself she seemed, like a bobbysoxer, a girl from the fifties.

"Hey." Nic looked at her.

She smiled back. Peaty green eyes, broad cheeks, a dimpled smile; she looked a little like Marcia Brady. She reached into her purse and pulled something from it, slowed and brushed her hand up against Nic's as she passed, murmuring, "Hi."

I'd seen him do this so many times. I watched him unfold the phone number she'd just passed him, the tiny quartered slip of paper.

"Have you ever seen that girl before?" I said. "How do you do that?"

He shrugged, an aw-shucks-I'm-just-a-good-Midwestern-boy smile. "Comes naturally."

We walked up the street, and into a Chinese restaurant that was one of the few places he'd eat in Columbus, being vegetarian. We sat in a booth, the familiar red-and-white color scheme of Chinese restaurants across the country. A curl of flypaper twisted lazily from the ceiling. A smell of grease and steam. The proprietress ambled over.

"Did you get the egg drop soup I sent you?" she asked.

"I did. It worked. Thank you."

"I told you," she said. Reaching out and patting his cheek. "Good for cold."

Every mother's son, and father's nightmare. A transistor radio in the kitchen played the Smiths. *If they don't believe me now…will they ever believe me?* A moment later the girl we'd seen on the street came in. She sat down next to me in the booth, facing Nic. She wore that pie-eyed, loopy and submissive expression she'd offered Nic on the street.

"Hi."

I looked from him to her and back again. This wasn't charisma, it was mind control. Her eyes seemed to dilate as she stared.

"You're Nic Devine."

"Yeah."

"Can I have sex with you?"

She was my age, but not my tribe. Her skirt ended just above the knee, and there was something stupid about her smile.

"I'm sorry," I said, into the awkward silence that ensued—because I honestly thought she was going to strip right there—"Do you two…know one another?"

"Yes," she said.

"Yeah." Nic burst out laughing. They both did. "God*damn* you are gullible!"

I blushed. Set up again, apparently. He flipped me the "note," which was blank. But how could I ever know when he was being serious, and when just pulling my chain? He said, "This is Erin. But you get to call her Marcia."

"I do? Why?"

"Because she lost a bet. She has to do anything I tell her to for the next twenty-four hours."

"She does?"

"Yeah. What's with the stupid questions?"

She got up to massage his shoulders. What must it have been like, I wondered? This was as close as I'd come to knowing, to seeing him in what passed for domestic life, and I was no closer to understanding a "real" Nic than I'd been at the start. The proprietress brought us our food, spicy bean-curd for him, chicken for me.

"How can you eat that shit?" I offered him a piece of chicken. "Sure I can't tempt you?"

Nic snickered. "I'm incorruptible. And besides, 'Man gave names to all the animals.'"

"Sure, according to Bob Dylan." Erin got up to use the bathroom and I said, "What am I gonna do?"

"About what?"

"Felice," I said. "I can't even find her."

"How hard are you looking?"

"What d'you mean?"

He leveled me with a stare. "You say you're in love, but…are you really?"

I nodded. A ceiling fan whirred overhead, reflecting itself in my soup. Round and round, round and round. I didn't know if Nic was a good role model or advisor for such things. The power of hypnosis wasn't necessarily the one I needed. I said, "Are you in love, with that girl?"

Nic looked down at his plate for a moment. "Sometimes."

"Sometimes? That's not how it works."

"It is," he said, and for a moment I thought, maybe he's right. Or maybe he might envy me too. "Sometimes, that's exactly how it works."

What was it like, I wondered again? Every year, the freshman girls rolling in like the sea and seeming to get younger, while he stayed the same, while the days stayed long and the summer never ended for him. I couldn't imagine it otherwise, though it must've been. He just sat there, spooning his soup, nodding and smiling. If what I wanted from him was wisdom, this seemed all he had to give: an eternal youth, who'd never been bothered to look for it in the first place.

****

We parted from Erin just outside the restaurant. I have to go matriculate, she said. And as he and I walked home together afterwards Nic turned to me.

"Listen, man, I don't know if tomorrow night's gonna happen."

I stared at him. "What? What are you talking about?"

He shook his head. "I dunno. We'll have to see."

He kicked at the ground a second, toeing the grass on the edge of a crumbling fraternity house lawn. We were less than a block from his place.

"You just told me you got Derek Whitefield to play guitar," I said. "You've been telling me this whole time you've got a band—"

"I do."

"Then what's the deal? Don't screw this up. It's the deal of a lifetime."

"Whose lifetime?"

We stood, facing one another like gunfighters. In the three o'clock heat, the summer seemed truly without bounds. From the porch of the house, a trio of pouchy fratboys—back early, getting a head start on the semester's drinking—eyed us from their deckchairs.

"We'll see," he said. "We'll just see what happens."

"You need this show to happen."

"You need it to happen," he said. "I'm happy the way things are."

"Oh really?"

He smiled. I couldn't tell if he was just shining me on or if he didn't want change, was happy leading a band that was largely apocryphal, great in rehearsal and in his dreams.

"What the hell's the matter with you?" I said. "You've got stage fright?"

He chuckled softly. "Nah. I just like to keep my options open."

One of the fraternity boys hollered at us, hoisting himself up from his deckchair.

"Hey faggots!" he yelled. "Hey fruit loops!"

Nic turned to look at him. Those guys were wasted, but they had both numbers and size on us. Sitting there under the crooked sign that read DEF.

"Excuse me." Nic took a step towards them. "Did you just call my friend and me homosexual?"

As ever, beginning with that aw-shucks routine of his. But his body language pulsed with casual instability, his fists curling. Like he was itching for it.

"We sure did."

Nic had on his black jeans and one of those blousy silk Sixties shirts he loved. Pink with peppermint stripes, like something Phil Spector might've worn on the back of his Christmas album.

"Gosh," he said, walking all the way over to the edge of the porch now. "That really isn't nice."

I wanted to stop him—the show definitely wouldn't happen if these guys squashed him flat as a bug—yet I was mesmerized. Again, rooted to the spot.

"It really isn't nice for you to dress like a girl," one of them—I decided it was the wit, the wiseacre of the group; he had pouty lips and a tan complexion, sandy hair sweeping across his forehead. The Quarterback, I thought, the Insurance Man's Son.

"It's not *nice* for you to stick your dick in another man's ass," the second, decidedly less-wiseacre said. "You oughtta get a haircut."

"Really?" Nic paused, as if to give this actual thought. "You think that's what we need?"

He stepped up onto the porch. I didn't see what happened next, it was so quick. Only the guy, the ringmaster, was suddenly on his back, writhing onto his side with an ice-cream-falsetto yelp. *Hey There, Lonely Girl*, I thought. The guy might've been a decent singer.

"We don't need haircuts," Nic said, sauntering off the porch. The other guys were too stunned to move. "They'd just make us look like assholes."

"What did you do?" I said, when he reached me.

A dead leaf had caught itself in his hair. He brushed it away.

"I hit him. Just once. Man, those frat boys are light."

We walked across the lawn, the heat clotting in our sinuses. For a long moment, silence was all there was. The half-harmonized rasp of his and my breathing, the dry scrape of our footsteps on the lawn. Earlier, when we'd left his girlfriend, he looked at me.

"You want a turn?"

"For what?" I'd said.

He'd just smirked. "I *am* the boss of her for twenty-four hours."

No thanks. I wasn't tempted. "Y'know you're kind of a pig?"

"Hey." He chuckled, and looked genuinely appreciative. "She's just a lot of fun and I'm really a great friend."

But what I wondered, as we walked away from the porch and that squealing redneck Nic had left up there—really, this was like *Deliverance* in reverse—was how he just continued to rotate, how I'd never know when he was serious or not serious as most of the time he appeared to be both—

"Uh, Nic?"

We'd reached the edge of the sidewalk, and just as we did I looked back and saw several Thick People crouching up on the porch. There were four more of them suddenly, and they were pissed. One stood up, pointed and shouted incoherently. Even at close range, I thought, these people were hard to tell apart. And it only took three of them to make a mob. I looked at Nic. I'd take my cues from him at this juncture.

"Hey buddy?"

He just stood there, perfectly still on the verge of the lawn. The hair at his temples was silky and lighter, soft like a girl's. I don't know why I'd never noticed that before.

"Hey—"

The four guys were closing in on us now, a lumpy phalanx, like an imperfect set of front teeth.

"Go on," Nic said, barely audibly. Twenty-five feet. Twenty. "I got this."

"The hell you say."

He wasn't moving. Still as a weathervane in the windless heat. I knew he wasn't Superman, that these four guys would cripple him and tomorrow night's show would be canceled. What a coward I was, thinking only of myself. Yet I didn't care. I turned and ran.

Except my foot got stuck in a sprinkler pit. I stuck and fell forward, twisting my ankle. As I fell I saw Nic turn and begin to run himself, with his long hair pluming out behind him. He was fast! The whoop that emitted from him was one of pure glee, like he was a truant and this was the first and not the last day of summer. He shot off across the lawn—barefoot, kicking off his Beatle boots so he could run faster—and I'd swear I saw him lift off the ground, vaulting over a low white fence that protected a neighbor's yard. Whooping and hollering, he vanished into deep greenery and shadow

I myself was not so lucky. The four guys gave up on Nic quickly—they were like buffalo, fast but not agile—and they took it out on me. The first one kicked me before I was even up on one knee.

When the first blow struck, all the feeling went out of my limbs. I felt it in my teeth, a numbness spreading as they kicked my shoulders, my side, my head. I folded over to protect my face with my hands as they just kept kicking.

Faggot!

One of them slammed a foot into my ribcage and I felt it crack. I heard it crack, and a sharp pain lacerated my side. I couldn't breathe, just gasped and took in what air I could. There was a sound, a great piercing siren's wail from up the block.

"Shit," one of them said. "Let's get out of here, he's had enough."

What was it? It wasn't a cop, nor a bird nor a plane. I heard an almost seismic rumbling, the sound of a perhaps familiar engine as it rolled throatily down the street. (Was it? I never asked. By the time it occurred to me, it was too late anyway.) The siren squawked again and the Thick People scattered.

"Fucked him up," one spat as they jogged off across the lawn.

The car passed. And I lay there listening to the Thick People's footsteps, their slapped palms as they climbed back up onto the porch. I could tell they'd taken it easy on me. I wasn't interesting enough to hit hard. They'd just tapped me back and forth like a soccer ball, until they were bored. My face burned. I rolled onto my side and tested my breath. Another pang shot through me. Blood trickled from my lips. I lowered my hands from my face and watched them slant away, indifferent. Grass and dirt scabbed the tip of my tongue, and my cheek scalded where the dry grass had scuffed my skin. I grabbed myself by the hair and pulled, just to be sure I was alive.

After a while I struggled to my feet. No one was coming. I limped across the street in the twilight. I was banged-up, but I'd live. In the distance the sun sank, its horizon line a band of gold. The familiar reek of creosote hung in the air. When I got home it would be Mara's turn to rush me to the hospital, experience too, rotating onto its side. Maybe this was what I got, for coming here; maybe it was all I got. The show would go on, unless it didn't. My ribs ached and my ankle buckled as I walked. My whole body hurt like hell.

27

I'm Not There

I waited on crutches with everybody else, outside the Marley Music Hall where I hoped to catch a glimpse of Nic Devine.

"Where the hell is he?" I fumed. It was 7:30 in the evening. Marcus kept me company. "And—who *are* all these people?"

Marcus scanned the throng with a look of bemusement. "Derek Whitefield must have a lot of fans."

"I guess."

Standing out here with us, in a line snaking off down High Street, was what seemed a very nation of Rip Van Winkles, wizened men—and alarmingly similar-looking women—with frizzy, discolored dos that stretched to their waistlines, droopy Fu Manchu mustaches and scraggly beards in the grayish, neutral-blonde shades of blasted oak and ash trees. They looked like Whitefield in other words, with their weather-beaten faces and bikerish black clothes, threadbare Grand Funk Railroad T-shirts and whiskey bottles doctored with iced tea. They clustered mysteriously in threes; a small group stood around toking next to a ghetto-blaster that played Lynyrd Skynyrd's "Saturday Night Special." It was Friday. The whole experience was exactly like that: a world moving out of sync.

"This is going to suck," I moped. "Even if Nic shows up, it'll be a catastrophe. These people don't want the future, they're dinosaurs! They're like a thousand years old."

"Take another one of those pills." Marcus chortled. "They'll calm ya down."

I shook my head. Two codeine, for my rib and ankle, had dulled the pain a little, but otherwise had no effect that I could tell. My chest was taped up tight, so I could breathe without agony. It was like wearing a corset.

"Where the hell is Felice, too?"

Marcus shook his head. He didn't know, but I could feel the reproach also. You fucked that up, he seemed to be saying. He was right maybe. I should've been there, or paid closer attention, listened a little harder perhaps. Something. I didn't care, I just needed to see her again before we left for Massachusetts. It was all I wanted of her now, a proverbial last dance before we left on Sunday morning to go back to school. Marcus fished a cigarette from his pack. A new brand, Export A. He offered me the green box.

"No thanks."

Marcus looked at me. "You still don't get it, do you? It'll be fine."

"That's easy for you to say." I felt he was humoring me, keeping me company out here for no reason. His fickleness extended in all directions. He was into Scott Walker now and the pre-disco Bee Gees, the industrial grunt of Test Department and the primitivist hilljack rockabilly of Hazel Adkins. Lords of Oblivion were a long-forgotten phase, as he'd sold his copy of "Crawl to Me" back to the folks at School Daze weeks ago. Gary Hauser snapped it up. "Felice is gone, my band is totally AWOL as of this morning—"

"You're on the surface of things," Marcus said. He stood with his feet in a "V," drew on his cigarette and plumed smoke towards the early evening sky, shell-pink now above us. As cool as he had ever been. "Really, it'll be fine."

I couldn't have been angrier at him, for bringing me here, seducing me into believing things that could never have been true anywhere in the world. Certainly not in this ordinary Midwestern college town filled with bored thugs and heshers, where the only things I'd gotten were a cracked rib and a mangled heart, a lesson in disenchantment. Where was everybody, where was Nic Devine when I needed him most? I looked out across the street at the closed grate of a barbecue joint; down at the stained, cigarette butt-studded pavement; up at the Music Hall's triangular black marquee. Some wiseass had thought to stick up there lettering that read *Derek Whitefield Returns!* No mention of the actual band he'd be playing in. I turned back to Marcus, feeling another seizure of annoyance to look at that pale, fake-innocent face, those shrewd, brown-button eyes.

"I can't believe you brought me here," I said. He just gave an abstracted nod and smiled.

"Ever get the feeling you've been cheated?"

"Yeah," I said. "Repeatedly."

If this concert didn't happen, if Nic messed it up I would effectively have come here for nothing. At the same time, I wondered, it was just a rock 'n' roll show. What did that have to do with anything real? How could I possibly have felt my life was riding on it? I turned away, scanned the crowd again for someone we knew. There was no one, except for Gary Hauser working the door. Lena was with her dad—free on bail but still facing tax evasion charges—while Invisible Dan had hightailed it back to Boston. Of everyone else—Kitty, Terry, Kris, Mara—I had no clue. I'd talked to Stevo earlier in the day. He said he'd be here in time to catch the second set. I doubted he'd be too thrilled to discover this "band" I'd hyped him on was strictly fictitious. And Donnie too, I thought. Where was he?

Yet just as I turned to Marcus to ask, Donnie came ambling along High Street. Speak of the devil! Here he was, our Priest of the Uncanny. He strolled up with his traveler's satchel over his shoulder, looking faintly perplexed. Also insouciant, not a care in the world.

"Hey." —I grabbed his wrist. "What's going on? Where have you been?"

He looked back at me. His hair had grown out a bit, and paled towards its natural brownish-blonde color, a wispy cropped-fuzz like a tennis ball's.

"What happened to *you?*"

"I got beat up by some Thick People. You?"

His face relaxed, into a loopy, euphoric grin.

"Negative. I got my result today."

He threw a weightless arm over Marcus's shoulder. Marcus nodded, like he already knew.

"Who are all these people?"

"They're here for my band, Lords of Oblivion." I looked at Marcus. "Why didn't you tell me?"

He coughed. "You didn't ask."

We stood there, the three of us, feeling stunned, embarrassed. Through me too there passed the giddiness of a reprieve. But was there no end to my selfishness, my self-involvement? At the same time I had that feeling that Donnie and I were not so much "friends" as we had done something else for one another, performed some other, greater office that extended beyond the bounds of simple friendship. I might not have liked Donnie but I was suddenly close to him: we were bound by experience, and by life itself. Your enemies, your rivals. In the end, you didn't want to be without these either. Donnie looked up and down the street.

"So this is that band you're so into, huh?" He chuckled. "Looks promising."

"They're not like this," I said. "The crowd is misleading."

I shifted my weight back onto my crutches. My ankle throbbed dully. I stood on my other, stronger foot—the good one—so it held me up. I said, "Where's Felice?"

He shook his head. "I can't tell you."

"You can't tell me, or you don't know?"

I searched him. He wouldn't tell me even if he knew, I thought. It was pointless really to ask.

"Come in," I said. "I'll cover your ticket."

He appeared to consider, but then shook his head. "Gotta go."

He shifted his bag, of soft brown leather, over his shoulder.

"You're sure?"

"Yeah." He surveyed the crowd again and laughed. "Looks like you're in for a night."

I looked at the bag, fingered the strap. "Is that brand new?"

"Nah." He looked at me strangely. While I stood on the good foot, lifting the other like a flamingo. "Same old."

He turned then, back out onto High Street. "I'll see ya."

I watched him go, his little stooped figure like a peddler or a merchant's, mysterious to the end as he vanished into the street's abstract distances. Same old. Was anything ever new, I wondered? It seemed like we'd been standing out here for hundreds of years. A hot wind blew after him, rippling the tattered bottoms of the fliers stuck to telephone poles. *Have you seen me?* The sky had turned a stark, infernal orange. I thought, perhaps we were "on the surface of things," as Marcus put it. Yet life had never seemed to me so mysterious, so eloquent and so strange.

"Why don't you go inside and see if your band's here?" Marcus said.

And maybe it was the codeine kicking in too, as my voice seemed to echo off the marquee's overhang, to carry its own faint trail of repetition. "Maybe they came in the stage door."

"I doubt it."

I'd checked earlier: thirty minutes ago, there'd been no sign. But I went inside anyway, limping ahead on my crutches, waving my wristband—the closest thing I had to a "backstage pass"—at Gary Hauser as I did. He grinned, that big, placid and stubbly face like a cow's as he tipped back comfortably on his barstool. He was having a great time, taunting the masses out front.

"No tickee no shirtee," he mocked. "Can't come in 'til I say so, sorry."

'Ha," I said. "You're here to see Nic, huh? After he talked such trash about you?"

He shrugged, stretching that grin a little wider. It was the same look he wore each day behind the till at School Daze records, on the one hand yokelish and slow, yet on the other never seeming to miss a thing. The joke was on me, again. He tipped his head, studying me the way you might a painting, up and down.

"It's not cool to hold a grudge," was all he said.

Then he waved me in, clicking me off on a little hand counter, with the other lifting a brown-bagged bottle of malt liquor to his lips.

"You counted me when I came in before," I said.

He shrugged.

There was that feeling again though. Everything seemed to be repeating itself, somehow. As though I were living not once, but twice.

****

The Marley sat at the south end of Campus, down where High Street tapered off into a nether region of laundromats and liquor stores, cinder-streaked brick tenements that seemed only half inhabited. Originally built in the 1920s as an opera house, The Marley had enjoyed a long and varied history—operating first under the name The Beacon, then The Red

Heron, then Charlie Brown's—that allowed it to call itself "The Midwest's Longest Running Rock Club." The room was too big for Nic, I feared, too overwhelming. Everyone from the Byrds to U2 to Metallica had played here, even the Rolling Stones on a small club date in 1978. I couldn't imagine him commanding the stage, which stood empty as I crossed the main ballroom. Purple velvet curtains parted on a platform which had the band's equipment set up—they'd been here just this morning to sound check—but right now there was no sign of them. Nic's Vox organ sat, small and toyish-looking, on a stand by his microphone. Whitefield's guitars, including a dread double-necker, sat in a semi-circle of guitar stands towards the rear of stage right. Even so it didn't look like nearly enough artillery for an arena of this size, the Dunkirk of our time and place. That is, assuming the band even showed up at all.

****

"You wanna tone it down a little there, buddy?" Nic had snapped while they were soundchecking this morning, "they" being just him and Derek. "Too many notes, man, too many notes."

"It's just music," Whitefield muttered. "Don't get your underoos in a twist, man."

"A twist, huh? I'll twist these fuckin' strings around your neck if you don't stop playing like Yngwie Malmsteen—"

It went just the way I feared it would from there, Nic deriding him until he snapped and stormed out in a huff. The others hadn't even bothered to show up. The bassist's blonde Fender—whoever he was, "some guy" in Nic's parlance—lay face down in a corner, where it looked abandoned and unhappy.

"Where the hell's your drummer?"

"Beats me," Nic shrugged.

"You should beat *him*," I said. "What good's a drummer who's never on time?"

"I should. I have." He sat on the edge of the riser, eating a sandwich.

Elbows planted on his knees.

"Who's your bass player? You're setting me up here."

He shrugged again. This was at 2:45 this afternoon.

"You're telling me you have no idea where your rhythm section is, your guitarist sounds like he's in a totally different band—the gig's in five hours!!"

Nic just smiled and took a lupine bite of his sandwich, whatever it was you put in one when you were a vegan who hated peanuts.

"A lot can happen in five hours."

"Like what?" I snapped. "You're gonna humilate yourself. You're gonna humiliate *me*."

"A little humiliation never hurt anyone," he said, as I stood up. These were my last words to him. I began limping towards the door.

"Y'know as a manager you suck," he shouted. "Five hours is a lifetime. You're supposed to believe in the band!"

****

So I was. So I did and so I had, but where had it gotten me? If only it was as easy to relinquish belief as some people said it was. *God is dead.* And Paul and John, and Jim Morrison too, even as certain conspiracy theorists insisted otherwise. What for? I went over now to the engineer, the sound man and the lighting guy who stood behind the soundboard. Another cluster of three, I noted. They were smoking and nodding their ponytails.

"Hey, you guys seen Nic?"

My voice carried through the empty clamshell of the ballroom. There were no seats, just the balcony that circled the second story catching and amplifying our voices. These guys were teamsters, gangsters. They were intimidating.

"Tcch," the sound man said. He was a blonde dude with the cool, 'stached face of a fireman, a ponytail roped midway down his back. "He took off a little after you did. I don't think he's coming back."

The other two guys just snickered. One had the stringy white hair, the albino features of one of the Winter brothers; another looked like Merlin the Magician. They seemed like they'd been around since the dawn of time. They burned incense and smoked butts, pinching them between thumb and index finger.

"Did you fix the thing I asked you to? The drum monitor was out."

"What difference does that make?" More snickering. "When you don't have a drummer?"

"Very funny," I said. "Just fix it, wise guy."

"Why don't you try backstage," the first one said. "I think there's someone back there."

I pivoted on my crutches, headed towards the stage door. Was there someone? Who, if not Nic? The engineer turned up his little transistor radio that sat on the mixing console. *I might like you better if we slept together*, went the song. Romeo Void. I limped around backstage, climbing up the short steps and then down the narrow corridor that led back towards the band's dressing room. It was dark, narrow—the lights were all out back here—and I groped my way along a wall that reeked of disinfectant and stale beer. Pipes hissed above my head. I could feel their heat while I grasped futilely towards a light switch. A faint glow emanated under the dressing room door. It was so desolate back here it was like spelunking or visiting the bottom of the sea, as the sounds of the radio and the engineers' snickering faded.

"Hello?"

My voice echoed off the walls. I wanted backstage vivacity, women milling around. Instead I had this ultimate solitude. I clawed at the sticker I wore, which Nic had stuck on my chest earlier as a joke. *Hi-My-Name-Is-MANGER*, it read, since he'd misspelled the one pencilled-in word, left out the "A." No matter. I hobbled towards the dressing room door where I could hear someone moving around inside. Hopefully it was Billy, who'd been lucky not to be around when Nic was trash-talking him earlier. *What's the difference between a drum-machine and a drummer? You only have to punch the information into a machine once.*

"Hey Bi—"

I pushed the door open. A guy was standing there, inside the tiny closet of the dressing room, all by himself. I recognized him. It was the bass player who'd snubbed Nic long ago, Archie's friend.

"What are *you* doing here?"

He shrugged. Either he didn't remember me or he didn't care, standing there in the middle of the room with an unamplified bass hitched up around his chest, playing by himself in the semi-dark.

"Waiting for my band."

"This is your band? I thought you said you'd never play with Nic."

He shrugged again. "I never said never."

He had, but that was beside the point. Now he recognized me, maybe. He squinted oddly.

"Did you quit the Hangman's Gang?"

"Nah. But, y'know…Nic made me an offer I couldn't refuse." He plucked a familiar chord pattern, staring down at his shoe tops. He had to stoop beneath the room's low ceiling to fit inside it. In the dim light—there were only votive candles and the circle of timid bulbs around an old vanity table's makeup mirror, feeble as Christmas lights—even his face looked squished, disproportionate behind those horn-rimmed glasses. He was ridiculous, standing there all knock-kneed in his plaid golf pants.

"Where is Nic?"

He plucked again. Day Tripper? I Feel Fine? "Went off to get Billy."

"Who is?"

He shook his head, tutting.

"Dude's got a little bit of stage fright."

"No he doesn't. Billy?"

This bass player—I couldn't remember his name, and wasn't about to ask—collapsed down on the couch now at the far end of the dressing room. "Far end." It really was tiny, barely bigger than a closet with that couch jammed up against the opposite wall taking up its entire width, and Nic's makeup table—laden with picks, tarot cards, makeup, an effects pedal and a bottle of Drambuie—took up almost half its length. It wasn't big enough for four people; it was scarcely enough so for one. A half-eaten cheeseburger, too, sat on the table, dribbling Russian dressing all over his set list. Whose was it?

"Everybody's got stage fright," the guy said, sullenly.

"Yeah, well. You gotta help me find 'em."

He just sat there. "I get paid either way. Nic paid me in advance this time."

Great. His name was right on the tip of my tongue again, but I lost it.

"Look," I began. He blinked back at me. "Forget it," I said. "I'll find them myself."

I turned. Spying Nic's set list, I saw what they planned to open with: a cover of the Hollies' "King Midas In Reverse." I loved that song!

"You're not gonna help?"

He just giggled shrilly, miming stage fright himself.

"Fuck that! I gotta get outta here, man!"

I reached over into the even-smaller closet behind the door to grab a beer from the twelve-pack which, along with a box of stale Ho-Ho's, were the entirety of the band's "rider" as I'd put it together. I didn't see what there was to do really, besides what bands, managers and audiences had been doing together since near rock 'n' roll's inception: get high. I reached into my pocket and dug out the bottle of codeine tablets the doctors had given me last night. I'd eaten my last leftover Vicodin from my wisdom teeth operation earlier, but I still wasn't feeling anything.

"What're those?"

"They're mine," I said, as I twisted away from his grasping hand. I could barely breathe back here, it was so hot and my lungs were taped so tightly. Luckily nothing was broken. I just had a stress fracture. I swallowed four pills, washing them down with the tepid beer I'd just taken from the closet. They were hard to swallow, chalky and bitter on my tongue. I drained the beer. Maybe I was a little high already. As I lifted the green bottle and looked through it, the emerald glass sweating profusely in the humid damp, the room seemed to refract. Me too, suddenly. I felt a chill wash through my body—anticipation, or fear—as I looked through the bottle, the familiar white-lettering with the number "33." Nic Devine, I thought, was not God or even Jesus. Nic Devine was 34.

****

"Hey, wake up, buddy! Wake up!"

I was still slumped against the wall. God knows how long I had been standing there, in the narrow passage that led from the dressing room to the stage. I was upright but folded over, forearms braced against my thighs.

"Oh…shit."

Nic snapped his fingers in my face. I'd been out! How long had I been out?

"You okay, pal?"

"What happened?"

"You passed out! You missed the whole thing!"

I stared at Nic, his face humid and glistening pink. His eyes were wild. His bandmates stood behind him, dripping, their hair matted with sweat. They looked wrung out, exhausted there in the dingy little hallway. Billy glowered over Nic's shoulder, his sticks chattering together as he wriggled them in his hand.

"Four encores, buddy. We killed!"

Oh my God!

"This asshole's the manager, man?" Derek Whitefield surprised me when he spoke. It was the first time he'd ever acknowledged me. His accent was strong Southern, Arkansas or Mississippi. "Where'd ya pick up this jackass?"

I rubbed my head. My tongue felt like it had a carpet growing on it, my skull seemed full of cement. Six codeine tablets had knocked me out cold! I'd missed the whole thing! How could I have been so—

Nic burst out laughing.

"God, you suck! Wanna buy a bridge?"

Whitefield's smile was deliberate, molasses-cool. "You was out for about twenty minutes, man. We ain't even been on yet."

He shook his head, still grinning. I brushed away my confusion, or tried to, pawing at my eyes like a woozy boxer. Nic said,

"You're so damn gullible buddy."

Then the whole band turned away from me—I was no longer of

interest—and headed, as one, towards the stage.

"We're gonna change the set around," Nic said, his voice drifting back down the hall, "on my signal."

They were all barefoot, I saw, except for Nic in his Beatle boots. I nearly tripped over Whitefield's cast-off sandal as I limped after them down the hall. I wanted to watch for a moment from the wings. What any of this meant, I couldn't tell you. Perhaps just that the entire band was country, except for the bassist who probably just couldn't find any shoes that fit his massive feet. They were like children, and yet a more ignorant cluster of hayseed motherfuckers was difficult to imagine. I remembered Nic saying, *Rock 'n' roll should be made by cavemen, total primitives*, and he was right. Billy Williamson had grown up on a farm in Coshocton, and spent his teenage years driving a tractor. If Derek Whitefield owned a pair of shoes before he was sixteen I'd have been half surprised. It didn't matter. These were the people I would live or die with, as they strode onto the stage and picked up their instruments as if at random, like primates fondling rudimentary tools. The PA played *Also Sprach Zarathustra*. I laughed out loud at Nic's twin senses of drama and the absurd. Gary Hauser had opened the doors finally and from where I stood I could make out a crowd of about a hundred people, if that, none of them seeming all that interested in this band. One's dreams when they came true were so marginal, so diluted and small. Others trickled in, but from this distance I didn't recognize a soul. Looking at the band again I wondered that these were the people that Nic, or luck or fate—whatever you wanted to call the principle that guides a life, for I knew now it wasn't just accident—had assembled to realize my dream. It didn't seem right. It wasn't right, but what was the alternative? They picked up their instruments and launched, without so much as a nod in the audience's direction, into the first song of their set. Not, as the set list had predicted, the Hollies, but instead the 13th Floor Elevators' "You're Gonna Miss Me."

You're gonna miss me! Once again, Nic seemed to be mocking me, teasing me—hadn't we missed everything, or hadn't I?—as he spoke the way your favorite band always does, directly to you and through you. He looked over at me and smirked—I recognized the song in two chords, the half-second's pause between the first and the second—as if to acknowledge he knew exactly what I was feeling. He always did. And as he stepped forward to the mic to let fly with that throat-shredding scream that was even more intense than the song's original singer's, I felt the music lift me up, drawing me over towards the stage.

28

Judas!

The band was tight. The mix was clear and bright and as they charged out of the gate, it seemed Nic had won the argument with Derek: there would be none of those epic, "radio friendly" solos that seemed designed with the purpose of giving DJs and programmers time to go to the bathroom. Nic was everything I hoped he would be, the moment he stepped to the mic and let fly with those primal howls, slashing away at his Gibson Cutaway while his hair streamed down to either side of his face. His profile broke across the spotlight. He wore black pants, his low-heeled boots and a blood-colored shirt with a swirling black paisley pattern. His guitar cord snaked behind him like a ringmaster's whip.

"You're gonna wake up one morning—"

The first words he sang were written, or at least stolen, by Roky Erickson, not long before he was confined to the Rusk Hospital for the Criminally Insane. Those words about the sun greeting the dawn, how we would look around and find him gone. The song was a modest hit for the Elevators late in 1966. They gave Roky shock treatment and released him after three and-a-half years, guilty as charged of marijuana possession.

"Awww—stop! No, stop, stop it!"

Nic whirled suddenly. The song tumbled into a chaos of botched chords and stumbling beats. Feedback shrilled off the monitors. They were thirty seconds into their first song.

"What the hell are you doing? Billy, are you deaf?"

I hung glumly on my crutches as I watched him change his mind again, that mind as fickle as the day was long.

"Goddamnit—He yelled to Derek off-mic, what I could hear and the audience couldn't probably—"This isn't Cream! You're gonna play that shit I'll put your head through Williamson's floor drum—"

As the song clattered to a halt, I turned away. I couldn't watch this, I couldn't. I fled back down the hall, so I wouldn't have to hear the scattering of boos that rose up from the tiny crowd.

"Judas!" someone yelled, parodying Dylan's famous heckler at Manchester's Free Trade Hall. An epochal moment this wasn't. I wanted a cigarette in the worst way, wanted more than that as I limped along on my crutches. My head felt light, light as a balloon thanks to those codeine tablets. My ankle didn't hurt, in fact I could barely feel my body at all! I spilled back onto the auditorium floor just as Nic was counting off a new tune. He'd removed his guitar and switched over to the organ. The indifference of the audience—who just wanted Derek Whitefield's lead foot to step on the effects pedal so they could party like it was 1979 all over again—was palpable. A few scattered claps, some booing. At least it was cooler out here. Nic stepped up to his organ and began with the transposed chords of—what else—"The Lion." His own worst song.

Oh, Nic, I thought. His betrayal seemed personal. As though he had sold me, and not just himself to the devil.

29

The Imposter

I moved towards the balcony. If he wasn't going to try, I wasn't going to watch. Felice was here somewhere, I could feel it. I could sense her presence, or else just knew she wouldn't leave me hanging. We were done as a couple, but unresolved. We weren't going to part on no terms at all. At last the place was beginning to fill up. I nearly collided with Kate Blum in the atrium at the foot of the stairs. We stood out on the worn checkerboard tiles, where the ceiling rose up like the nave of a temple. Gary Hauser sat on his stool and took people's tickets. He'd put on a pilot's cap, cocked over one eye. The pin on the front read *United*.

"Nice hat."

He smirked. "I finally found one that fits."

I reached over and grabbed Kate by the wrist. The beads in her hair clacked like a glass curtain as she turned.

"Seen Felice?"

"Nope." She shook her head. The sound out here was murky, reducing Nic's words—thankfully—to a churning mass of muddle-mouthed echo. God, this was a horrible song! "Lend me five bucks, so I can get a drink?"

"Sure."

I patted my pockets.

"Sorry," I said. "I'm tapped."

"Tapped, huh?"

"Yep."

She grinned, like I'd just said something funny. I turned and stepped over the staircase's velvet rope, the abacus-rattle of her hair—I could hear it even above the music—clattering behind me. *Tapped.* Like a keg, like a barrel. Or like someone in a game or a myth: *Dead.* I hobbled upstairs, feeling light, crooked, exhilarated. Where was Felice? Marcus sat on the landing, midway up towards the mezzanine floor. He wore a Walkman, sat alone under the crescent-shaped window that looked out like a ship's porthole over High Street.

"What the hell are you doing?" I yanked the headphones from his ears. "We came all this way to see the band!"

He smiled. This was the quietest spot in the whole club, the place where people may have gathered to have a smoke or a solitary moment. Down there in the distance—I could barely hear them, myself—the band ploughed into another song, a cover of Television's "See No Evil."

"You came all this way." Marcus shrugged. "I just came home."

"What are you listening to?"

"Elvis. The *real* King!"

Typical, I thought. He wasn't even into the lean, cat-like Elvis of the early, pre-army years. He preferred the sad, swollen face of the seventies, the fat and bloated demon who sang "Walk A Mile in My Shoes" and "In The Ghetto." Melodrama, melodrama.

"Where's Felice?" I shouted.

"She's not up there. I checked."

He bopped his head to the cha-cha beat of something doubtless designed to soundtrack little old ladies playing the slot machines in Vegas. A more infuriating "friend" was difficult to imagine. I hiked up to the top of the stairs so I could see for myself, peering over onto the balcony. All I saw was darkness, row upon row of empty seats. I went back downstairs and—for the moment, flummoxed—decided to watch the band. Really watch them, to see if I could judge them dispassionately. For now they'd settled into something like a "groove" (as much of one as they could muster with such a funkless guitarist, and such a clown for a bass player. From this distance, he looked a little like that other, fake Elvis, the one Felice loved so much). Finishing up the Television song, they plowed cleanly into "Crawl to Me," doubling up that initial organ riff on Whitefield's guitar so it sounded thick and powerful. Right on cue, I blinked and my contact lens popped out of my eye, falling down to the floor. Was I ever going to see this band? I dropped to my knees, thankful just this once the place was not packed, and groped blindly on the scarred wooden surface. Like a Muslim on the haj, a yawning cat I stretched my hands out in front of me while Nic—again—sang the words that were my life: *I wanna see you crawl, crawl, crawl!* So I did. So he owned me, as I grasped around on the floor and at last found it. I slid the contact back into place and straightened up, leveraging myself on my crutches, needles and pins rippling through my arms and legs: but I didn't need both crutches now, felt high enough that I could survive with but one. I dropped the other and limped a little forward. Finally, I'd watch the band operating in full.

****

They were amazing, sloppy in all the right ways. I focused on Billy Williamson's death's head scowl, watching him beat his snare and his tom with a grim deliberation. He was terrific. The band was too. But they were not what Felice's brother had promised me, Transcendence-with-a-capital-T. I wanted peak experience, transformation. Instead, they were solid, but hardly life-changing. The sort of band you danced to and then went home. It should've been enough. Wasn't it enough? Wasn't that—exactly that—what summer was for?

They played a bunch of songs in a row. I no longer remember the order, even though I have that set list (stained by the juices of that mysterious cheeseburger—what we all wanted!) still. Nic switched everything around. I remember they played "Flower Power," "You Bother Me," a small slew of covers. "Unoriginal," somebody grumbled, but was that really the point? The audience thickened. I recognized some people from Crazy Lady's, swaying like charmed snakes in that self-hugging, Gothic approximation of dancing popular at the time, a posture insular and melancholy, seductive and bruised. Terry Wheat was behind the bar at the rear of the main ballroom, pouring beers for the half-interested masses. I stood behind him and waited, watching from a distance. Too embarrassed to rush the stage. Most of the crowd simply ignored the band, apart from a few Whitefield worshippers shaking their devil horns in the air. Was there a devil here, I wondered still? Was that what this show was missing? Nic sang the Stones' "All Sold Out," spitting into the microphone with a peculiar venom. Then the Alleycats' "Nothing Means Nothing Anymore." He was taunting the audience, those cool, cruel Goths who didn't seem to recognize a great song—one I showed him, incidentally; how proud I was to have taught my idol a song—when they heard it. They simply didn't care. A pang of despair washed through me. It wasn't enough! Perhaps it could never be. It was only rock 'n' roll, and after all these years in which we'd seen and heard it all a thousand times, where was the transcendence in that?

But then, at the end of the first set, something miraculous happened. Nic had just rattled off a string of heavyweight covers: Eno's "Needles In The Camel's Eye" medleyed with, of all things, Funkadelic's "Free Your Mind (And Your Ass Will Follow)," then Mott The Hoople's "Death May Be Your Santa Claus." I watched Billy throughout the latter. He was all but levitating off his drum-stool, flexing his tattoo. *Run, Run Rudolph!* He was my Santa Claus, I thought. He brought the band to life. With hardly a pause they blasted into a Stooges song, and I felt myself too leaning into its excitement, knowing this was the band Nic loved above all others. As the band ripped into a scarifying, clangorous set of chords and Nic let loose with a tooth-loosening howl, someone from the audience climbed onstage. It was one of those hairy, lost-age Rip Van Winkles I'd seen milling around outside earlier, now carrying a saxophone under his arm. I started towards the stage—after all, it was my job to make sure no one fucked with my band's set—and yet Nic just nodded as if it had been prearranged, or he simply didn't mind the company up there. Then Nic stepped up to the mic.

Outta my mind on/
Saturday night—

It was "1970," song one on side B of the Stooges' *Funhouse* LP! Even Terry Wheat looked up—no one didn't love the Stooges—as they piled ferociously into the song and as the guy, suddenly, began honking away on his sax, wailing in a way that was instantly familiar. It was Steve MacKay, who played on the original recording! My God, I'd thought he was dead! Perhaps he was—I couldn't make a positive ID from where I stood—but it sure sounded like him. I doubt most people in the audience would've recognized him anyway, even as he honked, squawked and wailed like John Coltrane fighting his way out of a flaming cage, elevating the band to a whole other level. In that instant they were supreme, Billy walloping his skins like pieces of sheet metal, his sticks thunder mallets, Nic peeling off nightmarish squalls of feedback to surpass the original's hellacious intensity. All eyes were on MacKay, pot-bellied and barefoot, a long gray beard hanging over a black *UAW* T-shirt, on this Gandalf the Gray who'd hopped up to galvanize the band anew. The memory of that first, aborted song went crashing away into prehistory. This band killed. For two minutes, they were the best I'd seen: they flickered in and out of a song co-written by Sun Ra and the MC5, "Starship," using it to replace this song's bridge and then rocketed to a climax.

"Find a way out!" Nic hollered, repeatedly, achingly as the song rattled towards its zenith. He wanted out too, but—in the true sense—how was he ever to find it? The song, the band, the city—the world, maybe—was his cage. "Find my way outta here!"

A bone-rattling roar, the whole band collapsing on a single chord, before they stopped. Then applause, the crowd almost enthusiastic. Yet there were no cascades of flowers, no stage-storming frenzy like the band deserved. Ingrates! Nic's hair was drenched. All of them looked as though they'd stood out in a windstorm: disheveled, ruined, eyeing one another with these loopy, satiated grins, their expressions almost sexual. This was as close as the bassist might ever come to that particular sort of satisfaction, I thought. I watched him bonk himself on the head as he unstrapped his bass, then trip over his patch cord while he strode offstage. For five minutes though, they'd been the best band in the world, had delivered on the promise I'd glimpsed in rehearsal and more. Yet I had a feeling they'd never be able to sustain it. Maybe—if they could keep that up for, say, twelve times as long during the second set, when Stevo would be watching—there was hope, and they'd be rewarded with a contract, a chance at genuine success. I needed this for some reason. My own happiness seemed to ride on it still. Nic bowed slightly towards the sax player, an odd, unexpectedly formal gesture the latter returned before they walked offstage in separate directions. *Done.*

I ought to have been satisfied. But I wasn't. The house lights faded up, and with them some music, a Munchkin chorus singing "Follow The Yellow Brick Road." I laughed aloud! Nic had some twisted sense of humor, for a guy I suspected could never be satisfied himself, who would always find something missing from anything he'd just done. I went backstage to face his temper. I pressed through the crowd, scanning each face I passed, searching in vain for Felice.

30

Saved

I found Nic in his dressing room. He was taking off a string of beads, some weird pagan necklace he was wearing as he sat in front of his makeup mirror.

"That was great!" I said. "It was—"

"Shit." Thunder clouded his brow. "We sucked. The whole damn thing was a disaster."

"What are you talking about?" I said. "From where I stood you sounded great."

"So you say." He scowled. What does the audience really know, anyway? Who's it all for in the end? "I see differently."

He stood up, wheeled on his bandmates who somehow all crowded in here—they fit, as if into a phone booth—behind him. The bassist was sipping a Heineken from the mix 'n' match beer case in the closet. Derek was restringing his Epiphone Casino. I had a sinking feeling there wasn't going to be a second set, if he started in on them the way he was about to.

"All you guys suck," Nic snapped. "Only Williamson was in time! The rest of you were fucking awf—"

"Look," I said, leaping in front of the bassist before Nic jabbed that finger through his eye. "These guys are great, for a pick-up band. The problem is you, man."

"Oh you think so, huh?"

"Yeah, I do," I said. We glared at one another for a moment. "Go on, man. You're an artist, you're not supposed to be happy with what you sound like. Now stop acting like a diva and put your damn shirt on. Stevo's here."

"He is?"

He was. I'd just run into him at the bar.

****

"So…not much of a draw, this band, are they?"

"Not yet," I said. "Give them room."

He stretched and plucked a cigarette out of his own pack this time. Once more I had that sinking feeling he was up to no good, had come here in fact to claim Nic's soul.

"We'll see," he muttered. He struck a match and the glow played blue across the iridescence of his sharkskin coat. My ears were still ringing. His teeth gleamed in the half-dark. The PA played his band's current hit, with its big, dumb, electric chorus. *I'm a wolf child baby and I'm howling for your love!* "We'll see."

****

"He's here?" Nic said, now.

"Yeah. So quit pouting, pinhead, and get your shit together."

Derek grinned, that sly, stubbly sidelong smile that suggested he alone might be the guy who really knew the score. He plucked a few chords of the theme to *Jesus Christ Superstar*.

"Quit it," I said, "you're missing the point."

"Which is?"

"Not to make fun of your band mate," I said. "You're missing the point."

"Which is?"

I whirled suddenly, picked up a beer bottle—I was high as a kite—and flung it at Nic's makeup mirror. It exploded, both the bottle and the mirror, in a shower of foam and glass.

"Where's Felice?" I shouted.

There was a moment of stunned silence, then Nic, and his bandmates—the bassist especially—started to laugh.

"Man, you should be the singer," Whitefield said. "You got the right temperament for it!"

"Ya missed," Billy said, for the first time that I'd seen smiling, a look that cancelled his entire face. Contradicted it, somehow. "Nice try though!"

Nic shook with amusement. "Man, you're a hothead! Not so mild mannered after all now, are ya Tarzan?"

"I guess not."

"Where was that fire when those guys were kickin' your ass yesterday? You could've used it."

I shrugged. But I felt galvanized, alive! I was invincible. This was what the band could do to you after all. The pain in my ankle was gone.

Nic leaned over and blew out a couple of his candles, so it was even dimmer in here suddenly. What was up with that, besides? Why did he seem to prefer the dark, so? I looked around at my bandmates—his bandmates, but I was one of them now—and felt a chill, a premonition . Where was Felice?

"Hey—"

I looked at Nic, who was busy once more preening in front of his half-shattered mirror. He'd picked up two of Billy's donuts and was gazing through them like monocles, binocular-lenses, twisting his arms around upside-down. It was a gesture I'd seen somewhere before, what Brian Jones did on the original "Jumpin' Jack Flash" 45's picture-sleeve. Was everything a quotation with him? Maybe that guy in the crowd was right. Did it matter?

"That sax player at the end of the set," I said. "That was Steve MacKay, wasn't it?"

"Yep." Nic mopped powdered sugar off his eyebrow. "That was him."

"Oh, bullshit!" How many times was he going to pull one over on me, anyway? "I don't believe you."

"You don't believe me?" Nic said. "Have a little look at the autographed record sleeve on the table over there."

I picked it up: the original gatefold of the Elektra LP, sure enough autographed with a black sharpie. *Hey Nic, love your band! Especially since I'd never heard you guys till tonight. Luv, Mack.*

("Luv?" I wondered? Couldn't anyone in this town spell?)

"Wow," I said. "How'd you pull that off?"

"I met him when the Dawgz played the Second Chance in Ann Arbor in '79," Whitefield said. "*I* set it up."

"The Second Chance, huh?" I said, "What'd you hock to make that happen?"

"Nothin'."

I stared at the LP, the heavy cardboard foldout, its picture of Iggy and his three bandmates melting, deliquescing into a bath of what looked like molten lava. "Y'know," I added, "you can really get lost in these things."

"I know," Nic said, "the old gatefold."

I turned it around in my hands. Kaleidoscopic, the picture was. Its proposed meanings were infinite. "You keep thinking you know what you're seeing, but then it changes."

Nic snorted. "You should try it on peyote."

He'd changed now into a white shirt. I thought, drugs really were redundant when you were confronted with the reality of a thing. Anything at all. Belief, disbelief, in a sense the world beggared them both. I set the record down.

"You ready?" I said. "You finally gonna get your bandmates paid?"

"Yep."

"I always get paid," Derek muttered, as he pushed past me on his way out the door. "Fucker."

"I'm not—"

But there must've been some confusion. The band headed past me, Williamson tapping me on the shoulder with his sticks as he passed. ("Let's get it on," he muttered, quoting Grand Funk Railroad more probably than Marvin Gaye. These guys were such hairballs, marooned in the semi-distant past.) They stepped across a river of beer that trickled across the doorway, looking and smelling like piss. As I'd crowded through the door I'd kicked over a champagne bucket in which Nic mockingly chilled a 40-ouncer. I looked back at him, as he headed out towards the stage behind his bandmates.

"Knock 'em dead," I said.

"I will," he said, "I have."

I added, I don't know why, "Give me a reason to keep watching."

He glared. "Oh there's a reason. There's always a reason."

I stared into the gloomy cage of the dressing room. Its flickering candles and half-shattered mirror, ringed with a few last working bulbs, its towels and rags wet with sweat and makeup. It looked like the dressing room of some dissolute old actor, dingy and grimy and cysted with experience.

"Why's it so damn dark back here?"

"Hey, you're the manager, pal. You got a problem, you should call Con Edison yourself."

"Con Edison, huh?" I stared at the jagged mirror where I'd smashed it: the gaping hole where my reflection should've been. *Unseen, unseen.* "Maybe you mean Monopolated Light & Power?"

He didn't say anything. I said, "Where's your girlfriend, anyway?"

I thought I heard him laugh, although maybe I imagined that against the murmur of the auditorium beyond him. His voice echoed back to me through the simmering dark.

"Where's yours?"

31

What's My Name?

When the band hit the stage, they picked up right where they left. In sixth gear. They launched into a smartly chosen cover of another Mott the Hoople song. "Sucker."

Hi there, your friendly neighborhood sssss—adist wanna take you for a ride—

I looked out from my place in the wings—I was beaming, ecstatic— and saw Stevo, right where I needed him to be. He was standing way up front with his jaw hanging open, his fists thrust up into the air. Right, I thought. *Sorted.* The guy had signed a hundred bands both more popular and less talented than this one. I could smell his excitement from here. His recklessly tousled hair seemed to stand straight up on end, and as I followed the exclamatory line of his lanky pogoing body straight up towards the balcony, there she was. Resting her arms on the balustrade, gazing down to cast a cool eye upon me and my band. As she leaned upon the rail, half smiling, pale against the blacked-out seats behind her, she looked regal and distant. I couldn't tell what she was thinking or feeling, but in that moment I didn't care. Maybe she saw me too and maybe she didn't. Just then, I wasn't sure I wanted her to see me, was so happy just to look at her undetected. Maybe that was what I'd wanted all along, I realized. Not to be seen, so much as to see someone—someone else—clearly, to view the world as if I'd already left it. That was my power, if I had one. It was what made me feel—paradoxically— most alive. To be not the storm but the eye of it, all hole and no donut.

The band careened into its next song, an original unfamiliar to me. I wound my way along the backstage corridor and out onto the floor. The others were here now too. I saw Lena, Donnie—he'd come back after all— Mara. The place was semi-crowded, in fact half full. The audience seemed to swell through the hall like a gas, a newly-formed universe. I limped along through it on my one crutch, my taped and bloated ankle. Still, I felt no pain. Nic was having a ball, blasting into another original, "The Art Goblin," that was probably the best thing he'd played yet, ruthless and electric, raw and exciting. Its relentless drive pinned the audience—who'd begun to push forward now—a good five feet back from the stage. *Fine young minds all dressed in blaack*, he hollered. Another taunt, to the Goths in the audience. It was like he was protecting himself from them, somehow. His whole body seemed to quiver, like a sapling in a storm, and that's when it happened. I was still trying to get to Felice, elbowing my way through the thick of the crowd—there was Krist Cooley, pop-locking on the floor there to the left, lost in his own private world—when I looked back at the stage and Nic leapt off it, soaring into the air.

****

Do you trust your eyes? Do you? I'm not saying you shouldn't, nor am I saying I don't trust my own, merely that Nic revealed himself to me in that moment, in that glimpse I had of him from the corner of my eye while I pressed my way back towards the stairs. I saw him clearly. I saw His face. As he leapt off the stage, I knew this time He wasn't going to come down. Oh sure, he arced forth in a perfect swan dive and his body fell like anyone else's, as the crowd caught him and bore him up on their hands. That much could not have been otherwise. Yet Nic Devine was Risen. Without irony, without parody, in utter and complete sincerity—who knows, maybe it was the other way around and the crowd healed him—I tell you, Nic Devine was God. For a moment, and for longer, everything I'd wanted this band to be, everything I'd dreamed of this place was inviolate, intact, and real. And so long as I was with him, I thought, I was immortal too. I fought my way through the crowd and up the stairs, limping still on my numb leg, and I found Felice standing by herself on the landing. Marcus had gone downstairs at the half. I'd seen him out there too, watching the band. Felice was alone, staring pensively out the window. She turned to look over at me, just before I reached her. A thin shaft of moonlight fell on the floor between us, seeming oddly solid as it passed through the scythe-shaped window.

"Hey." I was out of breath. "Where've you been? I've looked all over—"

She looked at the floor. Not at me. My words, too, sounded hollow. I didn't quite believe them myself.

"I called your house."

"I don't have a house anymore."

"Yes, before," I said. "Where were you?"

"You didn't believe me." Her face burned with injury, anger. "About my brother."

"No," I said. Gesturing downstairs. "You didn't believe me, about my band."

I took her hand. She withdrew it. She stared at me with her arm hanging limp at her side.

"Where were you?" I said. But she said, "Where were *you*?"

I knew what she meant. All summer long, where had I been? Really, where had I been? Everywhere perhaps, or nowhere.

"I'm sorry," I said, but she shook her head. It was too late for that.

"You should've been here." The thin layer of moonlight seemed to waver between us; it seemed almost refractive, like water. "Maybe this wouldn't have happened."

"What? What did I miss?"

"I was with someone. Since you ask."

I took this in. For a minute, I didn't know—rather, didn't want to know—what she meant.

"With...Donnie? Kitty? You were—"

"I was with someone. Else."

She stared back out the window now. I was still one step below the landing, lingering on the stairs. I hesitated, feeling the weight, the repercussion of what she'd just said: someone. A person. A man.

"Who?"

I stood where I was. Down below the band was roaring. Otherwise her words might've knocked the wind right out of me, hit me harder than those football players could've. Her face creased now with regret. She reached towards me, and I leaned away.

"Who?"

Downstairs the crowd jubilated. The band had wrapped up Nic's tune and were plowing into a riff I recognized. It was their cover of "What's My Name?"

"Does it matter?" she said.

I twisted away, because it did, or I thought it did. I started limping down the stairs. She said, "You were looking for it. All summer, you kept suspecting me. It was like you wanted this to happen."

I shot back over my shoulder. "Looking for it and wanting it aren't the same things."

I went on down the stairs, staring down at that worn carpet that would've seen everything, teenage lovers fighting, kids who were drunk and sick and disappointed, opera lovers, flappers and philosophers. There wasn't anything I could say that hadn't been said, or anything I could feel that hadn't been—perhaps more intensely—by someone else before me; not that that mattered or helped either. I walked away. She chased me.

"It isn't important," she said.

"Bullshit!"

"It isn't!"

I turned to face her. We were at the bottom of the stairs now, where the worn scarlet carpet gave way to chipped white tiles. I said, "You fucking cheated."

"You didn't?"

"No—yes, but not in the same way," I admitted.

"So? You loved something else, more than you did me. That's not cheating?"

I shook my head. "That's sophistry."

"Is it?"

We stood where the band was louder, overpoweringly so even as we stood outside the ballroom in the lobby. A chandelier trembled overhead, and Felice and I too, with our agitated shouting, fought to be understood, fought to make our muddled feelings clear, like instruments ourselves. Felice said, "I did it because you were missing."

"That's not a good enough reason."

"No, it isn't."

She reached down and grabbed me, my wrist, fingers circling it like a handcuff. This time, at least, I didn't pull away.

"It isn't. I was angry, I was jealous," she said. "I'm sorry."

I stared at the floor.

"I'm sorry," she said again.

"Who was it?"

She looked away. Either, she wasn't going to tell me or—I had a feeling—she couldn't, for some reason. I said, "It wasn't—tell me it wasn't—"

"No." She shook her head. "Not Nic."

"Thank God for small favors," I said. Because I'd begun to believe it might've been anyone, Donnie, Terry, Marcus, Professor Plum or Colonel Mustard, anyone and everyone. I turned and walked back towards the stage. This time she didn't follow. She said, "Your band—"

"Yeah?" I didn't turn around this time, either. "What about them?"

In front of us, the ballroom was seething. The lobby floor was sticky, and Gary Hauser had abandoned his post. A few stray souls were dashing past, searching for bathrooms. The rest were inside watching the band, which was where I wanted to be. Felice had betrayed me. She'd sold me out. What was left to say? I'd betrayed her too, perhaps, but who cared? I'd missed enough, all summer long. I'd missed enough. You could be in the thick of an experience, and still miss the meat of it.

"They don't suck," she said.

I grimaced. "So?"

I couldn't help it. I stopped. There was also the pleasure of being right, of hearing from her the apology I wanted. She caught up with me again. I said, "I don't need you to tell me. They're amazing."

She searched my face. "Yeah. They are."

I knew what she meant, just then: they are, you are. I looked back, at her pale and strangely innocent face—somehow more innocent, now that she had finally committed the crime I'd merely suspected all along—and said, "I don't forgive you."

"I'm not saying you should. I don't forgive me either."

For a moment then it didn't matter, who it was or even that it was. My band, she liked my band. In a way, this was all I'd wanted from her all summer, the agreement for which we'd been searching. It was our truce. She took my free hand, and this time I didn't shake her away. She said, "I'm sorry."

I nodded. In the next room, Nic and his band had finished mauling the Clash, were piling into something unfamiliar to me, wild and electric.

"Are you in love with this guy?"

She hesitated. "Does it matter?"

Maybe, I thought. And yet—maybe it didn't, after all. We'd had our summer. Wasn't that enough? You wanted to live forever, you had to live right now. You wanted to be "someone," you had to be anyone, everyone, no one. For a second, I felt, what Felice had done really didn't matter: it passed right through me. At that moment, she could've said anything, could've said, *She said, I know what it's like to be dead.* Because in that moment, we knew everything we could, perhaps even everything there was.

I took her arm, and we went on together into the next room. I hadn't forgiven her, not really. I didn't love her yet. But as we stopped by the bar, I took her in my arms for a moment. A long moment. Since that was all we were given anyway.

****

"Together in the darkness!" Nic yelled, again and again. "Together!!"

It was the refrain from a song called "Come Together." Not the Beatles song, but one of the same name by the MC5. Whitefield and the bassist stood at opposite ends of the stage, their backs to one another and with Nic in the middle, where he'd been cast up by the crowd that had yanked his shoes off too. He stood there in stockinged feet, disheveled, with a sly, shaggy-dog grin flickering across his face as he glanced over at his guitar player. He'd forsaken his organ for this set and was playing one of Derek's guitars, the '58 Les Paul Cutaway. He was playing the E, A, D chords that belonged to that MC5 song, and to half the Stooges catalogue. Suddenly, he snapped, "When will I ever learn?"

And the band kicked into one of his own: it was that song, the one he'd rehearsed that day in Coshocton. For all I knew it still didn't have a name, but it was without question his best. That mountainous riff came crashing down on our heads—half "Mission Impossible Theme," half "Search and Destroy"—and it was perfect.

"All my life I've lived in the dark—"

He'd changed the words slightly this time, from "half" to "all," but it was the same song, the one it seemed we'd all been waiting for—every one of us—all our lives. The fact I was the only one there who'd heard it before didn't matter. Everyone seemed to know it. (What was it called? The name of the song seemed to rest on the edge of my tongue, but perhaps it didn't even need one, anymore than anything else you truly loved really did.) I'd have sworn people were singing along, the chorus I'd committed to heart that one afternoon in Coshocton, how everything lasts as long as you let it. So it did, even though Nic leapt into the crowd again midway through the song and lost the second half of the lyric. It didn't matter. The smile on Nic's face was worth the cost of admission alone, worth everything it had taken to get me here to see it. Eventually he wound up back onstage while the band—sounding like they'd just learned the song, themselves—somehow managed to keep it alive. I glanced over at Felice. She didn't seem to be interested in watching the band, was watching me instead. What of it?

Onstage, Nic leaned down and shouted something in Stevo's ear— Stevo who'd been one of his chief pallbearers, as he'd toured the crowd on his back—and the latter flexed his mouth into that mirthless and sinister grin and gave him the thumbs up. He was shirtless now, his pale and skinny torso gleaming with sweat. Nic signaled the band and they launched into the signature riff that began "School's Out," which then morphed instantly into a different Alice Cooper song, "Desperado." He sang the words about being a killer, being a clown and I for one believed him. Both times.

The rest of the set was a blur. It went on for more than an hour, with a mix of originals and covers. "Love is a Spider," by the Phantom Movers, Sonic Rendezvous Band's "City Slang," "Street Waves" by Pere Ubu, all according to the set list though I don't remember any of these. I remember a heavy thrashing of the Nazz's "Open My Eyes," a slow, prowling take on "Little Red Rooster" that was based on the Sam Cooke version, and a handful of originals whose names are forever lost. They roared through the Dawgz' second-worst song in "Livin' Too Late," then played the Hollies cover originally intended for the set's beginning. *You wouldn't want to be me*, Nic sang, and I wondered, did we have a choice? He capped it all off with a second Television cover, "Prove It." (*Just the facts.*) And then he lifted off his guitar and dropped it to the ground. Just let it fall casually at his feet. He'd done all he could with it. He stood facing the audience for a moment and applauded us, almost mincingly, like an actor. It was as if he was making fun of us—"taking the Mickey," as Stevo might've said—had pulled a fast one none of us would ever come close to understanding. Then he left. Derek Whitefield had time-traveled back to 1975 and was up there with his double-necked guitar slung below his waist just like Jimmy Page at the Long Beach Sports Arena; the bass player bowed awkwardly and spun around in circles trying to untangle himself from his instrument, then blew a kiss into the crowd. *Hubba-hubba to you too, handsome.* Watching him, I felt something, some pang I couldn't place before they were all gone and the stage plunged back into darkness.

Of course there would be an encore, there'd have to be, but I turned to Felice.

"Let's go backstage."

"Nah."

"C'mon. We have five minutes. I'd like to be the first one to tell Nic how amazing that was."

We were standing again by the bar, having been swept back by the frenzy and force of the crowd up front. The house lights were down still, the air shrilling with a malignant hum, the instruments still feeding back as they leaned against the amplifiers. They were coming back. In the meantime, Stevo climbed up onto the lip of the stage. His clothes had been ripped clean off, and he stood up there in his boxers. He'd gotten his hands on a little squeezy-bear of honey—it was there to soothe Nic's throat between songs—and he began to slather his chest with it, prancing and sticking his tongue out. *W'alright!* I supposed there was a little bit of Iggy Pop in each of us.

"You go," Felice said. "I'll wait."

I did. Knowing she wouldn't want to see Nic anyway, the guy who'd stolen me away from her before she even had a chance. I looped around towards the door at the side of the stage, where I ran into Lena. She had her video camera with her, hanging slack at her side.

"Hey," I said, as we embraced. "That was incredible! Did you get any of it?"

I could've kissed her, in the clumsy half-hug we shared there in the darkness. Our cheeks brushed against one another as I spoke into her ear.

"No film," she said. "I got maybe five minutes. Just the beginning of the second set!"

I could smell her breath, its cinnamon sweetness. She kept her hands upon my forearms and we stood like that a second, swaying. I could feel the transgression that was—forever—only a half step away.

"How's your dad?"

She shook her head. "Not great. But thanks for asking."

"Health-wise?"

"He'll be okay. But he's not too excited about going to prison. Confinement really freaks him out."

"I know the feeling."

We eyed one another. Had we learned anything? Perhaps we were only ready to be fooled differently the next time, by the obvious, the unseen. Invisible Dan, the apostate, was the only one missing now. Everyone else was here. Invisible Dan, I thought, my likeness, my brother. Perhaps it didn't matter who sold you out. Maybe the worst thing that ever happened to you was still better than having it not happen at all. Lena turned and walked off with her camera (didn't it figure that she'd run out of film? Yet even if she'd caught the band on tape, even if she'd filmed the entire concert, she'd have lost them, would have had just the document and not the reality), then turned to go backstage. I squeezed down the narrow hall, edging down it almost sideways, just as the band were emerging from their dressing room.

"Hey."

"Hey." Nic was leading the others out, smoking a cigarette. Something I'd never seen him do. "We're not finished."

"I know. Still, congratulations. Stevo's eating out of your hand. He looks like he's ready to have your baby."

"'Fraid he's outta luck." Nic chuckled. He tugged on the cigarette and offered a strange, skeptical look.

"Just go out there and finish him off. He'll have you on the radio all over the world."

"Yeah," he said. "Great."

I moved aside to let them pass. There in the dimness of the hall, a stampede of warm skin and sweat-drenched hair. I did a little two-step, a three-step with that bass player. *Who's On First?* I thought. I might be Abbott to his—

"Why don't you come out and introduce us?" Nic said. "Like Hamish Grimes on *Five Live Yardbirds!*"

"No thanks."

I looked at the bassist, as he strode right by me.

"What's the matter, buddy?" Nic glanced back at me. "You look like you're gonna pass out again."

The bassist was making his way down the hall. I took a step after him. My ankle buckled, and Nic caught my arm.

"Easy there, pal. What's wrong?"

"Nothing," I lied. I braced myself against the wall. "I'm fine."

"Yeah?" Nic's eyebrows lifted skeptically. "More girl trouble?"

I didn't answer, just watched the bassist as he disappeared down the hall. *Him*, I thought. Of course. Who else? Nic searched me a second.

"These things aren't worth it," he said, before he let me go, went on his own way out towards where the crowd was waiting.

"Which things?"

For it seemed to me nothing was worth it, if you weighed its cost strictly against what you lost, not even if what you gained was greater. This band had given me everything, yet they'd taken something too, in what was not actually a fair exchange no matter how I sliced it. Nic followed his bassist down the hall and for the moment I watched him go.

"You coming?" Nic called. His voice echoed down the hall from its far end. "We could use a tambourinist too."

"Nah." I didn't move. "You'll do fine without me."

Three songs was what we got. I watched from ten feet away. Less, from the bassist who'd stolen the girl I loved all summer, but for the moment I just stood and watched him play. Why? Looking at him from up close, he seemed just as clumsy and ridiculous as ever, pogoing away like a spastic weasel in his approximation of a "funky dance." What Felice saw in him, I'd never know. Fucking chump. Loser. But for as long as the music held him he was untouchable, as much a part of what I loved as the nexus of all my hatred.

I watched as the band tore through their finale. A singalong "Flower Power" (*Every minute, Every hour!*) A gleeful, messy romp through—what else?—"Jesus Loves the Stooges," and then at long last, as Nic resumed his rightful position behind the Vox organ, a familiar set of pulsing chords began. Could it be? Williamson threw his sticks in the air and caught 'em, kind of. All the lights went on at once, the house lights, the overheads and the ones in my skull as Billy toppled off his drum chair, kicked his floor drum hard, a movement like a dog's reflex leg-action. My God, I thought! "Kids in America!" It was Kids in America, the worst and most wonderful drunken sea-shanty manhandling of that song I could possibly have imagined.

Friday night and everyone's moving—

(*Finally*, I thought. Someone had it right.)

I leapt up and down: my ankle didn't matter, with the room all ablaze like a—Christmas tree, really. The yellow floodlights revealed everything as they played, the whole crowd roiling up and down in a frenzy. You know the words. Or if you don't, just chant the title (*We're the kids! We're the kids! We're the kids in*—) over the antiphonal roar of your car's engine at full throttle, since that's about as much like the original song as it sounded. Williamson played the drums with his feet. The bassist played the way he always did, hunched over his instrument like Cousin It, and Whitefield soloed like he'd been lost in the wilderness for years, and had just now found his way free. Nic dropped to his knees for a moment (yes he did!) and prayed in Derek's direction. *Introibo ad altare*. He and Nic faced one another at the end, after it had all broken down to raw chaos, just noise, and they bowed to one another. Exactly as Nic had to the saxophonist, whoever he was. And the song stopped, where it was barely any longer a song at all: just ringing feedback from Derek's guitar and the last toppling of whatever objects were left for Williamson to kick over. Then they walked offstage together, ignoring me completely as they passed.

I stood there, stunned. My ankle was killing me but I didn't care, anymore than I did about the bass player or anything else. Standing there with my jaw hanging open and my dream complete. This was what I'd wanted, this moment right here. As I stared out at that decimated stage, its tipped-over amplifiers and smashed instruments, beer cans and shattered bottles, abandoned picks and strings. Smoke hung over it from all the cigarettes in the audience, a soft fog drifting in the stage lights. Through it, I could see Felice out there in the distance, as blurred as if I were looking through a scrim. I stood there, waiting, until I was sure of what I already knew. This time, they weren't coming back.

"You—"

Backstage, I grabbed the bassist by the shoulder and spun him around. "You fucked my girlfriend!"

I drew my arm back to hit him, but Billy clasped my wrist and held me from behind.

"Hey, hey—take it easy champ."

"What the—what did I do?" the bassist sputtered, while Derek moved over to restrain him in turn. "What are you talking about?"

He glared at me. I said, "Felice. Hello?"

"Shit!" He smacked his forehead dimly. "*You're* the guy Felice was talking about? I knew I'd seen you before, but didn't remember where. She kept talking about some guy—"

"That was me," I said. "Some guy."

"Oh." He looked at the floor, hung his head. "Sorry."

Sorry. How poor were our apologies: his, mine, Felice's. They had so little to do with what actually happened, seemed to belong to a whole other order entirely. It was like she and I had disappointed one another out of sheer reflex, like it was something we needed to do, even, in order to feel the things we did. I went slack in Billy's grip. He let me go.

"I didn't know she was your girlfriend." His voice was thick.

I hesitated. "I'm not sure. Maybe she was never that, quite."

I reached out and cuffed him with the flat of my hand. But maybe she wasn't; maybe she was only ever my dream. Behind his shattered makeup mirror, Nic snorted.

"Girl disputes," he said.

"Fuck you. Is that mascara you're wearing?"

He brushed glass off the table with his forearm. Picked up and sipped a beer he'd mixed with lemonade, another of his sugary drinks. He'd slipped on a fresh bowling shirt, white with green sleeves and trim. Bob, read the name in cursive, above the breast pocket.

"Nice palindrome. Whatcha drinking there, pal? A shandy?"

Nic grinned and shook his head. "You mess with the bull, you get the horns."

A girl came in and started talking to Derek. A few other well-wishers from the audience drifted in before Stevo, at last, arrived. He was dressed, now—or semi-dressed—with his khaki pants tugged on backwards, his zebra-striped shirt half-shredded to rags, American baseball cap turned sideways: he looked like a B-boy from the future.

"Oi, Nic? Stevo." He stuck out his honey-covered hand and Nic shook it.

"Pleasure."

There was no room in there for all of us, so I moved out into the hall a moment. I didn't trust the guy for one second not to take advantage of Nic's vulnerability, so I stayed close. I loitered just outside the door as he began raving about the performance.

"That was fantastic," he ranted, while I leaned there against the pale bricks, the whitewashed walls of the corridor. The lights were on out here now too. "Great look, great band, great drummer. What about your original material, then?"

"We played originals," Nic said.

Billy came outside. He shut the door behind him. Like me, he didn't want to hear Nic's contrarian reasoning, was too afraid of what might or might not have been happening in there. I supposed he couldn't have trusted himself to put forth a more articulate argument on the band's behalf either. He said, "Elvis is gonna get offered a record deal, huh?"

"Maybe. You think he'll take it?"

Billy's weary smile—there it was, he almost managed one—told me what he thought.

"I been waiting for him to make an album for five years now. I ain't holding my breath."

Through the door I heard Nic's low, polite, Midwestern voice countering Stevo's swift English patter, but I couldn't make out the specifics. For a moment their voices were heated, but then I heard Stevo's hyena-like laugh. I couldn't decipher it though. My ears were ringing. They only spoke for a few minutes before Stevo left. Arms swinging, face illegible. I pushed back in.

"What happened?"

Nic shook his head and smiled.

"He offered me a deal."

"And?"

"I said I'd think about it."

"You said you'd think about it? What's the hell's wrong with you?"

Sweat, and a little black mascara, ran down his cheeks. He mopped his face with a towel.

"Were the terms unreasonable? Was he trying to screw you?"

"Uh-uh. He was just a little concerned about the lack of original material in the set."

"So? You have the songs. I know you do. Who cares if you played them?"

Nic mopped his face again with the towel. He stared at the spot where the mirror would've been, smiling inscrutably.

"I dunno buddy. Some people do. Some people think you gotta reinvent the wheel every time."

He tossed me the towel. I knew he wouldn't sign, just knew.

"Was it a bad deal?"

"It was alright. He didn't ask for anything that isn't already lost."

He cackled. I watched him. It took me a minute to recognize I wasn't angry, but I wasn't: I understood too that this band's blossoming mightn't be for public consumption. Perhaps the best of it had already happened, and might continue to happen, inside Nic's head. Perhaps it was meant just for the Happy Few all along. Nic could be late, or early, yet he was forever right on time when it really counted. I said, "What's with the mascara, anyway?"

"It's an homage."

"An Amish?" My ears still rang. I picked up a towel and swabbed them out. He repeated himself.

"Right," I said. Picturing Alice Cooper's kohl-rimmed stare on the cover of *Welcome to My Nightmare*, or *Love it to Death*. "What isn't?"

I stood for a moment. It seemed we had little to say to one another anymore. It had all been discharged during the performance.

"You leave tomorrow, huh?"

"Yeah, in the afternoon."

He stood up. We shook hands. Nic wasn't the kind of guy you embraced, even if I wasn't sure I'd see him again, if or when. I looked at the shirt, the name embroidered above the pocket. I said, "Hey…What does the "A" stand for, in your name? I've always wanted to know."

He blushed, unless it was just rouge. "Can't tell you. It's a state secret."

"No?"

"Nope."

"You sure?"

He hesitated. A long moment. Finally, he said, "Arthur. It's Arthur. But no one's called me that since I was a kid."

I burst out laughing. I couldn't help it. "Just like the Fonz, huh? You can't stand being called—"

"Hey, there's nothing wrong with it," he said. "It's a good rock 'n' roll name. Arthur Lee, of Love. Art—"

"Art? Is that what your mom called you?"

He hung his head. As if this, finally, was something to embarrass him. Arthur, or Art. The One True King, after all. But no name could do justice after all to his strange and stolen originality, the originality that was his because it was borrowed, the only kind of originality that counts. Insofar as we are like words, and we come into this world trailing clouds of association, is all. And it is almost impossible to speak, act or be without quotation. Perhaps that's a function of what some call "belatedness," but I doubt it. I suspect it's been thus for a very long time. I glanced back at Billy.

"Nice stick work," I said.

"Thanks."

"Where'd you learn to play like that? You didn't go to Berklee, did you?"

"Nah." He grinned, then. "I went to school here."

"Really?" This took me aback. "Where?"

He leaned back on the couch a moment. Scowling as he tore open another package of his favorite pastries.

"I went to art school, dummy. Columbus College of Art and Design."

"Yeah? What'd you study?"

"Architecture." He spoke through a mouthful of icing and crumbs. "I studied architecture."

I couldn't help but laugh. He sat up and tossed the crumpled wrapper towards a trash can. Missed.

"Something funny, college boy?"

"Nah."

I bent down and picked up the wrapper, which had landed at my feet. *Ho, ho, ho.* The last laugh belonged to the band, and to Marcus, perhaps to life itself. Since to live *was* to be fooled, no matter how you vowed otherwise, again and again and again. By what was obvious, and so, hidden; by what was impossible and so, perhaps, inevitable. I stepped out of the dressing room and left them, guitarist, drummer, singer and bassist (to whom I would remain forever blind: I just couldn't see the attraction) behind me. I walked off down the hall, the band's voices filtering out behind me as Derek heckled the singer.

"What're you always drinking them sugary things for, man," he asked. "They're for chicks!"

"Ah, they're good," Nic chortled. "They grow on you."

I walked on. My ankle hurt, but less. I tore off my sticker—the one that did not quite say 'manager' on it—and slapped it on a heating pipe. My own small contribution to this place, which would go on until some custodian found it, or else it would remain forever like the old graffiti: *Kilroy Was Here.* I made my way out of the wings and onto the floor of the now nearly empty theater, where Felice—Heaven by any other name—was still waiting.

33

Everything Lasts

We walked home alone, in the dark. No one was out now, the streets swept of Thick People and cops, the traffic lights flashing yellow down the long corridor of High Street. Eventually we just sat at a bus stop and waited for service to resume, so Felice could get back to Kitty's place and I could go home to my apartment alone.

"What d'you want to do?"

"Do?" I looked at her profile, halo'd by a streetlamp as we sat on the flat plastic bench. "I thought we'd discussed that. I thought we were done—"

"Not you and me. What d'you want to do? With your future."

"My future? What are you, my dad?"

"No. I was just curious." She sat with her palms at her sides and pressing against the plastic, like she was going to lift or levitate off the ground. "We never discussed it, you know, I mean, not really. It was always about me and England, or Trinity—"

"Yeah."

"So what about you? You're a literature major. What else?"

I looked at her, and she looked back with that same mysterious, indulgent smile she'd trained on me earlier from the balcony.

"What else is there?"

"Oh no." She laughed. "You're not getting away with that, Mr. Duck and Weave, Mr. Evasion, Slip Kid—"

"Alright, alright." I smiled. "Haven't I told you everything?"

"Everything?"

"Yeah."

Day was breaking over the store fronts opposite, and over a small, blasted-looking park, just a rectangle of grass with a sandbox and swingset. We were in that nether region between Campus and Clintonville, another part of town that wasn't anywhere really, past Nick's Nook and The Second Hand, just staring across at an antique shop and a hair salon. A world untransformed—finally—by acid or rock 'n' roll, just another blowsy cowtown suburb anyone could take or leave.

"I don't know," I said finally. "I haven't thought about it."

"No?"

"No." I suppose it was true, I hadn't. "I just wanted to get here." She laughed.

"Don't. It isn't funny. You're trying to get out of here, but you're also trying to get here still. To Columbus as I believed it would be."

"Did you find it?" She cocked her head sharply. Squinted into the sun that was spiking, painfully, into view. "Did you find what you were looking for?"

We could've talked in circles like this forever. Even when we were not fighting, our words hurtled 'round and chased themselves, over and over, rotating the way my favorite thing in the world did. I lifted my hand.

"What do you think?"

"I think you did," she said.

"I think you're right." I chuckled. "But I only think so."

Hours after the fact, after all, my dream had faded: did I see that band? Or did I just think I had, was it only—after all this, was it only—my imagination? Of course I had. But it was still my imagination, even after I had lived through it. Even then.

"I think you're brave," Felice said. And believe it or not this, seeming non-sequitur, was the last thing she ever said to me. A bus pulled up and took her away, in what felt like the middle of our last conversation. It arrived and we stood up and for a long moment were alone before it opened its doors. She flung her arms around my neck and squeezed once, hard, before she scrambled onto the bus and left me standing where I was. My whole body rang with regret as the doors hissed shut and the bus pulled away down High Street. I stood where I was, staring after it, but Felice knew better than to look over her shoulder. I was gone and I was gone for good. Her hair hung straight past her neck, her profile stared straight ahead. I willed her to look back. She did not.

You're brave, she said, but I didn't see how. I didn't understand a thing as I turned away and began the long walk back to my own apartment, which Mara would keep after I left but which I would never see again either.

Day broke. I walked along High Street with my hands in my pockets, tracing Felice's progress back to Wilkerton in my mind. Now she's at home, I thought, now she's asleep. But how did I know? I never saw her, or any of these people besides Marcus and Lena, again. Even those two became people with whom I shared a distant and embarrassing secret. Silence overtook us. It was never really the same.

But if it wasn't, did that mean it never had been? I stopped in an A&P to buy a cup of coffee, watched the steam curl off the top of that tasteless brown muck we'd been drinking all summer. If I'd lost my friends I'd gained something else, something I knew even then would never pass. *Everything lasts as long as you let it*, Nic sang, and wasn't that true? I thought it was.

I walked home by myself, watching High Street wake up, watching traffic increase and people unlocking grates and raising them, disappearing inside shops. The whole street was like a face raising out of sleep towards consciousness, an ineffable brightening, the whole stitchwork of muscles and nerves working in concert until it finally opened its eyes.

Nic had certainly opened mine. I traversed a gas station, its fumes thickening in the morning air and making me feel giddy. I passed School Daze records—still closed—and the cemetery where Felice and I'd had our last fight. This place belonged to me now. It was mine if it was anyone's. On a street corner I lifted my nose into the air and inhaled, felt the warm wind, the breath of the city hastening back to meet me. And for a moment I was transported, back to that farmhouse in Coshocton where Nic and Billy were fighting and rehearsing, rehearsing and fighting, twin processes that never seemed to end.

"Play it faster," Nic said, taunting his drummer, as though it were possible for time to move any quicker than it already did. "Can you play it a little faster there, ace?"

"Faster?" Billy furrows his brow—for I am there now, just as I am still on that streetcorner, just as I am everywhere the sun never sets—and looks at the singer. "Shouldn't it be slower?"

I see it clearly, so clearly now, the two of them over in the half-shadowed portion of the barn while I sit, invisible to the naked eye, in the sunlight that washes over the beaten and neglected couch in the corner. Dust swims in the air between them, and Billy taps his sticks impatiently, eager to get it right.

"I'll tell you what," Nic says, laughing. "Why don't you just play that part of it backwards. Just that fill there?"

"Backwards?"

Billy's looking at his bandmate like there's something he doesn't understand, then begins to, that crooked smile spreading across his face when Nic says, "Yeah, genius, backwards. Just turn it around again and invert it. You turn things around a bit and that's how you get it to sound like—art!"

I am there now, just as I am there on that street corner, that smell of diesel—and recently-mown fields, horse shit and honey, all those warm, midsummer smells—rising to meet me. Billy knocks his sticks together, that sound like the crackling of embers, to underwrite Nic's impatience, his eternal rage.

"Let's play then."

Somewhere in the distance, I hear a chime like a school- or a church bell. It's nine o'clock in the morning, or three in the afternoon. I start walking again, skipping cracks in the sidewalk as that song—without a name and yet known to everybody—begins playing in my head. I cross against the light, and then turn up 13th Street. People are unpacking their cars, students arriving and moving into campus houses, tramping their heavy boxes and crates across the lawns. Summer's over, but it is never going to end and while I walk the final steps to my apartment I know it's true: school's out, forever! It's still summer. I am free! And Billy taps his sticks together one last time in my head so I know, being older but not one jot wiser, no matter how the hits just keep on coming, the singer had it right from the start. This is never going to end, never going to end, never going to end.

Acknowledgments

Lindsay Amon, Xandra Bingley, Mick Divvens, Marc Gerald, Caroline Greeven, Jonas Heller, Nancy Heller, Katherine Howe, Jacob Hoye, James Linville, The MacDowell Colony, Maryse Meijer, Johanna Ratner, Pamela Robinson, Patricia Sanders, Fred Specktor, Allison White, The MFA Program at Warren Wilson, Dierdre Wood

Special Thanks to The Salivating Ear, for efforts above and beyond the call, and, of course, to "A. Nicolas Devine" and all Lords past, present & future.

About the Author

Matthew Specktor was born in Los Angeles. He has received a fellowship from the MacDowell Colony, and his work has appeared in Open City, Salon, and various anthologies. He holds an MFA from Warren Wilson College, and is currently completing his second novel.